Murder at White Oak

Marko Realmonte

Marko Realmonte

For Will Kir & Lorri Eddings

ACKNOWLEDGMENTS

Novels take time, effort and persistence. I draw strength from my friends, both old and new. I send my love and thanks to Dylan Bruno, my Chinook Lane gang (Judy & Mrs. Hoang), my surrogate family at the Crow's Nest (Kevin, Matt, Jesse, Martha, Kerrie, Tay, Jose, Jason, Carlie, Ryan, Chaley, Marissa, Chaney…and everyone else!) Blake Adams, Collin Boetel, Matt Pekel, Rachel Luckhurst, Matt Bell, Barbara Fogerson, Karen Swan, Eric Hoang, Bridget Lee, Jamie Muller, Ronda & Cecil, Joel Gartland, Joe Trimmer, Tom Pe, Evan Adler, Ronnie Kroell, Jesse Barnes, Josiah Becker, Tobias Reuter, Carla Barbosa, Sara Aluffi, Blaine Nagley, Rik Boere, Lee Mark Hamilton, Susan Hoisington, Keith & Derek Brewer, David Commons, Kyle Gorsuch, Janet Rader, Patrick & Payson McNett, John Duarte, Danny Jacobson, Alan & Dona Love, Kevin Clarke, Hampus Marcussen, Ethan Rill, Hamilton Von Watts, Theresa Arteaga, Brandon Tyler Williams, Terry Fetterman, Dan Rothwell, Betty Ashlock, Jordan LeFever, Ethan Rill, Christian Gisbert, Katie Baker, Dan & Dylan Black, Ian Tevyaw, Justine Iadiano, Don Jessup, Mark Tydell, Matt Abraham, Cole Williams, Tim Courtemarche, Clayton Takacs, Kene Lawrence, Laura Rochelle, Adam Martin, Ezri Heij, Josh LePage, Tom Polley, Graham Larue, Kyle Carlson, Richard Nolthenius, Robbie Dice, Erik Thomas, Mark Calkins, Tom Fulton, Michael Bruno, Lisa from Cabrillo and to Travis with the amazing tattoos.
(also in fond memory of Cassidy, Matthias, Billy and Janett)

PROLOGUE

Every story is a love story, but this one has a murder and a ghost.

CHAPTER 1: MANHATTAN

Mr. Abbot stands patiently at the edge of the pool until the boy notices his shadow in the lane. He stops swimming and pops his head out of the water.

"How kind of you to visit," Jake says, removing his goggles.

The butler bows. "I'm afraid this isn't a social call, Master Jacob. By the way, you seem to have forgotten your swimming trunks...again."

He grins. "I wouldn't say I've *forgotten* them. I find that Speedos rather constrict my endowment, thus shrinking my enjoyment of the water."

Abbot frowns slightly. "Quite, but a gentleman is always properly attired for the event at hand, and I believe the Olympics will require a swimsuit."

"Thanks for the reminder, so what can I do for you?"

The butler picks at some non-existent lint on his sleeve. "Not to be indiscrete, but your father and step-mother are speaking to a lawyer in the drawing room."

"And what is the topic of conversation?" he asks.

"Your fate, I'm afraid. I thought you might like to weigh in on the matter before it's decided."

He climbs out of the pool as Abbot modestly holds up a thick terrycloth robe. "What would your advice be?"

"Get as far away from this estate and these people as is humanly possible. Europe is my recommendation."

Jake laughs, swinging an arm around the gentleman. "And why don't you follow that same advice, sir?"

"Unfortunately, I made a promise to your grandfather to look after the Weston family, at least until you inherit... which I can assure you is not an easy pledge to keep in the current environment."

"We could kill them, you know. A little arsenic in their morning coffee, a bit of nightshade mixed into the croissants...and we could put the blame to Monsieur Dezo in the kitchens."

They walk to a marble-tiled changing room where Jacob puts on a white cashmere sweater and skinny jeans.

"Ah, if wishing could make it so. But I'm fairly certain it's considered a breach of the servant's code of conduct to poison your masters."

"Probably right. And the butler is always the first to be suspected." He checks his look in the mirror and winks at his old friend and mentor. "Let's just keep that plan in reserve in case everything goes tits up for me downstairs."

Mr. Abbot smiles at his charge. "Very good, sir."

CHAPTER 2:   JACOB

As soon as I enter the lavish, wood-paneled sitting room the conversation abruptly stops. The telltale sign. My father's lawyer holds a bone china teacup precariously in his lap with a stack of brochures and papers beside him.

"Ah, Jacob," my father says, "we were just discussing your future. You remember Mr. Caldwell, don't you?"

I regard the overweight little attorney with a curt nod. "Hello."

My stepmother has a smug look on her face which hints that I will strongly dislike whatever scheme they are about to suggest.

"As I was telling your parents, there are several fine military academies on the east coast where you can continue to train, and also complete your educational requirements before moving on to university. Camden is our first choice; they have a fifty-meter pool."

I smile and walk over to the bar, pouring myself two fingers of Macallan sixty-four, which I quickly swallow. "Do they?" I ask calmly. "I won't be attending any military establishment."

My father's face begins to redden and he looks as if he's about to stomp his feet. "You're sixteen young man and you will go where I tell you."

Abbot knocks twice on the door and enters carrying a silver platter with scones and biscuits which he deposits on the coffee table. He then stands resolutely next to the grand piano.

"Abbot," my father implores, "what do you think? Wouldn't the discipline of a military environment do Jacob some good after his disgraceful expulsion from Trinity?"

"Only if your desire is to heap further embarrassment upon the Weston name, sir."

"What? What are you saying, man?"

It is a marvel to watch Blake Abbot work a room. He cuts an imposing figure with his perfectly tailored suit and closely cropped salt-and-pepper hair. "People need both time and space to forget the scandal young Master Weston ignited at Trinity. Sending him to a military academy in the vicinity, which he will undoubtedly despise, will only bring about more, possibly worse, antics. Enroll him somewhere he will thrive, and more importantly, somewhere far away from here. Eton, or Harrow...something along those lines."

You can see the cogs and wheels moving in my father's puny brain. He relishes the idea of an ocean separating us. "Caldwell?" he asks.

"Yes, naturally we contacted the top UK boarding schools. Because of Jacob's exceptional academic scores and athletic abilities..."

"Not to mention all my money," my father interjects.

"Yes," the lawyer chirps, "and that. Eton would welcome him for the Lent Half, which begins in mid-January. Their academics are legendary, and their athletic facilities are second to none."

"But that's months away," my tiny, bat-faced step-mother complains.

"I'm sure I can find plenty to do around here to amuse myself," I say, combing my wet hair with my fingers and looking out at the view over Central Park.

My parents exchange worried looks.

"There is White Oak," Caldwell says quietly. Abbot glances at me and signals his approval.

"White Oak?" my father asks.

"A charming school with extremely high standards. It's about fifteen miles outside of London in the countryside. Quite exclusive. They have agreed to enroll Jacob immediately if he commits to finishing his Sixth Form with them. He would be preparing for A-levels."

"And his training? We need him to stay in top shape for competition."

Caldwell consults his notes. "White Oak has a twenty-five-meter pool and of course, Jacob can make scheduled workouts at the London Aquatics Center in Stratford. It's less than twenty miles away."

My father turns his gaze upon me. "Will you behave?"

"I'll do my best, sir."

Out of the corner of my eye I can see our butler smiling.

"Caldwell, make the arrangements," my father orders. "Abbot, get him whatever he needs to look like a proper English gentleman. I want him on the plane by the end of the week."

CHAPTER 3: FULTON

It's rather unusual to be called up to the Headmaster's cottage on a Saturday for afternoon tea so I simply assume that he wants something...and of course I'm right. His attractive, young wife Barbara serves us and makes a quick exit to her winter garden.

"Gentlemen," Rothwell says, smoothing his manicured beard, "so good of you both to join me."

"Not at all, Headmaster," says Michael Blackmore. The Housemaster at St. John's is a scrawny, nervous academic and an avid boot-licker. I place a biscuit on my plate and gently stir my tea.

"We'll be admitting a late arrival to White Oak this week and I need you to help him find his sea legs." He hands us each a file on the boy. "You'll find he's a cracking lad. Exceptional in every respect."

"From New York City?" I ask.

"Precisely."

"Jacob Weston," Blackmore says aloud. "Is he one of *the* Westons?" which is an obvious question, even for a history professor.

"The heir apparent," Rothwell motions.

"Excuse me, Headmaster," I ask. "Why is he coming to us mid-half? He'll be at a disadvantage from the other boys."

Rothwell stands and places his hands behind his back. The Headmaster stays fit; he could still play rugby with the lads. I watch him as he looks out to the steeple of the old stone church. His wife is outside trimming some vines. "Confidentially, Gentlemen, he was recently expelled from one of the best prep schools in the United States."

Blackmore looks intrigued. "On what grounds?"

Rothwell considers us intently. "Let's just say, Conduct Unbecoming and leave it there." At those two words I feel droplets of sweat dripping down my side. "I'm assigning him to St. John's which is why you are present, Mr. Blackmore."

"But we haven't any vacancies this term."

"Being Headmaster, I am aware of your occupancy." He takes up his prized cricket bat and touches its smooth, polished wood. "Mr. Weston's father has generously taken over the lease at Brigsley Cottage for the duration, and St. John's is the nearest house."

"Nice accommodations for a sixteen-year-old," I mutter.

Blackmore shakes his head. "If you don't mind living with the ghost."

Rothwell sighs. "Please don't fill the boy's head with all that tosh. You are excused Michael."

As Blackmore quietly leaves the Headmaster pours himself some more tea; he waves at his wife through the window.

"So why am I here?" I ask plainly.

"This young man is a genius in an unconventional sort of way, T.J. I'm told he has a real affinity for literature. I want you to guide him in his pursuits."

I stand and reach over the desk to shake his hand. "I'll certainly do everything I can to help."

"I'd appreciate that, Mr. Fulton."

"Just one other question: Are we paying special attention because this lad is brilliant, or because he's exceedingly wealthy?"

Headmaster Stillman T. Rothwell silently gazes toward the chapel again and grins.

CHAPTER 4: JACOB

He's young for a professor, I think. And not bad looking, if he'd shave that ridiculous mustache. TJ Fulton. Recipient of the Clarendon Scholarship at Oxford where he was in Magdalen College, graduating with high honors... He will do nicely.

"I hope you'll be happy here," he says, leading me into the Victorian lecture hall where a group of boys are already joking around with each other. "Gentlemen," he shouts to get their attention, "I'd like you all to meet Mr. Jacob Weston, who comes to us from *New* England."

The group seems welcoming, and I'm used to being the odd boy out at boarding school; certainly I could take any two of them in a brawl.

"Mr. Ashlock, you are in St. John's, are you not?"

And that is when we are introduced. Timothy James Ashlock, a boy so pretty he could make an angel weep.

"I am, Professor," he answers.

"I wonder if you wouldn't mind taking Mr. Weston here under your wing until he's up to speed."

"With pleasure, sir." He ushers me to the carved desk next to his, halfway up the creaky wooden amphitheater. We shake hands along the way. "Jacob, is it?"

"Jake," I say and he smiles. He's so distracting I may forget what day it is.

"I know the setting here is a bit much, but we try not to take ourselves too seriously."

"Thank God."

I steal a sidelong glance at him. His hair is as dark as a raven's wing, his skin as pale as a glass of warm milk. Ah, the English lads.

"We've been delving into some twentieth century French authors: Jean-Dominique Bauby and Saint-Exupery who you'll want to get a handle on because there's no bluffing your way out with Fulton. He knows his onions when it comes to modern lit."

I chuckle.

"What?"

"He *knows his onions,* does he?"

"Welcome to old England."

Fulton stands behind the lectern and looks up, and then directly at me.

"In honor of our newest arrival, the next author we'll be studying is an American." There is a murmur among the boys. "Can anyone guess who I think is the most influential American novelist of the twentieth century?"

A chubby boy in the front row raises his hand.

"Mr. Ferguson."

"Melville?"

"Oh, please. That would be far too obvious."

"Twain," another boy shouts out.

"No, Mr. Wood, and raise your hand next time."

Timothy raises his hand.

"Mr. Ashlock, and it better be good."

"F. Scott Fitzgerald."

"That is good, but no." Fulton catches my eye. "Mr. Weston, you are our honorary American, and although you don't know my tastes, would you care to wager a guess?"

"Salinger," I say without hesitation.

He cocks his head and is silent for a moment while he considers me. "You are correct. Extraordinary. How did you work that out?"

I look back at him, debating whether to tip my hand or not. Finally, I give him what he wants. "You're under thirty, wanting to be the trendy professor with the mustache and the red sports car. What could be cooler than to teach a bunch of teen posh boys a novel where the protagonist is a sixteen-year-old prep school dropout? Not to mention the judicious use of the word *fuck* throughout the book."

This seems to stun the class. Even my new friend Timothy is staring at me with his mouth agape.

"You know Salinger then?"

"I do, sir. But I don't think *Catcher* is his best work."

"Interesting. And what, in your learned opinion, is his best?"

I'm enjoying this Socratic exchange.

"*A Perfect Day For Bananafish*, Professor."

"Okay," Fulton says. "Let's all read Mr. Weston's favorite Salinger piece by Guy Fawkes Day. That's next Tuesday, gentlemen."

***

After class we gather our things and head to the dining hall (nicknamed The Buttery) for lunch. A few of the lads pat me on the back and introduce themselves while we're queuing up for the day's fare, which is lasagna. Timothy and I head for a window table, facing the Great Lawn.

"You honestly are quite mad, Jake," he says, tucking into his meal with abandon.

I shrug. "I like Fulton, otherwise I wouldn't have given him the time of day."

"Well, I've never heard a boy use the word *fuck* in front of a beak."

"Beak?"

"Teacher. A beak is a teacher. And then to get him to assign the short where Seymour Glass blows his brains out in the last paragraph. That's blinding work on your first day."

I smile, studying his cheekbones, waiting for the sparkle of his clear blue eyes. "You already know the story then?"

He rolls those eyes. "You're not the only one with a brain."

"Here and I thought you were just another pretty face," I tease.

"Not just," he says and winks.

I could die.

CHAPTER 5: TIMOTHY

I'm not exactly sure what to make of him yet. He seems to genuinely like me, but that might be just because he's gay. He doesn't even try to hide the fact, which you've got to admire a bit. Most of the St. Johnnies are so thick they haven't realized his dark truth...not yet anyway.

Jake is certainly unique. No one can catch him in the pool, no one. He's as fast as a dolphin and as strong as the senior lads. He's younger than me but nearly twice my size. He's smarter than the beaks and richer than God Himself. What the bloody hell is he doing at White Oak Academy? You'd figure him for Eton surely, at least I would.

I'm trying not to like him too much. I know more than a few rich toffs. They are careless with their toys and easily distracted. I don't want to be gluing back together my broken heart while he's boarding his private jet.

CHAPTER 6: ROTHWELL

Paddy Lester, the groundskeeper and I are up early for the hunt. We like to thin out the population of deer that roam the property every winter looking for food.

"Seen a group drinking from the river yesterday at dusk," he tells me. We head toward the bridge.

"Any bucks?" I ask hopefully.

"I'm sure you'll find something suitable for your wall, Stillman."

He knows me too well. "Have you thought about my proposal?" he asks.

"Yes," I answer. "What you grow in the lower greenhouse is of no concern to me...just make sure I get my full cut of the profits. And if by some strange happenstance you are found out..."

"I know, I know," he says. "You had no idea what your groundsman was doing. You're a broken record."

We crouch down and watch. The mist is slowly rising. Lester takes aim, fires and a tremendous white-tailed doe drops down dead. "And you, old man, are a stone cold killer," I tell him.

"That will be fine eating," he says, taking out his ancient Buck knife. "Now why don't you help me do a field dressing on that beautiful animal like I taught you when you were fifteen."

CHAPTER 7: TIMOTHY

The common room at St. John's is decorated for All Hallows Eve and Guy Fawkes tonight. The power has been coming on and off all day, so no one really knows what's going to happen during the festivities. Matron Finlay has been recruiting decorators from among us so the hall is strewn with orange and black balloons, cutout spiders, witches and crepe paper streamers. She seems pleased with the results, as random as they are.

Blackmore loves to think that St. John's has the most *esprit-de-corps* of all the houses, but that's highly debatable. Someone has dug up a bunch of Fawkes masks, which I personally think are creepy...like clowns.

Peter Chadwick, our Head-Boy, is running around giving orders while in full costume. He's come as Braveheart, complete with kilt and blue-painted face. It's a good outfit, but he wears it every year. He was born to be a military leader like his father and grandfather. Chadwick is intent on games...more precisely, on winning them. He's acquired massive wooden barrels and filled them with water for apple-bobbing.

I've come dressed as Austin Powers. Lame, I know, but I'm skint so it's all I can afford. I had the thick black glasses already, and a frilly white shirt from one of the string ensembles I play in.

Blackmore is a wizard, which may seem a bit cliché but every boarding school in England has a bit of a Hogwarts vibe, what with the houses, robes and endless stone passageways.

I'm curious if he'll come; I wonder if anyone even bothered to invite him.

The first year's are scrambling around like madmen all hopped up on sugar. There's going to be a prize this year for the Best Costume.

Chadwick and Blackmore start to arrange teams. We'll be playing darts and bobbing for apples.

Matron Finlay pours me a cup of hot cider. "You look nervous, Timothy," she says.

"Do I?" I notice myself fidgeting with my shirt. "I guess I'm just excited for the party."

It would be rude if no one invited him and he's just sitting in that cottage all alone, right?

"First years! All you little shells. Time for the apple bob," Chadwick announces. We use our blue and black striped neckties to bind the hands of the participants behind their backs. It's pretty funny to see ten-year-olds trying to get their mouths around apples.

I'm thinking I'll just pop over and see if he wants to visit the party. I'm halfway out when Jake strides in. All he's wearing are gold wrestling boots and a matching Speedo. He's put a bit of oil and glitter on his muscles to maximize the effect. He barely gets one foot in the doorway when the wolf-whistles and cat-calls ensue.

"Better not leave yet, *Austin*," he says to me grinning. "The party is just getting started..."

Chadwick rushes over. "What the hell are you supposed to be?"

"Don't tell me you haven't seen *The Rocky Horror Picture Show*? It's a classic Halloween film," Jake says, "unlike *Braveheart*."

He looks fantastic. I mean, if you've got it, flaunt it. "You must be freezing your stones off," I mention.

"It's the price one pays for shock and awe, Mr. Powers."

Blackmore looks like he may faint.

"Hello Professor Blackmore, you look terrific. Dumbledore, is it?" I mean, honestly, it's a surreal moment. I'm wondering if Jake will have us all doing the "Time Warp" before the party is finished.

"Weston," he says. "Your costume is highly...exotic."

"I'm taking that as a compliment."

Billy, dressed as Spiderman, cannot stop laughing as he pats Jacob on the back. "This party is knees up, best one I can remember."

Jake turns to me. "Knees up?"

"Add it to the list," I say.

The only one who doesn't seem to be having fun anymore is William Wallace. Blackmore announces that they have reached our block with the bobbing. The Sixth Forms are those of us from age sixteen to eighteen. I think it would be fun to go against Jake.

"You and me?" I ask, pointing to one of the barrels.

He smiles broadly. "I'll kick your ass. Tie my hands!"

When we are set, Blackmore places us on either side of the barrel. "You've got this," Chadwick says to me.

"Go!" he yells.

Jake shoves his head into the water and in two seconds comes up with a red-delicious clenched in his teeth. I pull my dripping face out and smirk. "Impressive."

Peter quickly pushes me out of the way. "Tie my hands," he demands. "You and me, Weston. Right now!"

"I've got my apple. I don't want to play again," he says.

"Coward!"

Jake just chuckles. Blackmore says, "I'd remind you, Chadwick, that you are two years Weston's senior."

He's seething. "I've got an idea. A wager," he says.

Jacob looks intrigued. "You've got my attention."

"Boys," Blackmore interjects, "you know we don't allow gambling."

"A thousand pounds!" Chadwick shouts. "Loser gives a grand to the London Food Bank!"

Blackmore consents. "A worthy charity."

"I'm in, let's do it," Jake says, hands still bound.

"Not bobbing for apples," Peter says. "You're supposed to be a glorious swimmer. Whoever can hold their breath the longest."

Jake's eyebrows raise. "Are you sure, Chadwick?"

"Absolutely."

They position themselves over the barrel. Weston is taking quick shallow breaths in preparation. We all look to a clock over the doorway and when the second hand reaches the top, Blackmore shouts, "Begin!"

Both boys plunge their heads underwater and the room goes still. The first minute passes without either of them moving a muscle. When the time closes in and the second minute elapses, the Housemaster looks decidedly concerned.

"Perhaps we should call it a draw, gentlemen."

Neither budges. The boys watching have started to whisper excitedly to one other. I stare as tiny bubbles break the surface and Chadwick begins to dance around. I think this challenge is coming to an end.

At two minutes, forty seconds Peter comes up gasping for air. His face is crimson...and yet Jacob remains submersed. Every boy in St. John's is mesmerized.

"It's some kind of trick," Peter barks. He's really keyed up. He stands behind him, and then loses his mind. He pushes Weston's head further into the barrel, forcing him to stay underwater. Jake thrashes and jerks around, his legs twitching and then he goes completely limp.

The clock hits three minutes before anyone does anything! I run full-tilt at Chadwick, pushing him away. Jake is motionless.

I reach in and pull him out of the barrel and lay him prone on the floor. He's unconscious and I'm thinking I'll have to perform CPR.

His eyes suddenly pop open and he exhales loudly. "Did I win?"

Everyone starts cheering. I can't believe this bloke. Meanwhile Blackmore is giving Chadwick a furious dressing down, flapping his arms wildly in his wizard garb. I catch the terms: *unsportsmanlike* and *dangerous* before drifting away.

We go over to get some chocolate cupcakes from the Matron. "Were you about to go mouth-to-mouth on me?"

"Maybe."

"My hero," he jests. "I'd have stayed dormant if I knew that was coming."

"How in God's name did you manage it?"

He shrugs. "I'm a freak. But being completely still underwater is easier than swimming. Swimming uses up oxygen fast."

Chadwick reluctantly comes over. "Suppose you heard him slagging me off. Blackie won't let it go until I apologize... So..."

"Accepted," Jake says instantly. "Hey, mate. No hard feelings. Truce." He holds out a hand.

Chadwick bows politely and shakes. "Bygones be bygones."

"I'll tell you what," Jake offers, "I'll add my grand to the food bank...if you show us what you've got on under the kilt."

Peter looks at once confused, offended and then amused. He lifts the skirt up exposing his bare bum.

"Degenerate," he says.

We laugh.

"Money well spent," Jake says.

CHAPTER 8: BRIGSLEY COTTAGE

He gets up in the middle of the night to stoke the fire. The northeasterly wind has been blowing wet, polar air down from Scandinavia, resulting in an ice storm that has downed the power lines to all of White Oak.

It's strictly candles and flashlights for awhile. He pads around the cottage which is far too big for a boy alone. Truth be told, he misses his mum, and Mr. Abbot. He'd call the old gentleman if his phone battery hadn't died four hours ago.

The hair rises on the back of his neck and gooseflesh covers his arms as he senses that he's being watched. A cold draft wafts through the cottage filled with the smell of night jasmine and chimney smoke, moss and the evergreen forest.

"Hello?" he calls to the darkness...but no one answers.

He approaches the leaded windows at the front of the living room while frozen rain pelts the glass. The inky blackness is impenetrable. Jacob reaches his hand out, placing his fingertips on the cold panes.

"Hello?" he whispers again.

Thunderclaps roar as a sudden flash of lightning reveals a boy outside, drenched to the bone, gazing in. Jacob jumps back with a muffled scream.

"Jesus Christ!" he yells. He sprints to the door grabbing his raincoat and flashlight from the sideboard. Standing in the open doorway, with the wind howling through the trees, he casts the yellow beam back and forth, revealing no one.

"Come inside and get warm," he tells the darkness, "come inside."

But the other boy has vanished, and Jacob's invitation (at least for now) remains unanswered.

CHAPTER 9: BLACKMORE

One feels a sense of responsibility, and frankly honor, to have a boy like Jacob Weston under my care. As the Housemaster it's really my duty to check in on him every day, and I try to, but Brigsley Cottage is such a bother...still, he's only sixteen and needs my supervision.

I knock at the door, which I really needn't do, and let myself in. The boy is sitting on the floor wearing only pajama bottoms.

"Professor Blackmore," he says, getting up and grabbing his robe, "I was hoping you'd come by."

"How nice of you to say, Weston. We missed you at breakfast and I hear you did not show up for your swim workout, so I'm here to see if you're feeling alright."

"Ah, yes. I'm fine, just didn't get much sleep," he says. "May I offer you some Earl Grey?"

"That would be grand," I answer. "You were quite the hit at the party last night. The boys are still talking about it."

He laughs and I see him glance over at his Best Costume trophy on the mantle. "It was fun."

The old-fashioned kettle has been rigged over the fire. He's a resourceful lad considering he's worth billions.

"This storm has truly cut us off at the knees. The Headmaster is saying that power will be fully restored today." I watch as he bends and pours me a steaming cup. He's much bigger than the other boys in his form. Americans, honestly. He looks like a fashion model with his chiseled features and long blond hair. I'm told he's headed for the Olympics. "So how are you settling in?"

"Quite well, sir. Thank you."

"Missing home, I imagine?"

"A bit," he nods. "Does the electricity often go out?"

I sigh. "The school is 400 years old, so we have our share of leaky pipes and blown fuses. The Buttery has a backup generator, so we can always seek refuge there."

"I'm thinking of sending out to London for one of those myself," he says. Cheeky monkey.

"I understand you've hired a professional coach to help with your training."

He looks absently through the windows to the bare birch trees beyond. "Oh, yes, the Headmaster has agreed. It's my father's doing, I'm afraid. I'll go to London twice weekly. They are trying to get me prepared for competition."

"How exciting it would be," I say, "to be an Olympian."

He looks rather bored by the prospect. "That all seems a lifetime away."

I take the key from my pocket. "Headmaster Rothwell instructed me to give you this."

He turns it over in his hand. "What's it unlock?"

"The White Oak pool, of course, Ducker. You now have access anytime, day or night."

"Thank you, Professor."

"You're one of only three students that possess a key, so please don't abuse the privilege or it will be revoked." I stand up. "I guess I'll leave you to it. You have Latin and Philosophy this afternoon?"

"Yes."

"Don't miss class. And please have your dirty laundry bagged and near the door by six. Tonight there will be a mandatory assembly at Deerfield Hall observing All Saints Day. Eight sharp. You represent St. John's, so press your tails and arrive shipshape in Bristol fashion."

He stares at me, and I can tell that something is troubling him. "Sir," he ventures.

"What is it?" I ask, "what's wrong, lad?"

I sense his reluctance. "It's nothing, just that last night during the storm, I saw a boy outside my window."

"What hour?" I demand.

"Half past three, I suppose."

"Impossible," I say.

"Impossible?" he asks.

"Well, *improbable* at least. Did you recognize him?"

"No. And when I ran outside he had disappeared. His uni was soaked through and through."

I touch his shoulder. "May I tell you something in the strictest confidence, Weston?"

"Of course."

"What you may have seen is a ghost."

He laughs right in my face! "Professor Blackmore, that is utter nonsense. It has to be some Halloween prank because I'm the new arrival."

"Perhaps," I say, just as two boys come charging through the doorway. William Redgrave and Colin Hunter.

"Oh excuse us sir, we didn't mean to interrupt."

"I was just leaving, Redgrave. What mischief are you lads up to?"

"No mischief, just thought we'd have a run into the woods and show Jake the tree."

I place my teacup down on the table. "A fine idea for a chilly morning." Leaning toward Weston I whisper, "Try lighting a few candles and watch what happens. There are more things in heaven and earth..."

CHAPTER 10: JACOB

"What the hell was old Blackie doing here? Checking up on you, was he?" Colin teases.

"It's his job," I say. "I am a St. John's boy even if I'm not under the same roof."

"Spawny for you," Billy says. "They got us packed like sardines over there. Poor Timmy is locked away in the turret like bloody Rapunzel."

"Freezing his arse off while he tortures that fiddle. At least you have a fireplace, mate. Count your blessings."

"I do," I say. "So, what's all this about a tree?"

***

I rummage around Brigsley until I find a pair of mostly-clean sweats and my trainers. Even as sleep-deprived as I am, I know a brisk run will do me good.

We take off following an icy trail that begins right behind the cottage fence and leads out toward the Tydell river. I glance around hoping for some sign of last night's visitor but all I see are birch and alder trees growing so closely together we can barely run side by side. Our breathing fogs the cold air, as our laughter shatters the morning stillness.

Billy is in St. John's so I see him often enough; boys usually hang around their own houses. Colin is in Exeter, but he's a good athlete and I've noticed him lolling about the pool. It's hard to miss his flaming red hair and freckled torso. I know this outing is meant as a test. They see that I'm a big guy, but they probably wonder how strong and fast I truly am. Billy only knows that I can hold my breath for a long time.

I allow Colin to set the pace, but as we get to an incline I decide to step it up a notch. Five minutes later I've soundly outdistanced them both as I hear the panting, spitting and cursing of adolescent defeat. It's then that I see the tree.

It's still a quarter mile on, but it's distinct. An English oak, sitting alone on a knoll, the branches as white as winter snow. I sprint the rest of the way to it. A short time later the lads have joined me.

"You run like the Devil himself is chasing you," Billy says and Colin heartily agrees.

"Rothwell would certainly be chuffed if you joined rugby."

"I've got enough on my plate with swimming three hours a day, thank you very much," I say. "What do you reckon makes it so white?" I touch its pale, twisted trunk.

Colin quickly slaps my hand away, shaking his head.

"Dunno what gives it this pallor," says Billy. "One story says it was struck by lightning a century ago. Others say it's a freak, an albino, or possibly just dead."

"It's a *ghost tree*," Colin whispers.

"What did you say?"

Colin stands close enough to me that I can feel the heat radiating from his body and smell his sweat. "Ghost. Tree," he repeats crisply in my face. "As in, white as a ghost."

I stretch my hamstrings out, trying to appear nonchalant. "It's just odd that you use that particular word because I think I saw a ghost at Brigsley last night during the storm." I wait for them to laugh (or mock me) but the fact is they both look a tad uneasy.

"Was he a skinny little chap dressed in the school's kit?" Redgrave asks, and Hunter shoves him.

"You know what we were told," he warns.

"Crikey though, he saw it on All Hallows Eve! Bloody Thump the Door Night! It seems unsporting not to give fair warning when he's sleeping in the haunted fucking cottage every night. He's our new mate, after all."

"Are you two having a go at me? Because I can take a good punking the same as the next boy. I mean, well played gents, but it's over. Come clean."

Billy pulls me aside. "Listen Jake, I've been living at St. John's since I was eleven-years-old and I've had the shit scared out of me every halve. Can't be sure of it, but seems like you saw Tommy Walker." I look in his wide brown eyes and I can see his pupils are dilated. Billy is frightened and he's telling me the truth. "And trust me, there are worse spooks than Tommy rattling around this old school."

We both watch Colin's red hair wagging as he sprints back down the hill. "Just remember that I never said a word," he shouts back at us.

CHAPTER 11: FULTON

Speaking as a teacher, you meet a mind like his just once in a generation. His ability to compare works of literature from different periods and distill similarities of theme and significance are like nothing I've seen since Oxford. He's started writing his first novel, titled, *Brilliant Flames*. But young Jacob Weston is troubled. He's fixated, obsessed even, with suicide.

CHAPTER 12:   JACOB

Deerfield Hall is a Gothic monstrosity of the Perpendicular phase, as I was told by Oliver Morgan, the prefect that gave me the tour nearly a week ago, (although I don't think he used the term monstrosity).   The polished wood and stone trappings are meant to be both imposing and uncomfortable, which they are.   Deerfield is one of the few venues where all 500 of the happy White Oak campers can get together to give speeches, sing songs, and pray for those less fortunate than ourselves.

It's truly odd to see everyone in one place.   The professors are wearing long black robes and sit together like a murder of crows near the dais. All of us boys are togged up in striped trousers and tailcoats trying desperately not to feel as ridiculous as we look.

Like most boarding schools in the UK there are color designations to ties and waistcoats which denote special achievement or talent.   Top athletes are awarded black bow ties and grey waistcoats, while great musicians and artists get maroon ties and vests.   There's a whole other realm of accessories for prefects and monitors which I can't keep straight and don't give a shit about.   The privileged faces around me are at once both innocent and worldly.   There's some bizarre hierarchy in the way we are seated too, but I can't for the life of me tell which seats are more holy than others.

The musical director is a fussy little man named Veltie Gartland, who leads us in a dissonant rendition of the school anthem: *Boys of White Oak Through the Land.*

I'm not kidding.

Our priest, Father Hodgson, gives a brief invocation. He looks old enough to have known several of the original

Apostles. He's just marking time until Death comes calling his name.

Next up is Headmaster Rothwell, who searches the place trying to make eye-contact with me, which is just weird. His speech is so boring I can barely remember five words of it; something about martyrs, and Rayed Manus Dei.

Thankfully, I've managed to work my way next to Ashlock, who is proving to be a harder nut to crack than I'd first anticipated. I love it when they play hard to get. We are sharing one of the White Oak hymnals so my fingers brush up against his every now and then...accidentally of course.

"You must come 'round to my cottage later," I tell him.

"Must I? Whatever for?"

"Because you're beautiful and brilliant and obviously rather poor... all the things I'm attracted to," I whisper.

"This is an expensive school, what makes you think I'm poor?"

I press my shoulder against his and lean in. "Your shoes have been resoled and your jacket has been mended twice. You're far too thin, which means you don't eat here year round. It's nothing to be ashamed of, Ashlock. We are all victims of circumstance. And anyway, if you were just another posh tosser I'd have no use for you."

His cheeks redden a bit and he laughs quietly to himself. "But aren't you just another posh tosser, Mr. *Weston*?" (my last name getting that extra little shove of sarcasm).

"More or less," I answer, "but I don't pretend to be anything else."

***

When the All Saints Day observances draw to a close, Timothy and I sprint directly from Deerfield to Brigsley Cottage. It's begun sleeting and we've both managed to forget our brollies.

"I've always wanted to see the inside of this place," he says.

I rub my hands together as we enter. "I'm chilled to the bone and wetter than a beaver's hat. This formal wear isn't intended for use during ice storms."

"That's why they call these jackets Bum-Freezers," he explains.

I throw two logs onto the dying embers of the fire while he admires the room; touching the furniture, the lamps, the books. He picks up a framed photo of my mother and me.

"Your mum?"

I nod thoughtfully. "Yes, mugging on the observation deck of the Empire State Building. Happier times."

"You're so young."

"I remember that day vividly. I was twelve. Three weeks later she was dead."

I run upstairs to my room and grab two sets of sweats from my dresser. I toss a pair down to him. "Here."

We both strip all our wet gear off in front of the open hearth.

"It's not polite to stare," he mentions.

"You're bruised," I say.

He twists his back so he can see his own ass. "Courtesy of our Headmaster. I take it you haven't been introduced to his infamous cricket bat yet."

I look away. "My God this place is medieval. What on earth did you do?"

"It doesn't matter," he sighs.

"Light the candles and I'll make us some snacks," I say. "There's something we need to discuss."

Thankfully the electricity is up again so I prepare microwave popcorn. The real surprise is something I've been saving: a decanter of Louis XIII Cognac smuggled over from France. I pour two double-shots into tumblers.

"If they catch you with that you won't be able to sit down for a week," Timothy warns.

"Then we best finish off as much as we can tonight." We clink our glasses together.

"To all the dead saints and martyrs," I toast. The mantle clock strikes ten.

"This really is awfully kind of you," he says softly, looking positively devastating in my old NYU hoodie.

"Generosity is the essence of friendship," I quote. I pour us two more shots.

Tim lifts his glass. "Your health," he says.

"All Hallows, then All Saints," I count off, "and tomorrow is All Souls, right?"

"You are correct, old chum. Cheers." He downs the cognac. "This has a lovely warming effect," he says, inspecting the color of the liquor, "I can feel it down to my toes."

"I'm glad you're enjoying it." I stoke the fire. "So you play the violin."

"Did you deduce that from the callouses on my left hand?"

"Not exactly," but now I am looking at his elegant white fingers. He bites his nails. "I'm dying to hear you play."

He scoffs. "I'm sure you'll be forced to. They make me fiddle for my supper around here. I'm on a musical, slash, academic scholarship."

"You must be exceptionally gifted."

He blushes.

"You can be the judge. The lads in St. John's say it sounds like I'm strangling a cat."

I sit down beside him.

"So tell me what you know about Tommy Walker."

He laughs out loud and stuffs his face with popcorn. "You're joking, right?"

"I saw him last night...on All Hallows Eve."

"Probably some blokes having a laugh on your account," he says.

"That was my theory at first...but not anymore."

"Then you've gone round the bend, mate," he sings, *"Tommy Walker wandered...into the darkened wood..."* and chuckles. "I thought that was just a rhyme they told first years so they wouldn't venture too far away."

"It's folklore then?"

"Entirely."

"But was he a student here? Did a Tommy Walker exist?"

"Who knows?" he shrugs. "The story, as I heard it, was that he wandered off, or was snatched, and was never heard from again. So his lonely spirit haunts the school, specifically Brigsley Cottage. It's a load of tripe."

"Really?" I ask. "How many candles did you light when we came in?"

He quickly glances around the room. "All of them."

"Yet now two have been blown out."

We both stare at a pair of extinguished tapers leaving thin trails of smoke curling into the air.

"You're barking, Weston, you truly are."

"He never lets one stay lit for more than an hour," I state matter-of-factly. I've done my research.

"I'm sure it has nothing to do with the drafty nature of old cottages," my skeptical new friend remarks. I walk around and turn off the lamps so we are left in candle and firelight alone. It's rather romantic.

"Tommy Walker," I call, "if you can hear me, blow out the rest."

A sudden gust of chilled air sweeps through the room taking the flames from all the remaining candles leaving only the fireplace as illumination. We share a tense moment as I watch shadows dance across Tim's worried brow.

"Bloody hell," he whispers.

CHAPTER 13: TIMOTHY

Jake has decided to walk me back to St. John's... I think we're both a bit trollied. For some ungodly reason he wants to see the hovel I call home.

The turret which Blackmore assigned me to isn't even a proper room. Originally, it was meant as a sort of military fortification, perhaps giving the old building a defensive posture should the Vikings ever decide to invade England again. There's just enough room for a single mattress and a small desk. My clothes are all folded in neat stacks because there isn't space for a wardrobe. The violin case and a loose pile of sheet music sit atop the only chair.

"Please don't mock," I beg.

Jacob takes a look around. "Sweet Jesus," he says, "you barely have enough room in here to cuff the carrot." He smirks.

"Is that your definition of *not mocking?*"

"Sorry. No we are here for the good of science, Ashlock." He's brought along a candle which he quickly lights and holds aloft.

"Tommy Walker," he shouts, "if you can hear me... blow this out."

Of course nothing happens.

"Interesting," Jake notes.

"Apparently I am phantom-free. That certainly takes a load off," I say.

"What is a ghost anyway?" Jake asks, blowing out the flame himself.

"Historically they are troubled souls."

"Exactly," he agrees, putting a drunken arm around my shoulder. "Restless spirits. Imagine this scenario: A White Oak lad goes missing, meeting some gruesome fate, and now he's forced to wander about Brigsley for all eternity... he seems to be confined there."

"Perhaps he just prefers it. Maybe it was his home," I venture.

Jake trips on a stack of my uniforms and then leans against my desk, he's far too big a bloke to be in this confined space. His feet are enormous. He opens the violin case and inspects my instrument. "That's a decent hypothesis," he says. "Of course, if we refer to our Poe, perhaps Little Tommy is buried under the floorboards...or even in the walls."

"Don't be morbid," I say. "In literature spirits almost always have a purpose. They are out for vengeance, trying to right some wrong inflicted upon them in life. It's personal. There's always a bit of unfinished business, which is why they don't willingly cross over."

Jake smiles, threading his fingers through his thick blond hair. "You're glorious, Ashlock, you little ripper," he says. "You know what we're going to do?"

"I'm afraid to ask," I mutter.

"We're going to solve Tommy Walker's murder."

CHAPTER 14: JACOB

Yes, I'm smitten. He's charming, clever and just a bit sad. I find him irresistible.

"I have a plan," I say.

Tim's refolding a stack of sweaters that I bumped over. He looks up. "Let's hear it then."

"First, pack up all your gear. You're moving in with me."

"Absolutely not."

"Not afraid of ghosts, are you, Ashlock?" I tease. "Listen, it makes perfect sense. The cottage is a piece of this puzzle, and I need you around to bounce ideas off. You have far too little space in here, and I have far too much over there. Brigsley has three bedrooms, for Christ's sake!"

"Perfect," he says, "one for you, one for me and one for Tommy Walker."

"Hilarious. What's stopping you?"

"First, Blackmore will never sign off on it. He enjoys my misery here far too much."

I scoff. "Leave him to me. What else?"

I know where he's about to go.

"Second, I'm not going to sleep with you. I like you Weston, but I'm not gay."

I laugh at him. "Mon Chéri," I say, "hardly anyone is *Gay-gay* anymore. It's all about being bi-curious or simply not being placed in a box. Don't let others define you because to allow definition is to limit! You may not be full homo, but you're definitely on the spectrum, less so than I am, sadly, but your sexuality is fluid."

"Maybe so," he admits, "but if I move into Brigsley you'll be keeping your *fluids* to yourself."

"It's a deal," I say. "Pack your duffel while I go downstairs and give Blackmore an Oscar-worthy performance."

"You're not going to pay a call on the Housemaster when you're steaming drunk, are you?"

"He'll be none the wiser. I can hold my liquor, mate."

CHAPTER 15: BLACKMORE

Half past eleven on a blessed feast day and there's a knock at the door...there truly is no rest for the wicked. I'm surprised to find it's Jacob Weston calling.

"Sir," he begins, "I'm sorry to disturb you at this hour, I just have a rather pressing matter that I need your help with."

I usher him into my quarters and put on the kettle.

"Of course, my boy," I say, leading him to the parlor, "how can we be of service?"

He looks upset. "You were right Professor, about the ghost I mean. Tommy Walker won't leave me alone."

"I was afraid there might be an issue," I tell him. "We simply don't have a vacancy in the dormitory rooms or I'd put you up here immediately, I assure you."

"I understand completely. It's just that I was speaking to my father on the phone. I didn't tell him about the ghost."

"Please don't mention it," I say.

"No, he wouldn't understand. In fact, he'd probably have me out of White Oak tomorrow if he knew. Anyway, he was concerned about my living arrangements. You see, I spend so much time by myself training at Ducker, and then I'm alone again in Brigsley Cottage. He feels I'm not getting the authentic English boarding school experience."

"I see," I say, pouring hot tea, "so you would like me to assign a roommate?"

"I would, sir. I think if there was another flesh and blood boy about the rooms we'd have less trouble. I've mentioned the poltergeist to Timothy Ashlock and he doesn't seem to mind."

I really can't imagine Ashlock rooming with the child of a billionaire. I mean, he's a musician!

"Weston, that cottage is far too posh for the likes of Timothy Ashlock. Between you and I, he's one of our charity cases."

I watch him trembling as he holds his teacup. He must have had rather a fright, the poor child.

"Sir, Ashlock is in my form and he's been tutoring me in English. I know he's not my equal socially, but perhaps he could be a kind of valet in exchange for being able to let a room. I'm sure my father would greatly appreciate it if he knew I was being treated as a proper gentleman."

There's sound logic to that, of course. And I can see the terror the lad has of spending another night alone in that strange cottage. Perhaps this will even mean a bonus from old man Weston if he finds I'm doing my upmost to look after his heir. I try to appear as if I'm giving the matter careful consideration, when really I've already decided in his favor.

"You're a bright lad, Weston. Let's call in Matron Finlay and make her aware of the new arrangements. I'm confident she will appreciate the extra help with the chores at Brigsley."

"Thank you kindly. I'll sleep much better tonight."

Indeed, the lad seems to have had a burden lifted off his shoulders. He looks positively joyful.

"Not at all," I say, patting his back. "I hope the next time you speak with your father, you'll mention that you're being treated properly as a St. John's boy."

"I certainly will."

CHAPTER 16: LONDON

A Rolls-Royce Phantom VIII is waiting outside the iron gates of White Oak on Monday at five AM as Jacob comes sprinting down the path to meet it. He's wearing red Adidas sweats and carrying a leather workout bag.

The young chauffeur exits the idling car to open the door for his new client. He's heard of this family and he wants to make a good impression.

"Master Weston," he says, tipping his cap, "let me take your luggage." He reaches to place the bag in the trunk.

"Good morning," Jacob says, "and what is your name, if I may be so bold?"

"Ethan, sir. Ethan Polley at your service," and he bows.

"And you are to be my regular driver, twice weekly, at this ungodly hour?"

"Indeed, sir. I'll be taking you to the London Aquatic Center in Stratford and back."

"Okay," Jacob says. He shuts the back door of the sedan and opens the front one himself and climbs in. "Let's set a few ground rules, shall we?"

"Anything you please."

"Perfect. First, you can pull into the school and drive up to my cottage from now on. Secondly, when we are alone, which obviously will be most of the time, you are to call me Jake. No sirs or misters. I'll sit up front with you and we will converse like civilized gentlemen."

The chauffeur smiles. He pulls away, beginning the drive toward London.

"Anything else, Jake?"

"Yes," he continues, "a vehicle like this has a sizable trunk, correct?"

"It's as big as my first flat in Soho," Ethan remarks.

"Perfect! I'll occasionally need to store an item or two back there, with your permission; there will be substantial bonuses for my extra needs."

"Nothing illegal, I hope?" he asks with a worried look.

"Don't fret, Ethan. Nothing that will get you into any hot water, but I will need to make side excursions on our return trips from time to time...just shopping and the like, and I do require your complete discretion. Do you have any problems with my requests?"

"None, mate, none at all."

He pats the eager, young driver on the shoulder. "You and I are going to get along like a house on fire. So, whereabouts are you from?"

Ethan glances over at his new boss. "Manchester, but I live in Southwark now."

Jake motions. "I don't see a ring...not married?"

"Nah, not anymore. Married my childhood sweetheart when I was nineteen, but she told me to piss off a year ago."

"That's a pity," Jacob says, watching the countryside go by. "Still, there are plenty of fish in the sea."

CHAPTER 17: JACOB

My life from five-thirty to eight-thirty every morning belongs to Poseidon. The water has been my refuge ever since my mother passed away four years ago. I love the muffled sounds of the underwater world, where distractions all fade away and my mind can be free. The acrid smell of chloramines has become a perfume to me. The pool is my safe haven and it has become my truest home.

People knew early on that I was freakishly fast in the water. I seem to have been built for slicing through the liquid world. My father breeds thoroughbred racehorses so speed is something he notices. Here, finally, is an aspect of my life that he can comprehend, and even appreciate. Trophies and medals began to pile up. Experts were brought onto the payroll; coaches, doctors, dietitians. I learned the physics of swimming. The science and economy of a perfectly angled stroke and a well-timed kick. Seconds were shaved away from the heartless clock and people began to whisper the words Commonwealth and Pan Pacific until the Olympics became the final goal.

When I was fifteen I could hold my breath for over three minutes. Along the way the powers that be decided that the 400-Meter Freestyle would be my race. I would own it. The Australian swimmer Ian Thorpe is my hero. He won five Olympic gold medals, including the 400-M. They called him *The Thorpedo.* Ian Thorpe is also gay.

There is comfort in knowing that someone who understands the profound isolation of the pool; the countless, repetitive hours spent traveling thousands of kilometers in that wet embrace, also understood the lonely life of being a gay teen. When my lungs are burning and I can feel every heartbeat against my eardrums; when I really want to chuck it all, I think of *Thorpy* standing on that podium and waving. So maybe I can be a role model for some young swimmers in the future too.

I'm about to meet my new coach, an Irishman named Dylan Lir. I hope he knows his onions about the 400-M. Of course, when it comes down to it, I'm all alone in the water...and in the world. I've always thought that drowning would be a lovely way to die.

CHAPTER 18: DYLAN LIR

The new boy is on time, and that counts for something. I've read his splits and watched video on every race he's ever competed in. He's got a shot and there's no denying it, but money doesn't get you through the water any faster. I've got to test the lad, challenge him, and see what stuff he's made of.

He comes out of the locker room wearing one of the new Fastskin LZR Racer suits I've bought for him. It's a wonder of modern technology. A swimsuit with the sleek, hydrodynamic properties of sharkskin. The body-length version of this suit is banned from FINA competitions for giving an unfair advantage but swimmers can still compete in the jammers and it's my job to shave every millisecond for the boy. I blow my whistle and he comes running over, holding out his hand.

"I'm Jacob Weston, sir."

I refuse to shake. "You can call me Coach, or Coach Lir. Nothing else."

He grins at me.

"What do you think you're smiling at, Weston?"

His expression turns serious. "Absolutely nothing, Coach. Thanks for the first-rate suits, by the way."

"Yeah, yeah," I turn my back on him. "You can thank your rich daddy for the magical Speedo jammers, but a bit of reduced skin friction isn't going to buy you a gold medal. Jump in the water."

He smoothly enters the pool without a splash. "So let's watch the rich boy swim," I yell.

His expression just changed. It was subtle, but I saw it just as he was adjusting his goggles...he's embarrassed about the money. That's a bit of leverage I can use. He's slicing through the water and Jesus, Mary and Joseph he's fast with a really clean stroke.

I check my stopwatch and blow the whistle twice. "You call that swimming? Get your ass in gear you rich toff!"

He accelerates. Excellent efficiency. Fine technique. Straight lines in the water, very little head movement. He doesn't skim too high or too low. Tons of focus. After two laps I blow the whistle again. "Enough!"

He stops and wades to the edge.

"Come here," I command.

He lifts himself out of the pool and moves to get a towel.

"No towel, Weston, grab a water bottle instead. Hydrate."

He doesn't argue. Maybe he has the mental strength for it. Swimming requires fierce dedication and a staunch work ethic...an iron will. It's not for the faint of heart, and I can't abide any hint of backtalk or complaining. He's drinking his water.

"That display was pathetic," I say.

"Thank you, Coach."

He's dripping and shivering. "Was that a six-beat kick you were using to gain speed?"

"Yes, Coach."

"It's effective for you. You fancy yourself to be the next Ian Thorpe, eh?" His eyes glint and the smile returns. "Oh, so you do!"

"He's a legend," the boy says.

"Yeah, he is and you aren't. You're just a lazy, rich poser who's five pounds over-weight."

I look in his eyes and I can see it. He wants it. He can almost taste it.

"Is this truly important to you, son?" I ask softly.

"It is," he tells me.

"Okay then. Grab a towel and sit down. We don't want to muck about and waste each other's time. Let's make a plan and get you to the fucking Olympics. We've got about two years."

CHAPTER 19: TIMOTHY

Ghost or no, Brigsley Cottage is a damned sight better than that dank little tower I was rooming in. Apparently, I'm to be Master Weston's valet, that's how Blackie explained the arrangement to me, as if we were in an episode of *Downton Abbey* or something. I'm not whinging, mind you. I'll gladly polish Jake's boots, if that's what it takes. The back room is acoustically perfect for music. He comes in wet-haired and flushed from training.

"How was Stratford?" I ask.

"Amazing," he says, "I really like my new coach, and the facility is top shelf. You should come along sometime. So, did you do it?"

"Of course I did," I say, enjoying the moment where I actually know something he doesn't.

He's slicing half a dozen apples as a morning snack. "Come on then, what of it?"

I'd gone to search the school archives on the pretense of writing an article on famous White Oak graduates. The secretary, Mrs. Devon, was more than happy to let me peruse the rolls and ledgers. I didn't have much to go on, aside from the rhyme, but I decided to start with the present and work my way back.

"It wasn't easy, you know."

Jake is smirking. He's guessed I've found something.

"I knew Brigsley was only 150 years old from the date carved on the cornerstone."

"Clever," he says, and he looks ready to burst.

"But Walker is a right common name in Britain. The uniform you described was modern though; you did say he was wearing a waistcoat, right?"

"For the love of Christ, tell me what you found!" he shouts.

"Don't get all miffed," I say, "1976."

Jake drops an apple slice on the floor. "Are you certain?"

"Thomas H. Walker, 1976. He was on the books for Michaelmas and Lent but his name doesn't appear on the Summer rolls, so logic dictates..."

"That he went missing sometime during the Lent halve in 1976!" Jake grabs me, hugs me and gives me a spin. "You know what that means, don't you?"

"What?"

"It means his killer could still be alive."

"It's feasible," I calculate, "not likely though."

As I finish that sentence a lightbulb explodes in one of the back bedrooms.

"Okay, definitely possible," I say. "The Lent halve begins mid-January and ends right before Easter."

Jake stares into the hearth, poking the embers gently with a fire iron. He pops another section of apple into his mouth while he thinks. "We need a photo to confirm it's him."

I shake my head. "They won't give us access to confidential student files."

"Don't you boys do yearbooks here?"

I slap my forehead. "Why didn't I think of that?"

"Where?" he asks.

"Kyler Library, mate. Bound to be one there."

CHAPTER 20: JACOB

It's a colossal old relic of a building which makes me think the library might have once been a monastery. The school's massive stone bell tower adjoins it. There are statues and stained glass and, of course, thousands of books. In the large atrium, skylights let natural light stream down to the large oak reading tables two floors below. Iron ladders must be navigated to access the higher shelves.

Timothy knows Kyler like the back of his hand. I suppose when you've been living in a turret you find other places to spend your time.

He waves to Mrs. Jessup, the silver-haired librarian behind her desk, and off we go. Down three flights of stone stairs to the lowest level of the basement. It smells like dust, old leather and mold.

"You certainly seem to know your way around," I say.

"I like to explore."

He glances in my direction as he stares up at the stacks. "The internet is spotty at White Oak on its best days, as you've probably noticed. Truth is, I've always preferred real books." He's climbing a rickety ladder to reach a high shelf.

"Me too," I say quietly. I feel myself falling for him as I watch his methodical search, his hair hanging down in his face, his eagerness to find our prize. How lucky I am to have met him at all.

"That's odd," he mumbles.

"What is?"

"It's missing. The annual for 1976 is gone."

Timothy is crestfallen.

"All right," I say, "White Oak starts enrolling boys at ten, he's probably in one of the earlier books."

He frowns as he reaches further out. "I thought of that too, but they're all absent. They jump from 1969 to 1977. Everything in the middle is missing."

"What the hell?" I'm getting a bit freaked out and so I climb up next to him and start searching the stacks myself. I can feel his warm breath on my neck. "I don't suppose there's a Thomas H. Walker in the 1969, is there?"

"Nope."

The bells suddenly start to toll and I flinch. Tim grabs me by the waist so I don't tumble off the ladder. We can feel the vibration of the bells from next door.

"Time to go to class," he mumbles.

"What are the odds?" I ask. "Missing boy, missing yearbooks?"

He climbs down and wipes his hands on his trousers. "Someone at this school has tried to erase this lad entirely."

CHAPTER 21: ENGLISH LITERATURE

It's a gloomy, dark day and the lecture hall is drafty and cold. Jacob is bundled in a thick blue fisherman's sweater. The only remnant of the school uniform he's wearing is a woolen beanie bearing the White Oak crest.

"Gentlemen," Mr. Fulton addresses the class, "Happy Guy Fawkes. I've been reviewing your themes for the term paper." He glances up for a moment, making eye-contact with Jacob. "I will say that your proposals are creative. Unfortunately, I must reject a few based on subject matter. Mr. Wood, you may not write about: *The Origin of Pornography in Modern Literature*, as interesting a topic as that might be for us to read."

The group snickers.

"Please confer individually with me before you begin your grand endeavor. Remember you must reference at least five authors from the twentieth century. This paper counts for thirty percent of your grade, so attempt to dazzle me with your literary prowess."

Timothy stretches his legs under his desk, gently resting his knee against Jacob.

"So, back to our earlier conversation. I hope you all had a chance to read about the untimely demise of Seymour Glass. What can we take away from Mr. Salinger's short story?"

Several hands go up.

"Mr. Redgrave."

"He has obviously gone dotty in the war," Billy says.

Fulton considers this evaluation. "Possible. There certainly seems to have been evidence of erratic behavior. PTSD we'd call it today. His mother-in-law was fairly concerned on the phone."

"If I'd have had that wife and mother-in-law I'd have shot myself too."

Fulton looks over to Ian Wood, a red-faced boy whose father is in Parliament. "Insightful, Mr. Wood, even if you didn't raise your hand. What do the adults, other than Seymour, represent in this story?" Fulton asks the group.

"Mr. Ashlock?"

Timothy takes a sideways glance at Jacob. "Materialism. They are selfish and shallow, and like the bananafish, their appetite is insatiable."

Fulton is smiling. "Bravo. You're exactly right. Europe had been devastated by World War II, but when Seymour returns to America from his service, he witnesses that unbridled materialism, even with his own wife."

Jacob nudges Timothy, showing his approval.

"Mr. Hunter, can you tell us what the little girl Sybil represents?"

Colin looks unsure. "Freedom?"

"Close," Fulton says, "Mr. Weston, you got us into this, what are your thoughts?"

Jake sits up. "Sybil represents innocence. The curious, pure world of children and their imagination."

Fulton bows. "Why then does he kill himself?"

Jake continues. "There is a theme of Zen Buddhism that runs through Salinger's work. Seymour's death may be a calm and accepting step toward spiritual enlightenment."

The class begins to murmur. "Have you something to add, Mr. Chadwick?"

"Only that Weston's theory is absolute twaddle," he says.

"How so?"

"Who knows why a man would choose to hop the twig? Maybe Seymour was depressed, or shell-shocked. Maybe he just got tired of living."

Jacob blinks his eyes several times as he thinks. "Peter may be right," he admits. "There's a nineteenth century poem that is a favorite of mine titled: *Richard Cory*. It's about a privileged man of wealth and status who goes home one night and puts a bullet in his head, much like Seymour. Gazing around this room I can make out a lot of gentlemen like Seymour Glass and Richard Cory. Rich, white toffs who are handed everything in life on a silver platter."

"Yourself included?" Fulton asks.

"Absolutely, sir. Who knows how many of us will end up one lonely night holding a revolver to our head?"

Timothy abruptly stands and bounds down the stairs without looking back. "Excuse me Professor," he mumbles as he flees the building.

CHAPTER 22: FULTON

That afternoon I stop by Brigsley Cottage and ask Jacob to take a walk with me. "I'm sure you've worked out why I wanted this chat," I begin.

Jacob stretches and looks up at the dark clouds. "Is it about the theme of my term paper?"

We walk down a path that leads toward the river, patches of ice melting along the banks. "Ah, yes, *The Suicide Authors*. It's an intriguing concept."

He picks up a stone. "I could change it, you know. I could call it, *The Homosexual Authors* and have an eerily similar list of names."

"You'd have to remove Hemingway."

He scoffs. "A terribly over-rated writer. All that macho bullshit about bulls, war, women...in terse, artificial prose."

I laugh.

"If you ask me, the best thing Ernest Hemingway ever did was put the barrel of the shotgun into his mouth."

"You're pretty critical for a boy your age," I say.

He looks at me, and then throws the rock at a tree, hitting it squarely. "Haven't you heard? Teenagers know everything."

I put my hands in my pockets to warm them. "Do you know why your flatmate left class so suddenly during our discussion?"

"I wondered about that. He said he desperately needed some air."

I sit down on a bench facing the river, it's freezing. "I shouldn't be telling you this, but his brother died around this time last year."

He comes closer. "I know that. He was British Royal Navy. He died in Afghanistan."

"No Jacob," I say, "he came home from Kabul. He shot himself at home in Hackney."

"What?"

I watch the color drain from his face. He turns away but he's obviously started to sob. "How could I be so flippant? God, I'm a pompous ass."

We are silent for awhile, just listening to the rushing water and occasional call from a moorhen. He slowly pulls himself together, wiping his nose on his sleeve. He points at a trail leading into the woods. "A couple of guys took me for a run through there to see the famous tree."

"Hmm, what did you think of it?"

"Very *Minas Tirith*."

"Tread lightly, Mr. Weston. Tolkien was an Oxford don. He's like royalty to me."

"Yes, I'm aware."

He blows warm air into his cupped hands and we walk a bit further down the icy trail. The clouds have blocked the sun entirely, and it looks like more weather is heading our way. It's going to be a bloody cold and wet Guy Fawkes Night.

I'm duty bound to ask him directly. "Do you often think about suicide?"

He smiles at me. "Constantly, darling. Doesn't everyone?"

I stop him, placing a hand on his shoulder. "Be serious, Weston. You're brilliant, athletic, good looking and heir to an immense fortune. Why would you want to take your own life?"

"Oh, I don't Professor. I'd never give my numpty step-brother Denny the satisfaction. He's a cabbage. And I'm still far too curious about this life to jump prematurely into that next place."

He pauses for dramatic effect. "But do you know what the leading cause of suicide is for boys my age?"

I look into the river. "I believe it's sexual identity."

"Yes, Professor. But being queer isn't the issue. The problem is the way we are treated by the ignorant straight majority. Disowned from families, excommunicated from churches, and bullied at schools like this one. That's what drives young boys to find daddy's gun, even in this century."

I can see he's felt that pain, perhaps is still feeling it. "So, your 'incident' at Trinity?"

"Two other boys and me caught literally with our pants down in the choir room. *In Flagrante delicto,* as we say in Professor Silver's Latin class."

"Embarrassing."

"For my family, yes. For me, not so much."

I'm working it out in my head. "So, your father sends you to an all-boy boarding school, in a country where the age of consent is sixteen...as a punishment?"

"My dad is nothing if not ironic."

I laugh out loud.

"I think my father finds my gayness inconvenient. In his mind it's yet to be determined if I will make him proud through my accomplishments or just continue to disgrace the family name."

"Like many other boys, you must be under a lot of pressure to succeed," I say.

He grins. "I suppose I'd feel some stress...if I wasn't so head-and-shoulders above everyone here," he jests. "So you think I'm good looking."

I close my eyes and sigh.

"Race you back," he shouts, tagging me, and he is off like the wind.

***

Five minutes later I make it back to the cottage and Weston is sitting outside, drinking a Pellegrino from a straw. "It must be dreadful to grow old." He hands me a bottle of water for which I am grateful.

"Funny," I say, "I felt so young this morning."

He's regarding me with a measure of sincerity. "Thank you, sir, for everything you said today. You're a good man, even if you are a beak."

"Learning all the slang, I see."

He winks.

"Listen Jacob, this much talk of suicide sends a flare up in a place like White Oak. You'll have to talk to a councilor or they will have me drawn and quartered for being remiss."

He puts a hand over his heart and bows. "I wouldn't want you to get the sack over my little fixation, Professor. Please, do what the law requires."

This boy is a unicorn. "I'm going to have you talk with Dr. Rowland next week. I think you'll like her."

CHAPTER 23: JACOB

Storm clouds are building again to the north. I watched them moving in during my tete-a-tete with Fulton. I've been living in England for two weeks and have barely seen the sun for two hours.

When I enter the cottage Timothy is at the table surrounded by open books. My laptop sits rejected to one side. He's furiously scribbling away.

"Busy?"

He looks up. "Doing preps," he says.

I come closer to the table. "Any headway on our project?"

He shakes his head. "I've an idea, but I need to get online. The net has been down all day. No wifi, nothing. No bars, as you yanks say."

"Okay, first off, no one ever says that. It is curious though. I need to give the situation some thought." I move toward him. "Stand up for a second."

He looks wary but puts down his pen. He starts to stretch, but as soon as he's up I grab him in a massive bear hug.

"Settle down, Mr. Weston, what's all this about?"

He pulls himself free.

"I've been an insufferable prat. A tactless wanker. Can you ever forgive me, mate?"

He turns away. "He told you then, did he? About Henry?"

"Yes," I answer, "but why didn't you?"

"We all have secrets, Jake."

"Bollocks," I say, and he chuckles.

"You're quite the anglophile."

"I am indeed," I admit, "but that's beside the point. True friendship can afford true knowledge, and I will always be your friend. I'm so deeply sorry about your brother."

He looks at me, tears welling up, and the sight of him makes me emotional too.

"So are we both going to blub now, like a couple middle-school girls?" he asks.

We laugh instead and fall into each other's arms. "Remember," I say, "one loyal friend is worth ten thousand relatives."

"Who said that?"

"Euripides," I answer.

"Exactly how clever are you?"

"The jury's still out on that one. I certainly missed the scent when it came to your brother."

He sits back down, cracking open another book. "There's no way you could have guessed. It was a shock to mum and me both, we didn't have a blessed clue. Looking back I suppose he was depressed; and I didn't admit it to you simply because I didn't want to put any more dark thoughts in your head."

I begin rummaging for food in our pantry. "I do have a fascination with the subject."

He rolls his eyes. "You don't say?"

I take out a box of Hobnobs.

"Promise me something?"

"Anything," I answer with a flourish.

"You'll never actually do it. No matter how gutted you get. You'll speak to me first." I can see how determined he is. "I can't bear to stand by and lose anyone else."

I touch my hand to his cheek. "You have my word as a gentleman."

"Right," he says, "I'm glad that's sorted. Let's go to the bonfire."

***

Of course I know about Guy Fawkes. The Catholic traitor who tried to blow up the House of Lords and kill the King. I just don't understand what all the fuss is about. It would be like having *Benedict Arnold Day* in America and that would simply never fly.

So fireworks, striped shirts, burning crosses and 500 adolescent boys...what could possibly go wrong?

They've built an immense bonfire in the middle of the Great Lawn, far enough away from any structures to be relatively safe.

Blackmore, being the history beak, is actually trying to lecture the crowd on the failed *Gunpowder Plot of 1605* while standing on a chair, but no one is paying him any mind. Some clever boy has successfully attached a dozen firecrackers to the back of Blackie's robes, and when they go off, he runs yelping into the crowd. It may be the first time he's ever received a round of applause.

Paddy Lester, the head groundskeeper, is in charge of the fire. He must be seventy-five years old. I suppose it's his chance to burn a season's worth of underbrush and other discarded flammables. It's like he's never heard of composting. Anyway, the old boy is a true pyromaniac at heart.

I lay on the lawn and watch the lads jump and yell, circling the giant pyre. I'm tired and cold, even sitting this close to a fire. Tim is running with the boys. They are all chanting, *"Remember, remember, the fifth of November, The Gunpowder Treason and Plot."*

By the time they are burning a giant effigy of old Guido the rain has begun in earnest. Paddy must be devastated. His bonfire will die an untimely death tonight.

I've had enough British revelry and rioting so I head back to the cottage but Ashlock is nowhere to be found.

CHAPTER 24: TIMOTHY

The merriment of Guy Fawkes Night is coming to a soggy conclusion. It's colder than a well-digger's nappy outside and to make matters worse, the sleet has begun. I'm heading for home when I see something odd.

Near the edge of the lawn I watch Billy Redgrave giving Paddy an envelope. Money, was it? Whatever it is, the two of them look guilty as sin.

The groundsman puts his hand on Redgrave's shoulder and they stalk off on the trail together, so I decide to follow.

It's easy enough to track them since Paddy is carrying a lantern, but the weather is truly horrific. I'm wearing a slicker, but it does nothing against the cold.

After twenty minutes of tearing through a slog of thorny brush on a muddy little trail, they head toward a dilapidated old barn. Lester's cottage is out this direction, but I don't believe I've ever seen this shed before. I watch him unlocking the chains and they both go inside. I can't get close enough to peer into the tiny windows without being seen, so I sit and wait.

Mother of God it is freezing!

Fewer than five minutes later Billy comes out alone. He runs up the path not ten feet away from me, using the light on his cell phone as a guide. He's carrying something...a package of some sort. Whatever were they up to?

CHAPTER 25: JACOB

The power is down again. I've lit two dozen candles but with Tommy around it's a full-time job to keep them glowing.

Attempting to read *Ossa Latinitatis Sola* (The Mere Bones of Latin) by flashlight is proving to be more than I am capable of doing tonight.

It's past eleven and I'm worried about him. He's probably just out and about somewhere with the St. Johnnies, I tell myself, but having a flatmate is a lot like being married. A huge wave of relief washes over me when he comes stumbling in.

"Thank heavens," I mumble.

He's taking off his muddy boots and mac near the door.

"I'm frozen solid," he says rushing toward the fireplace, "were you worried?"

"A bit. Boys go missing from this cottage."

"Apologies, mate. You wouldn't have any of that cognac left for the frigid traveler, would you?"

"Coming right up," I say. I go to the pantry to retrieve our stash. "You know the last time we had a big storm like this Tommy Walker appeared."

I hand him his drink and take a sip of my own.

"You think there's some correlation to the weather?" he asks.

"I haven't the faintest. But maybe we should keep watch in case he makes an encore."

"In that case, I'll change into something more comfortable...and less damp," he says, walking back toward his room.

***

We sit in the dark together, huddled under blankets in our pajamas and robes, eating biscuits in front of the fire. Waiting.

"Some people would find this tableau rather ridiculous," he comments.

"You have a point," I say. "Get your violin, I require some music from my valet."

"We're supposed to be waiting for apparitions, not scaring them away."

"Please?"

He groans, picks up a candle and shuffles back to his room. When he returns he has put his tailcoat on over his pajamas. I applaud and he bows gracefully.

The firelight reflects off the polished wood of the violin as he places it deftly under his chin. There is a moment of stillness, as if he is gathering strength, and when he begins it is miraculous. He makes the violin sing as if it's a living thing. The piece he performs is filled with longing, and melancholy and utter, raw beauty.

I am speechless. There are no words to describe his talent. By the time he has finished playing I am sobbing. Literally. He comes over and musses my hair.

"What was that?" I whisper.

"Tchaikovsky. I treasure that movement, it's so terribly sad."

He puts the instrument back in its case and fastens the buckles.

"I can't even tell you..." I stammer, "and I've heard my fair share of philharmonics. You are..."

"I know, I know," he says lightly. "I'd never admit it in public, but I'm wicked fucking good, right?"

We both start laughing hysterically.

"Yeah," I admit, "that's exactly what you are."

**

It's gotten late and we've fallen asleep on the couch...but then I hear something and it startles me awake. I nudge Tim with my foot.

"What?" he asks, still groggy.

"I heard something."

He sits up and his eyes widen. We hold our breath... and it sounds again.

"Did you...?"

"Yes, of course I heard it," he whispers back. "It sounded like someone tapping on the glass."

He grabs my hand. "It could just be a branch, you know. It's a gale out there."

The smell of jasmine and moss is pervasive. "Do you smell that?" he asks, and I beckon him to the window. "This is just the way it happened before," I say. I touch my fingertips to the cold glass and Timothy gasps.

"I see him!"

It's faint at first, just a grey mist dancing at the tree line...but he moves like lightning toward the window and comes into sharp focus only inches away from us. Tommy Walker. His long blond hair plastered wet against his face, his eyes two black holes. The school uniform hangs waterlogged and heavy on his frail body.

A book falls off the table and the sound of it hitting the boards makes us jump. When we look back out the window...he's gone.

"Cor blimey," Tim exclaims.

I sit back on the couch and look at the fire. "At least now I know I'm not mental."

"If you don't mind," he says, "I think I'll sleep in your room tonight."

CHAPTER 26: ROTHWELL

Kitty places her gloved hand on my arm and leans over, "Isn't that the Weston boy in the second pew?"

I crane my neck a bit to get the proper angle and see the top of his tall blond head. "So it is," I whisper.

"I didn't know he was a Catholic," she says. I have to wonder what a boy with his tendencies would be doing attending Sunday Mass. "We should ask him to brunch," she continues.

I watch the colored light streaming down through stained glass and listen to the glorious pipe organ leading the service into benediction.

After the blessing I make my way toward the pulpit. We've taken on a young chaplain named Tobias Gates who has been helping Father Hodgson with his duties. He's a handsome German man in his twenties with a strong jaw and a booming voice. I shake his hand warmly, and Weston catches my eye.

"Good morning, Headmaster."

"Hello. Don't get enough religion in the compulsory chapel services during the week, Mr. Weston?" I ask.

"Well," he motions casually, "there's nothing like the pomp and circumstance of a grand Sunday Mass, and since it's the Feast of All Souls, I thought I would honor my mother."

I'm impressed by his answer, but I sense insincerity. "We weren't aware that you were so fond of the Church." Kitty has joined me and is standing quietly by my side, waiting for an introduction.

"Oh, I've always adored the Church," he continues. "The rituals, the smell of incense, the sound of a young boy's choir," he says and winks at Father Gates. "It's just that the Church hasn't always been overly fond of me."

I sigh, touching the small of Kitty's back. "May I introduce my wife, Weston. Barbara, this is Jacob." She bows her head as if the boy is the Duke of Cornwall.

"So nice to meet a fellow American," she says, taking his hand.

"Are you from the colonies too then, Mrs. Rothwell?"

"Originally yes. My family is from North Carolina!" she says with pride. I watch the look of amusement pass over the boy's face.

"Barbara was wondering if you'd like to join us for Sunday brunch? I know it's last minute, so if..."

"I'd be delighted, Mrs. Rothwell," he answers quickly.

"All right then," I tell him. "We will expect you in about an hour."

CHAPTER 27: JACOB

I come dashing in, running up the stairs to my room, when I hear Timothy brusquely stop playing. He must have been practicing while I was out.

"Don't stop on my account," I yell down.

He comes up and stands in the open doorway, still holding the violin. "How was Mass? Did you confess all your sins?"

I'm putting on a black cashmere turtleneck and some Armani slacks. "That would have required the entire afternoon," I joke. "The service was marvelous, filled with excess, just the way I like it. All Souls Day, you know." I snap on a platinum Rolex that was a Confirmation gift, and spritz myself with a bit of Clive Christian Osmanthus.

"Do you have a date?"

"I do," I say. "Brunch at the Headmaster's."

Timothy looks bewildered. "You are full of surprises. This is not how I thought you'd be spending your Sunday afternoon."

"Purely reconnaissance, mate. Rothwell's wife is a social-climber, and I've got a few questions for them both. How do I look?" I ask.

"Like a billionaire's son."

"Well, if the Testonis fit..."

***

The Rothwell's cottage is far grander, naturally, then ours. It's named, *White Gables* which seems appropriate considering its complicated roof structure. A proper English garden encompasses the yard surrounding the estate and even in winter is charming. I wonder if this is how Barbara occupies her time. I knock and she immediately answers.

"Oh," she says, "how wonderful you look, Jacob!"

"Call me Jake. It's nice to spend a day out of uniform, Ma'am."

"You must call me Kitty, everyone does..." She's wearing a white cocktail dress with ruffled crepe shoulders and silver accents. It looks like a Jason Wu. She's at least ten years younger than her husband.

The Headmaster clears his throat. "He can refer to you as Mrs. Wright-Rothwell."

She slaps his shoulder playfully. "Don't be such a humbug, Stilly. Take the afternoon off for once."

Rothwell wanders toward the formal dining room.

"Come in and sit down," he says.

The table-setting is refined; Baccarat crystal and Fontaine flatware. A Lalique vase filled with fresh hellebore flowers. In fact, the whole cottage is extremely stylish. There is a painting over the mantle that certainly looks like one of Sisley's landscapes. Someone around here comes from money, and I think I know who.

"I would have brought a nice Bordeaux but the rules prohibit it," I say, winking.

"You wouldn't want me to catch you with alcohol, young man," the Headmaster warns.

"I wouldn't want you to *catch* me at all."

Two boys from Farrington House have been enlisted as waiters, which makes me uncomfortable. I recognize one of them from Professor Silver's Latin class.

"I hope you like turbot, it was just brought in fresh," Kitty says.

The boys begin to serve us. I wave at Micah Lang, the boy from Latin and he gives me a quick bow back. "I love it, Kitty, thank you," I say, turning toward Rothwell.

"Is serving at your table a punishment or a privilege?"

I see the boys grin.

"I'd say it's a bit of both," he answers. "It never hurts to have some skills, and perhaps a bit of humility, wouldn't you agree?"

"I wouldn't know about that," I say, "having never had any humility whatsoever."

Kitty giggles. "What a charming rascal you are."

The Headmaster seems somewhat less amused.

"From what I've heard, you're part fish yourself, Weston. They say no one can catch you in the water."

"I do my best, sir," I reach for some rolls making sure that everyone can glimpse my diamond-studded Rolex.

"We are certainly looking forward to the swim meet with Eton. We've never beaten their boys."

I snicker. "Well, place your wagers, folks. Those posh tossers won't know what hit them this year."

Micah nearly drops his tray laughing.

"I like your confidence," Rothwell says. "Eton's headmaster, Heath Fetterman, and I have a standing wager...I'd like to win it this year."

It's money in the bank, sir."

Kitty touches my wrist next to my watch. "How have you settled in, Sugar?" she asks. "Do you miss New York? I certainly would. Do you like Brigsley Cottage?"

I swallow some fish, which, by the way, is delicious. "I miss a few people, but not the place."

She grasps my hand, "I always say that home is where your heart is."

"Then White Oak is home for me," I say sincerely. "I've fallen in love with the people here."

The Headmaster gives me a dubious stare.

"What a fine compliment to your school, dear," Kitty remarks.

"Indeed," he says.

"And Brigsley is cozy. It's not as elegant as your cottage, of course. But I think it will be really aces once we get the ghost sorted out."

Kitty drops her cutlery.

"Ah, so they've gotten around to frightening you with those ridiculous stories," Rothwell says. "Our campus is apparently riddled with spirits. The boy in the bell tower, two lads near the tree, I've even heard one about a headless Headmaster...and of course, the famous *Haunted Cottage*."

I look directly into his eyes. "I don't know about the others, but I've seen Tommy Walker."

The room goes still.

"Codswallop," Rothwell finally says, wiping his mouth with his napkin.

"You've never heard of him?"

"We've all heard the rhyme, Weston...about a boy who went missing."

"He was a pupil here in the seventies," I say.

"Oh my!" Kitty exclaims.

"I wouldn't know. I've only been Headmaster here for six years," he answers, and I can tell he's lying about something. "Let's change the subject, shall we?"

The boys begin clearing our plates. A custard tart is brought out for desert.

"Your garden is lovely, Kitty. The best I've seen at White Oak," I mention.

She giggles. "How kind of you to notice. Since our three boys are all off to Cambridge I find myself puttering out there constantly. My empty nest syndrome. Your parents must miss you terribly too."

"That's unlikely."

"Oh," she laughs again, resting her hand over mine. "What a card you are. I've seen your father interviewed on TV. A *Titan of Tech*. He must be fascinating."

"You may be right," I say, "I really don't know the man."

Rothwell is scowling. "Might I have a word alone, Weston?"

We stand and he leads me to his den. It's very manly and pretentious with leather club chairs and the heads of dead animals on the walls. A big trophy case sits near french doors leading out to the garden.

"Just what do you think you're doing, young man?"

He must have been an athlete in his day. He towers over me as I try to look surprised. "I'm sure I don't know what you mean, Headmaster."

"All that talk of ghosts, and then demeaning a great man like your father. You have my wife utterly beside herself," he states.

"Then let me go apologize to her immediately," I say. "She's a fine lady, obviously coming from the same kind of wealth and breeding that I do."

Rothwell looks taken aback, which confirms my guess. She's the one with all the money.

"I do hope you realize that I won't tolerate any of the nonsense that got you booted out of Trinity here at White Oak. We aren't that way here."

I grin. We're in the thick of it now. "Statistically speaking, sir, about forty or fifty of the White Oak boys certainly are *that way*... but observation tells me that number is altogether higher."

His face reddens and his eyes narrow. "Stick to your studies and your training. And keep it in your trousers, Weston, because I'm watching you. I can see right through you."

I get up to leave. "Please thank Kitty for the lovely meal."

CHAPTER 28: TIMOTHY

I find Jake huddled with Professor Barnes in the computer science lab. I don't want to interrupt but he calls me over anyway.

"Please tell him," Jake says.

Barnes pushes his bifocals up the bridge of his nose. He's a nerdy professor with unruly Einstein hair and a pocketful of pens.   "As I was explaining, the school runs on it's own private network with its own servers. This allows us to create a firewall protecting student information from outside breaches."

I shake my head, not really understanding much of the jargon, but trying to put on a good show.

"And tell him about the cell phone coverage and wifi, if you don't mind, sir."

"Of course.   Cell towers can have a range of up to seventy kilometers, which puts White Oak within the scope of central London...but with all the thick stonework and other obstacles here our service is often sluggish and drops out. If we had a tower closer to the school I'm confident that our students would have a more seamless experience."

Jake gets up and pats Barnes on the shoulder. "I'm on it, Professor. Thank you so much for your time."

We leave to get some lunch at the Buttery.   "So what does all that mean?" I ask when we're walking down the breezeway.

"It means we need to go shopping," Jake says.

CHAPTER 29: JACOB

First things first. You'd think the son of a tech mogul would have arrived at this spot sooner, but there it is. I pay for the best VPN money can buy and set it up on my MacBook. Rather than using the school's wifi signal I create a personal hotspot using my Apple iPhone X. We'll be in business if the electricity stays on and I can keep a charge on all my devices. Hotspots quickly suck the life out of a iPhone, so I'll need more batteries and chargers too.

"Explain it again," Tim asks, scratching his head.

"The way White Oak is configured with dedicated servers and a private network...it would be incredibly easy for someone on the inside to snoop, if they wanted to, and I'm certain they do. Emails, text messages, browser history, photos, videos, everything. The administration probably knows every porn site Ian Wood has ever visited. I could have done that hack when I was eleven."

He looks impressed, if a bit doubtful. "Sounds like a bloody fantastic way to surveil the student body."

"Exactly. So every time we type Thomas H. Walker into a search engine someone might be watching...and blocking us."

"But you're beefing up our security?"

"In a substantial way. I've got Abbot working with Vodaphone in London. Weston Industries is going to be putting up a new cell tower three kilometers from White Oak Academy."

"You can do that?"

"It will be up by November fifteenth which should help with 3G and 4G cell coverage and speed. I also bought a bunch of wifi extenders and boosters. They may help in the short term, but only with the school's routers, which honestly we are trying to avoid. We may end up just giving those out as Christmas presents to the St. Johnnies."

I'm really cooking.

"I've set up a VPN..."

Tim gives me a blank expression like I've done a flyby over his head. "A Virtual Private Network. It changes our IP address every time we log on, and most importantly makes it so no one can spy on us. From this day forward it will look like we're surfing the net from Brazil. Of course, no wifi network is completely invulnerable, but it will be way harder to see what we're doing. I've set up new Gmail accounts for us and we'll be able to configure disappearing text messages through an app. I've also bought us untraceable phones."

He's put a bag of popcorn into the microwave. "It's all very MI6, but is it necessary?"

"Someone took those yearbooks, Tim, and I don't think the power outages and faulty internet are just about the weather here. I'm gutted that I've been jabbering about Tommy. That was foolish. I even mentioned him to the Headmaster! I'm getting us PO boxes in Greenknoll Village so we will be able to send things to ourselves, or to each other that we don't want going through the school mailroom."

"So is it safe for me to use your lappy?"

I push the MacBook Pro toward him. "It is now. Be sure to use only this computer though, and change all your existing passcodes tonight. What's your idea?"

"Tons of searching and researching, starting with the *British Newspaper Archive* where we can scour all the local and national papers that existed in 1976. It will take some time to do because I think the school may have tried to hush up Tommy's death. Even so, you have to think there was some kind of active physical search that happened right after he went missing, and that probably entailed some news coverage...primitive as it was in that era. Once we know more I may be able to access police records because there must have also been an inquiry and investigation. If there was anything published anywhere about Thomas H. Walker, I'll find it."

I grasp his shoulder. "We make a good team, you and me. Iron sharpens iron, so a friend sharpens a friend."

"Hang on," he says, "I know that one. It's from the Bible."

"Correct. King Solomon," I say. I'm nervously pacing around the cottage while he's working and I spot a flyer that's been left near the mantle clock.

"Hey, what's this?"

He glances up and grins. "Auditions for the pageant. We're doing, *A Christmas Carol* this season. I'm going to try out...You should too!"

"No thanks."

He's zipping over the computer keys. Jotting down snippets on a pad, then clicking the mouse and moving on. "Why not?" he asks. "I know you're not too bashful to make a spectacle of yourself."

"True enough," I admit, "but a gay boy hanging out with all the theater geeks is just too cliché for me."

He shakes his head, incredulous. "You might meet another gay boy hanging out with the theater geeks."

"That is a possibility... I wonder if that's where the term *drama queen* started." He smirks, then I point at him. "But what one really has to wonder is why a musician of your calibre would want to try his hand at remedial acting?"

"I just thought it would be fun for a change."

I'm watching him closely and I've just caught him fibbing. "Or could it be, Mr. Ashlock, because this pageant is a joint venture with Bentley Wood High School?"

"Is it?" he ask innocently.

"Yes," I add, "it says so right here at the bottom of the notice. I believe Bentley Wood is the local all-girl academy."

He smiles at me sheepishly. "Hmm, there's that, of course."

CHAPTER 30: ABBOT

Serving a great family is difficult enough, but serving a family that once knew greatness and has fallen by the wayside is tortuous. Every decent Weston is either dead or living abroad.

This woman Joanne and her idiot child are insufferable. They lack even the most basic social skills. Caught in the vice of materialism they seem to believe that their next enormous purchase will bring them happiness.

It will take a long time, (and millions of dollars) before they realize that money carries certain innate responsibilities, and while it can greatly enhance our existence, we cannot base our lives on the shiny possessions of this world.

But what do I know? I'm just the butler and it's time to bring the master his coffee.

Two quick raps on the door and I enter Paul Weston's den without a sound. I pour him some strong *Kopi Iuwak* coffee (beans imported directly from Vietnam) and place it on his right side. He makes a grunting noise that I assume is meant to thank me.

"Sir, pardon the interruption." I wait for him to at least acknowledge my existence.

"Yes, Abbot, what is it?" He glances at me then looks back at his computer monitor.

"I wanted to remind you that next month, on December twenty-third, Jacob will be competing in the Eton Trials. His new coach has asked if the family will be attending."

He sighs and I can almost discern a spark of humanity in the man. "I'm afraid we'll have to miss it. I have business in Asia that week and Mrs. Weston has her heart set on visiting Bali for Christmas."

This is so true to form.

"Sir, I wonder if Mrs. Weston is aware that December is the height of the rainy season is Bali...and by rainy I mean to say tropical monsoons."

He smiles. "What can I do, Abbot? She is a determined woman."

I'm thinking Jake's arsenic plan is looking brighter every day. "An understatement...as you know I'll be spending Christmas with my sister in Cardiff. Perhaps if I am allowed to leave a few days sooner I could go watch Jacob's swim-meet and represent the family."

If he imagines that I'm going to spend my yuletide in an Asian monsoon he really has another thing coming.

"That's a splendid idea! See how the boy is shaping up and get a first-hand look at this school. What was it called again? White something?"

"Yes sir. White Oak Academy. I will devote enough time to make a thorough evaluation of the school, his coaching and his living arrangements and give you a full report."

"Good man, checking up on my investments," he says. "I wonder if you'd do one other thing for me?"

"Yes?"

"Please send him my love."

CHAPTER 31: JACOB

It's therapy day and I couldn't be less in the mood. I'd considering playing it up as a deranged psychopath but that performance might get me expelled...and then committed. I suppose I'll have to resort to *angry gay teenager* as my default position, which is close enough to the truth most days.

Dr. Jane Rowland. I've Googled all her credentials and pretended to be another doctor so I could troll all her LinkedIn contacts. On paper she looks awfully mediocre, but Fulton thought I would like her, so perhaps she is greater than the sum of her parts.

I certainly won't be mentioning the haunted cottage, but I shouldn't have to. She'll feel she's put in a good day's work if she can save the poor homo from slitting his own wrists. Some mornings just aren't worth getting out of bed.

I decide to wear torn jeans and a Nirvana tee-shirt to the appointment. I know it sounds a bit on the nose, but I am worried if I wear my Elliott Smith she won't get the joke...one can't be too sure.

The office they've placed her in is certainly off the beaten path. It's above the student art gallery, beyond the cricket pitches. Perhaps White Oak is inferring that none of the boys here need therapy, or maybe it's just to hide the ones that do.

If I was suicidal going in, then walking through the art gallery only made me more so. It's pretty safe to say that none of our boys are destined to be the next Van Gogh. Then again, Vincent probably would have had an appointment on the second floor too. He did end up shooting himself, not to mention the ear thing.

Her receptionist is a Sixth Form boy that I've never seen before. His name is Kyle. Talk about a confidentiality breach! This lad could probably write a scandalous book from what he's seen and heard around here. I sign in and immediately get escorted into the doctor's inner office.

"Hullo," she says brightly, "I'm Jane, you must be Jacob." She's a nitwit.

"I am indeed."

"Well have a seat and let's get started," she motions me to a plush chair near a Buddhist fountain sitting on a little table. The gentle sound of water hitting pebbles is meant to be soothing, but it just makes me want to pee.

"No thank you, doctor. I'd prefer to look around first."

She seems surprised. "Okay," she says, seating herself behind her freshly-polished desk. There's nothing on the desktop except a tall metal vase containing a single white lily. Where the hell is her computer? Does she go out and use Kyle's when she needs to look something up?

She's rereading my file while I peruse her bookshelf, her furniture, her diploma. I touch everything. It's a notably sterile environment, a bit too sterile for my taste. There must be a therapist catalog filled with comfortable chairs and lavender-scented candles that they all use.

"You can tell so much about a person by the way they dress, or the way they choose to furnish their office...or their bedroom. Don't you agree, doctor?"

"I do," she says, but she's on guard already. I'm wondering if she has a button under that empty desktop which alerts Kyle. Maybe he has a black belt in *Krav Maga*, the deadly martial art.

"Well then it really would have been more productive for you to come visit me this morning."

She's overly thin. Her eye make-up is too smokey for this early hour, and her boobs are certainly fake. The outfit is Stella McCartney Ready to Wear, but I think it's a knock-off too.

"I'd certainly get a workout running around campus to all my appointments," she laughs nervously.

"You look like you get plenty of workouts," I say. "Smith College. That's impressive. Sylvia Plath attended there."

"It's an amazing school," she says.

"Of course, Sylvia ended up with her head in the oven...so that's not in the brochure. She met Anne Sexton though."

"Interesting. Both women committed suicide," she says and makes a notation on my file.

"Both women won Pulitzer Prizes too. Smith seems to attract suicidal girls...have you written any sad poetry lately, Doc?"

I can see she's had about enough of me, but I've collected all this ammunition so it would be a shame not to use it.

"You think you're clever, don't you?"

"Oh, I know so. I also believe that the only people that venture into the field of psychotherapy are those who are interested in analyzing themselves. It's the career of choice for those with deep-seated issues who aren't brave enough to make a damn appointment. The self-help refuge of cowards."

She smiles. Let's see if she can fire something back. "What you're doing now, Jacob, is called deflection. Trying to make me the subject so you don't have to examine yourself. But please, continue. What are my issues?"

And we're off to the races again.

"Judging from this office and it's austere decor, you suffer from OCD, since everything in here is a little too...just so." I moved a couple of things around on her shelves and I can already sense her anxiety building.

"I do think it's fascinating that an all-boy school would hire a shrink from Smith College, of all places, who doesn't know anything about testosterone-filled laddies. And you certainly don't look like Mrs. Jessup or the other maternal figures working in the offices or the kitchens on campus. You were hired to be an object of desire, a siren that young boys will tell their innermost secrets to."

She probably regrets this morning's make-up choice about now. I decide to go in for the kill.

"Your thin and fragile demeanor, apart from the fake tits, belie some deeper affliction...anorexia or some other eating disorder that you've barely managed to get under control. I'm sure you thought of yourself as *Daddy's little girl*, always trying to please, and never quite hitting the mark.

Straight A's in school, never drinking a beer or touching a boy...and yet, you seem the type who would sneak off with a juicy cucumber or other bit of produce, oiling it up and putting it where nice girls shouldn't..."

"That's enough!" she shouts. (Ladies and gentlemen we have a winner). "You don't know the first thing about me!"

I smile my most charming smile. "Perhaps not, but I have noticed an unusual amount of phallic symbols in your antiseptic little palace." I stroke the cylinder of her metal flower vase, and then move it a few inches to the left just for fun. "And when I started in about the cucumber you blushed...A simple blush. An uncontrollable sympathetic nervous-system response...which is the only honest exchange we've had between ourselves...Jane."

CHAPTER 32: MUDBALL

The rain has subsided. It's a bright sunny morning in England and William Redgrave is pounding on the front door of Brigsley.

"Wakey, wakey, hands off snaky!" he yells.

Jacob comes down the stairs wearing only bright red Dolce & Gabbana boxer briefs. "For the love of God go away!" he yells back.

But Redgrave is on a mission and continues to pound on the old wooden door. Timothy appears from the back of the cottage with his dark hair sticking straight up.

"Nice hair," Jacob says.

"Nice knickers," Ashlock replies. Jake opens the door and Billy comes rushing in. He's wearing rugby shorts and a St. John's polo.

"Hurry!" he says, "we need to be at the pitch in twenty minutes!"

"What do you want, you daft bastard?" Jacob asks.

Billy sits at the table, grabbing an apple from a bowl and taking a giant bite. "You must help us defend the honor of St. John's!"

Timothy is suddenly excited. "Mudball, is it?" He's scrambling to put on some clothes.

"Hurry, Jake!" he yells from the back, "it's mudball!"

"What, pray tell, is that?"

"It's a game," Billy says, "like rugby, but not. The houses play against each another. We're playing Exeter, and we never win. Help us mate! With you and Chadwick we stand a fighting chance!"

Jacob goes to his room and finds a passable rugby outfit and in ten minutes everyone is ready. As they are jogging to the pitch he turns to Tim. "I'm American. I don't know the rules."

"Doesn't matter," Timothy says, "they change a bit every year. Just grab the ball and run like mad."

***

The morning is clear and crisp and nearly all the boys have turned out. Some will play, but most will just cheer and jeer along the sidelines.

Blackmore immediately runs over. He has a whistle around his neck, and knee-high wellies to keep the gunk off. He hands them each shin and mouth guards.

"So glad you can participate, Weston. Please put on your boots and guards."

Peter Chadwick is smiling broadly as he comes running over. "All set, lads?"

"Absolutely," Jake says.

"Remember," Blackmore lectures, "White Oak football is a gentleman's game. We won't interrupt play because there should be no penalties."

"And the rules?"

Peter grabs Jacob around the shoulders. "Just follow beside me. Don't lift anyone up or throw any elbows and we should be fine. If I toss you the ball...run like hell."

"Pete, he's fast as a jet," Billy says.

Chadwick points out the base lines and poles but the pitch looks more like a muddy swamp. Jacob is smiling.

"You'll be our secret weapon," Peter says, "I hope you aren't afraid of getting filthy."

"It's what I live for."

***

The whistle blows, Colin kicks the large, odd-shaped ball from the middle of the pitch for Exeter and then it becomes all out pandemonium. Boys immediately start slipping and sliding, pushing and yelling.

In minutes it's hard to recognize who is who. Everyone is covered in dark brown slop, laughing wildly. An Exeter boy catches the slippery ball and yells, "Yards!" Jacob learns this enables a free kick. It's a confusing game.

Awhile later the lads form a "wall" trying to prevent access to the opposition. There is a lot of contact, but no one seems to get hurt in the mire. Jake thinks the whole outing is an exercise in British bedlam.

"Having fun?" Timothy asks, completely covered in dripping mud.

"Loving it!"

Chadwick continues to bark orders and point boys into position. Jacob trots by his side, trying not to unwittingly cause penalties. He's managed to keep his hair bright and shiny, but the rest of him is soiled.

"The Exeter lads are fast this year," Chadwick mumbles.

"Not fast enough," Weston says.

Peter signals. "Get ready, mate."

The chaos continues with the boys in a closely packed scrum. An Exeter boy causes a penalty by turtling. (grabbing the ball and sitting on it).

When St. John's breaks free, Chadwick is clutching it desperately. Together they run down field with a gang of Exeter boys in hot pursuit. Jacob looks back in time to hear Peter yell, "Weston!"

He catches the ball, puts his head down and runs like mad. St. John's scores and the crowd on the sidelines roar!

Jake gives the ball to the umpire and bends over, hands on his knees. His teammates surround him, yelling their approval and embracing. Chadwick congratulates him by rubbing a handful of sludge into his clean blond hair. "Well done!"

An hour later St. John's has defeated Exeter three to nil. No one is happier than Michael Blackmore who is prancing around clapping backs and trying not to get muddy.

"Glorious boys, glorious! Now clean yourselves up and we'll have pizza in the common room to celebrate."

***

Rugby, cricket and football at White Oak have an ancient athletic complex right off the pitches where the showers can accommodate thirty boys at once. It's much bigger than the locker room Jake is used to at Ducker.

Immediately the place is filled with steaming water and the echos of young athletes yelling at one another in their tiled fortress. Timothy has thought ahead, being a veteran of Mudball, and brought a duffle of clean, dry clothes for Jake and himself. Their dirty things lay piled in a heap as they all scrub to get the muck off.

There is the usual horseplay and foolishness that comes from energetic youth. Many of the St. Johnnies start hugging and slapping Jacob and Peter who have chiefly been responsible for getting a win for the house. They are the heroes of the hour and are basking in their wet, soapy glory.

Maybe it was the sight of Tim under the steaming shower, or just the contact of so many naked bodies that unintentionally got Jake aroused. He has never been embarrassed or in any way modest regarding his own nudity, but this is England.

The other boys begin to take notice, but it is Peter who makes the first comment. "Mate, it's bad form to have a full salute around so many blokes, they might get the wrong idea."

Jake shrugs. "Sorry, I'm a healthy, young, red-blooded American boy."

Billy Redgrave is laughing, but Colin, smarting a bit from Exeter's loss yells, "Looks to me like you're a Betty Boy!"

Hearing this Timothy starts grabbing some towels and tries to get Jake to leave with him before the taunting escalates...or becomes violent.

Other Exeter lads start in though.

"Knob jockey! Poofter!"

Jacob finds the scene amusing and the slang hilarious.

"I think you guys are just jealous."

Tim is getting worried however. "Jake, enough, let's go."

"I've got to remember all these phrases," he laughs as they are toweling dry. "My favorite so far is 'bone smuggler.'"

When they've managed to put on some trousers, Peter comes over. He seems disappointed, or maybe slightly betrayed. He leans in to Jake and whispers, "You truly are though, aren't you?"

He smiles and puts his hand on Peter's shoulder. "What if I am, Chadwick? What of it?"

Peter brushes him off. "You know we used to put people like you in prison."

"I know," Jacob says, "now you just send us to boarding schools."

CHAPTER 33: TIMOTHY

This won't just go away. He'll never deny it...he'd consider that disingenuous, and news like this will travel fast. I do admire him though. Jacob Weston gives exactly zero fucks what people think.

We have some celebratory pizza at St. John's and then beg off. He got the stink-eye from Chadwick and one or two others, but it doesn't feel like the story is common knowledge...yet.

At Brigsley we open up a bottle of Barolo that Jake recently acquired. It's delectable.

"We shouldn't be drinking wine in the middle of the day. People will think we're a couple of tosspots."

Jake scoffs. "Let's pretend we're in Italy, shall we?"

"Don't you have class?" I ask.

"Poly Sci with Mr. Blair, but not for another hour. You?"

"Chemistry with the new beak," I answer.

Jake swirls his wine. "Who is that again?"

"Kendel."

He opens a book and starts highlighting passages, then he looks over and raises his eyebrows. I must look like I need to talk.

"Spit it out, Ashlock. What's the good of being friends if we can't say exactly what we mean to each other?"

"The locker room," I say quietly, "your little secret will soon be out."

"It was never a secret, Tim, and I've always been out."

We laugh. "If you weren't so crushingly handsome unclothed it might not have happened."

I scoff. "Don't put this on me. You should have made that a colder shower."

CHAPTER 34: JACOB

Political Science isn't really a science. It should be called, *Political Theory.* I mean it's not like you can do a controlled experiment in politics...or economics for that matter. It's all history and bullshit, mixed with conjecture about human behavior.

What I like about most sports is the definitive outcome. Finish with the fastest time and win the medal, no debate required. Politics is all squabbles and deliberations. You might argue that voting provides an unambiguous outcome, but you'd be wrong.

I enjoy this class though. Eric Blair is a great professor and bit of an outsider like me. He was born in Australia and went to college at Harvard. God only knows how he ended up teaching at a boarding school in England, but here he is. Everyone agrees that the man is brilliant.

There are only twelve boys in our class. The other toffs probably think they are going to be MPs (Members of Parliament) and a couple of them might indeed find their place in government. Boarding schools like White Oak are known as the nurses of England's statesmen. Scott Fitzgerald wrote that these institutions create the "self-consciousness of a governing class," which is just a kinder, gentler way to say: Elitists Snobs.

I open the top of my desk to stow my backpack only to find that someone has etched the words, *Fag-Boy* into the soft wood. My expression must have registered my surprised on the crude moniker because Professor Blair instantly notices.

"Did someone leave a scorpion in your desk, Weston?"

I try to regain my composure. "You might say that, sir. Someone has left me an engraved message."

He wrinkles his brow, "And would you like to share it with the class?"

"Not particularly."

Of course now I've built up curiosity regarding the matter. Those who are not already aware of it will surely take a look as soon as I'm away.

"Please, Jacob," Blair says.

"It reads, *fag-boy*."

Most of the boys in class laugh, but my friend Lance Reynolds, one of the few black lads at school does not. He looks sympathetic and Blair does not look amused.

"An interesting term. Does anyone here know about the long history of fagging in Britain?"

We look to one another. Chadwick looks rather shamed, but he's too obvious a suspect. Perhaps Morgan did it; he's smart enough to know arcane phrases.

"Does it have something to do with smoking?" Billy asks.

"No. Although the British say, *let's smoke a fag,* which originated from loose strands of tobacco sticking out of a hand-rolled cigarette which like the frayed end of a piece of rope, known as the fag-end, which became shortened to 'fag.'"

Oliver does indeed raise his hand.

"Mr. Morgan?"

"I believe it refers to the practice of younger boys acting as servants to the senior boys."

Blair nods. "Correct. Senior boys were given both power over and responsibility for the behavior of younger boys...but there were well-defined rights and duties associated with being a fag-master and with being a fag-boy. It was originally meant to teach the aristocracy about service from both ends of the relationship."

"Sounds like an excuse to adopt a bit of slavery to me," Lance says.

Blair's gaze wanders among us. "Slavery is another politically charged word, especially for people of color like yourself Mr. Reynolds, but in this scenario the boys who are slaves are eventually promoted to masters."

England is such an odd place. Rank, position, and class are still important, in the US it's about money and celebrity, but it always boils down to power.

"And was fagging practiced here at White Oak?"

"An excellent question, Mr. Weston. It is my understanding that fagging went on here until 1981, when it was finally abolished."

"Why was it stopped?" Peter asks.

Blair turns to the chalkboard and boldly write the phrase: *Abuse of Power*. "The practice degenerated into harsh discipline and corporal punishments, including brutal treatment of the younger boys. Sexual abuse was not uncommon. What began in the sixteenth century as a structure for maintaining order devolved into a means for older boys to bully and torture the most vulnerable among us."

"The three B's," Redgrave whispers, but I have no idea what he means.

"What are the three B's, Professor?" I ask.

Blair walk right up to me and places a hand on my desk. "The famous three B's of boarding school: *Bullying, Beating and Buggery*. A sad legacy even for our most prestigious institutions."

This gives me pause. I am old enough and big enough that someone would have to be both foolish and bold to want to fuck with me, but there are scores of boys here who are easy targets for sadistic, entitled bastards. The bell sounds ending class, but I raise my hand.

"Weston?"

"Thank you, sir." I look directly at Ollie Morgan. "I just wanted to say that whatever coward scratched this message into my desk had better watch his step. I am no one's fag."

Eric Blair smiles. "Gentlemen, I think we can all now comprehend how the American revolution began."

***

When the lads have filed out Lance lifts the top of my desk so he can see the engraving. "That's messed up, mate."

I look at him. "I imagine you've had to deal with your fair share of prejudice and name-calling around here."

He chuckles. "They don't call it *White* Oak for nothing. Do you know how many black lads are at this school?"

"Fifteen or twenty?" I guess.

"Eleven," he says bitterly. "We're rather an exclusive club. Let me tell you...it's easier to be gay than it is to be black."

"Oh this is going to be good," I say. "Please tell me how you've come to that conclusion, my friend."

He walks to the window, looking down at the quad. "You have the power to be invisible. If you walk into a room full of strangers no one can tell just by looking at you that you're gay. You can fit in. If I walk into that same room, women are hiding their purses. I'm black everywhere and all the time."

I squeeze his shoulder. "That's true enough, Lance, but consider this: You didn't have to sit your parents down when you were thirteen-years-old and tell them you were black."

We stare at each other, imagining what it would be like to switch places. "Okay," he says. "Well played."

"Kids are rejected and thrown into the street by their own families for being queer...but you know what would be really challenging?"

"Yeah," he says. "Being queer and black."

"Exactly," I say and we laugh at life.

CHAPTER 35: FULTON

I see him leaving Eric's lecture hall and so I feign a chance meeting. I drop my briefcase as I walk past and then bend down to pick it up.

"Hello Professor," he says and I turn, as if just noticing him.

"Why Jacob," I say, "just the man I wanted to see. Do you have a minute?"

"Of course. I'm on my way back to Brigsley."

I match his pace. "May I tag along? It's something of a rather personal nature."

"By all means."

When we are out of earshot from any other students I come to the point. "I spoke with Dr. Rowland regarding your session."

He grins.

"What the hell did you do to her?"

He touches his hand to his chest innocently in a 'who me?' pose, but finds he can't keep up his innocent charade for more than two seconds before laughing outright.

"I simply gave her a taste of her own medicine."

"Well," I remark, "she doesn't think you're suicidal. She thinks you're brilliant."

He's still grinning. "It doesn't take a PhD to come up with that assessment."

We pause on the path near his house. "And she thinks you're a sociopath."

He looks up, blinking. "Maybe I didn't give her enough credit."

I place an arm gently on his shoulder. "I think you should cut the poor doctor some slack. She has her qualities."

He quickly turns, confronting me.

"Dear Lord, you've slept with her!"

I'm both shocked and, I must say, impressed. Weston's insights run deeper than words on the page. This boy is a teenaged cross between Sherlock Holmes and Oscar Wilde.

"If I had it would be indiscrete to admit it to a student. It's against the rules for faculty to fraternize."

He's shaking his head at me. "I suppose the old adage, crazy in the head, crazy in the bed, must hold true…but Fulton, old man, seriously…she has more issues than the *New York Times*."

We both begin laughing. "Please keep whatever squalid little theory you've fabricated to yourself. I don't need a scandal, and neither does she."

He seems to understand the implications and motions toward his heart. "I'm exceedingly good at keeping secrets, I'm just not very good at having any," he says.

We've arrived at the cottage and I'm ready to head directly back to my office. This is not how I imagined this conversation in my head.

"Fulton," he says, "one more thing."

"Yes?"

"Please tell Crazy Town that she owes me one."

CHAPTER 36: TIMOTHY

Professor Wayne Kendel replaced Professor Warren after his wife fell ill earlier this term. Kendel is overweight, sweaty and unshaven. I never feel comfortable around him, and it isn't because he's a Scot. He makes me self-conscious, like I have spinach in my teeth and everyone is noticing, but no one is saying.

Chemistry has never been my strong suit either. I'm concerned about blowing the lab up, or spilling something caustic on my hands.

It surprises me when he asks me to stay after class. I want to escape as fast as possible, but I always do as I'm told.

"Mr. Ashlock," he says, "you're one of our scholarship boys, isn't that correct?"

"Yes," I say, "academics and music."

He's almost completely bald; the small fringe of hair that he has might once have been red but is now close-cropped and gray. It looks oily and unwashed.

"So, we'd hate to send you back to the ghettos simply because you're failing chemistry, would we?"

"Sir?" I say, "I'm not failing."

His plump little fingers are thumbing through his grade ledger. "Not yet, but you certainly aren't excelling, are you lad?"

"I suppose I'll try harder through exams and trials, Professor," I say, starting to gather my things to make a getaway.

"I have a proposition for you, Timothy..."

I can feel his gaze. "I'm recruiting a teacher's assistant, someone who can help out with the lab work, cleaning up and so on...I'm sure you'd be a fabulous aide-de-camp..."

He's moving closer. He has me nearly pinned against the steel worktable and his hands have started to roam. He's quickly behind me and his whispers become incoherent. I start to feel dizzy, as if a fog is carrying me far, far away.

When he finally grabs my genitals I want to scream out, to yell accusations, but I find myself paralyzed and afraid; frozen like a deer in headlamps.

This isn't the first time something like this has happened to me, and it probably won't be the last.

When I am allowed to go, I bolt for the toilet to be sick. I think I actually told Kendel I'd consider the assistant's position and I may have even thanked him, I can't recall.

***

I jog the distance home sobbing all the way, (It's the only place I can feel safe). When I burst inside, I find Jake shirtless and doing push-ups in front of the fireplace. He's also conjugating Latin out loud.

"*Amatus sum, amatus es, amatus est...*" he looks up for a second when I enter and smiles, "*Amati sumus, amati estis, amati sunt...*"

I dash for my room and shut the door. I can't let him see me in this state.

"Hey," I hear him call. In a moment he is rapping on my door. "Remember me? Your flatmate and best friend in the world..."

I abruptly realize that he is *the* person I most want to be with. I only feel safe in this cottage because I know he's here. I open the door and embrace him as hard as I can. I bury my head in his chest and squeeze him just to prove he is real.

"What's this for?" he says, returning my hug. "My birthday isn't until the end of the month."

I just hold on tighter. "Can't a friend show a bit of open affection?" I ask.

"Certainly, but you Englishmen usually keep your feelings sealed up in a jar under the bed."

"I missed you."

He pulls away and takes my face in his hands.

"You've been crying. What happened? What's wrong?"

Nothing ever gets past Jacob Weston. He's far too clever for me to lie, so I tell him as much of the truth as I can remember...and he is bloody furious.

"I'll kill him," he yells.

"Please leave it alone."

He's storming the halls so I follow him into the living room. He locates his monogrammed silver flask from out of its hiding place and takes a long pull on it, handing it to me afterwards. I oblige. The whiskey is both smooth and warming.

"I'll have him killed then. Slowly, so we can watch him suffer."

It's impossible to tell how much he means and how much is in jest. "You've gone mad, Jake. I'll be fine."

"Bullshit," he yells, "the bastard will pay!"

I take another swallow of the smokey liquor. "If I screamed blue murder every time a bloke around here tried to fondle my wares...I'd have gone hoarse in a fortnight."

This news only seems to enrage him more. "Make a list...I'll slay them all."

I laugh. It's then that I realize just how much I am loved by this madman. Hearing him rant about morality, decency and protecting my honor. He would never allow any harm to come to me... not ever. He would die first.

I grab him by the back of his neck and pull him close. I kiss him as deeply and fully as I have ever kissed anyone in my life. My eyes close and the warmth of his mouth becomes my entire world. He doesn't pull away; he's tentative and gentle. Waiting to see what I'll do next. When we finally look at one another, he whispers, "Why?"

"Because you are stronger than I will ever be, and because you are utterly fearless and alive. I know that you love me and it's impossible not to feel something in return. You are an unstoppable force, Jake Weston."

CHAPTER 37: JACOB

I wake with Tim sleeping in my arms. We've crossed a rubicon and I'm worried that as time passes he'll want to slow things down, or cease the recent developments altogether.

All we've done is what I call *snuggle and snog,* strictly first-base maneuvers. It wouldn't have been right to do anything more after his traumatic day. Last night I worried as he pressed so closely against me that he would notice my excitement...but he was too much of a gentleman to mention it if he did.

I climb out of bed and dress in the dark, trying not to disturb him. It's almost five AM and Ethan will be waiting to take me into London.

I look again at Timothy asleep in my bed and just seeing his head on the pillow makes me feel like the luckiest person alive.

***

After practice I set my mind to the goal at hand. It takes me exactly thirteen minutes to hack into the White Oak servers.

My search quickly leads me to some encrypted folders, which I break into and copy. When I have all the evidence I need, I cover my tracks and head for his office.

Kendel answers my knock and his expression is both confused and pleased.

"Yes?"

"Hello Professor. I'm Jacob Weston."

He smiles and I smile back. "Weston, I don't believe you're in any of my classes, I'm sure I'd remember you."

He's taken over Professor Warren's old office and turned it into a disorderly nightmare. Books are stacked on the floor, papers and folders are piled high on the desk. Soda cans and candy wrappers fill the overflowing trashcan.

"I wasn't expecting visitors..."

I laugh as I look around. "Maid's day off?"

"Indeed," he says. I'm wearing the school uniform, but I've loosened my St. John's tie and rolled up my sleeves. I know these pants are way too tight; so yeah, I'm tempting him and I want to see him drool. The fat, old bastard. "So, what can I do for you?"

I lean over his desk, and give my long blond hair a quick shake. If he makes a move on me, he'll regret the day he was born.

"Sir, I'll be taking Chemistry during the Lent halve. I was wondering if Dr. Warren is returning to his post or if you will still be filling in."

He gives me another greasy smile. "I don't know for sure. It would be enchanting to have you in class though. You're American, aren't you?"

"That's right," I say, "I'm the billionaire's son."

A faint recognition passes over his face. "Ah, yes. The swimmer. I've watched you by the pool."

I grin. "I bet you have." He's starting to get suspicious.

"It's nice of you to drop by and introduce yourself, Mr. Weston. But if you'll excuse me, I really must begin preparing for my next class."

I bend over to tie my shoe so he can get a good look at my bum. "I'll just take up another moment, sir." I stare directly into his pudgy, red face so I can see the glint of lust. "You know, Timothy Ashlock is my dearest friend."

He looks a bit guilty. "Is he? Mr. Ashlock is one of White Oak's finest."

"Indeed, he is," I say. "Which is why I became so enraged when I heard that you were grabbing his naughty bits yesterday."

Kendel looks offended. "I don't know what vicious rumor you've heard, Mr. Weston, but let me assure you..."

"Shut the fuck up," I whisper.

"How dare you!"

"Listen carefully, Wayne. If you touch him inappropriately again, or make him feel uncomfortable in any way...there will be consequences."

"Really?" he say sarcastically, "And what might those be?"

I glare at him. "Hmm, I suppose eventually someone will find your body floating facedown in the Thames."

"I could have you expelled for threatening me!"

I cross my arms and smile. "You know, I have a talent with computers and earlier today I was playing around with the White Oak servers when I came across some personal folders of yours."

His eyes widen. "You must be mistaken."

"I'm quite certain you were in several of the images. One does like to keep mementos, I suppose."

He looks nervous. "All of my files are password protected," he stammers.

"Oh please," I scoff, "I copied everything and saved it to a thumb drive, just in case you decide to clean house, though judging by this office that seems unlikely. So here's what's going to happen: You will finish out this halve without touching another boy. At the end of the term you will give Timothy an 'A' in Chemistry, then you will slither away from White Oak Academy forever. Are we clear, Wayne?"

He knows when he's been beaten.

"Get out," he whispers.

CHAPTER 38: TIMOTHY

I'm at the Buttery eating at our usual table and he's late, which is odd because Jake never misses a meal. He constantly complains about the food here, naturally, but that has never stopped him from eating copious amounts of it.

I've got Billy to keep me company and it's fish and chips day, so everyone's in a good mood. Even the kitchens at White Oak can't muck up batter-fried cod. Finally we see him wander in and load a tray with enough food for two hungry swimmers. He comes waltzing up with a huge grin on his mug.

"All right, lads?"

Billy says, "All right."

I have to wonder what he's playing at.

"I'm hungrier than a hostage," he says, tucking in.

"Have you heard the news?" Billy asks.

Jake seems curious. "I guess that depends on what news you're referring to..."

"Tim and I both got into the pageant!"

He looks at me but I stare at my fish.

"Fantastic!"

"With girls!" Billy exclaims.

"Yes, I read about the female presence," he says. "How scandalous. Who will you two be playing?"

I laugh because Billy is twice as keen as I am. "We're both ghosts!" he exclaims.

"Is that so?" and he gazes at me with those piercing blue eyes.

"I'm the Ghost of Christmas Yet to Come...and Tim is the ghost of Jacob Marley," he states.

"*Jacob* Marley? What delicious irony." I press his foot under the table with mine.

"Why were you late for lunch?" I ask him.

"Oh," he says, turning to look at some lads kicking a ball outside. "I had a meeting with that new beak...Wayne Kendel."

Billy frowns. "He certainly never misses a meal."

I stare at Jake and he winks at me.

"I heard some news as well," he says.

"What's that?"

"Apparently a new cell tower went up right on the outskirts of White Oak Academy. Now the boys can stream porn on their phones faster than ever before."

Billy lights up. "That is good news!"

Jake directs all his attention to Redgrave. "Say, Billy, I'm having a little dinner party at Brigsley next Thursday. I'd really like it if you could attend. It's only for my best friends."

Billy smiles his widest, gap-toothed grin. "I'd be honored. What time?"

"About nine o'clock."

He bows. "I'll be looking forward to it."

CHAPTER 39: JACOB

This school day can't end fast enough for me. I've been looking forward to being with Tim all afternoon.

I stoke a mighty fire and light every candle. I've taken a shower and put on a cashmere sweater and soft cotton sweats. I assume he's at his string ensemble because his violin is gone. In the meantime I make some finishing touches to my Suicide Author's paper for Fulton.

My seventeenth birthday is coming up on November thirtieth, which happens to be another strange British holiday: St. Andrew's Day.

It's apparently a massive deal in Scotland, but all of the Commonwealth gets into it. At White Oak parents are invited to the school on St. Andrew's and there are a variety of activities, including concerts, which is why Tim is nervous. Also, his mother is attending...and I'm excited to meet her. The only activity I've signed up for is playing in an inter-house waterpolo match.

When Tim turns up he catches me in the act of making his favorite beverage...Irish coffee. I fill two big ceramic mugs and hand him one as he sets his things down on the table.

"You are a godsend," he says.

"How was practice?"

"Fine, I guess."

He looks like it was anything but fine. "Why are you making a face then?"

"Let's just be charitable and say that Seth Ferguson is no Yo-Yo Ma on the cello."

I sit by the fire and watch him take off his shoes. He comes over and sits in my lap, which is a new thing.

"I thought about you today," he says.

I smile. "I think about you every day."

"So what exactly did you say to Kendel?"

I sigh. "Nothing much. I threatened his life."

"You didn't!"

"Of course I did. The fat fuck. I don't think he'll be bothering you again, or anyone else for that matter."

"How will I ever repay you?"

"I'm sure you'll think of something."

He gives me a slow deliberate kiss. His mouth is wet and hot...then he gets up. "I need a shower. I smell like teen spirit."

I laugh. "No fair teasing me with just one kiss...but you do get points for the Kurt Cobain reference."

He walks behind the couch and bends down to whisper in my ear. "I found something on Tommy Walker."

I sit upright. "You were using my MacBook, right?"

"Yes, yes," he says, "I was on your VPN. It was all completely clandestine. Listen to this though, he disappeared on Monday, March fifteenth, 1976...and it happened to be storming like mad that evening."

I feel myself swallow. "*Beware the Ides of March...*"

"What?" Tim asks.

"It's Shakespeare. A soothsayer named Spurinna comes to Julius Caesar in the play warning him: Beware the Ides of March. March fifteenth, which is when Caesar was killed."

"You amaze me," he says. "You really should go on a quiz show."

"To win a bunch of money?"

He shakes his head. "Sorry, sometimes I forget that you're already filthy rich. The reference is just in the play though, right? It's fiction?"

"No. Shakespeare was using a historical fact. The real Julius Caesar was murdered on March fifteenth, forty-four BC."

"Do you think the killer is using literary references, or is it just some odd coincidence?"

"Beats me," I say, "but I hate coincidences."

"Hey, what's the deal with the dinner party on Thursday?"

I smile. "I'm tired of celebrating all your obscure British holidays. Thursday happens to be a traditional American feast day...Thanksgiving. So I'm inviting a few people over and we are going to eat the customary meal. I think you'll enjoy it."

"Doesn't that involve a turkey?" he asks.

"It does indeed."

CHAPTER 40: TIMOTHY

Mr. Blackmore is handing out copies of the play to the assembled cast while Mrs. Logan, a rapidly degenerating spinster, watches carefully. She has brought her birds over from Bentley Wood to begin preparations for the play.

"Today we will have a brief read-through to familiarize ourselves with the material and to get to know one another," Blackmore announces. "We have several weeks to put this up, which is plenty of time, but I think we all want to make it a smashing success."

Redgrave and the other boys seem fascinated with the five girls who've made the trek into our realm but I'm rather disappointed. First of all, they are dressed identically in the Bentley Wood uni which consists of an ill-fitting, masculine blue blazer, V-neck sweater and starched white shirt. It looks like a skirt might have been an option with this ensemble, but they're all wearing navy blue trousers.

I wonder if the girls are as disenchanted with us. We're a motley pack, no denying it. I think Mrs. Logan is miffed that we aren't wearing neckties. It's supposed to be a theatrical rehearsal though, not luncheon with the Queen.

We are to go around the room stating our names, our part in the play and then give one personal remark. It's a kind of ice-breaker but most of the personal comments are pretty mundane or silly.

"I'm William Redgrave, I'm playing the Ghost of Christmas Yet to Be, and I can walk on my hands."

I roll my eyes.

The girls are not much better. A tall girl with shoulder-length mousey brown hair says, "I'm Lily Wallace, I'm playing Mrs. Cratchit, and I can speak French fluently."

I have no idea what my tidbit will be. We get to a slip of a girl with short blond hair who says, "I'm Sam Milford, I'm playing Belle, and I'm an atheist."

This gets an immediate reaction from the room. It's a bold statement, after all. I think chapel is as mandatory at Bentley Wood as it is at White Oak.

Mrs. Logan seems flustered by her. "I'm sure you don't mean that, Samantha." She laughs nervously.

"Oh but I do, Mrs. Logan. I put God right up there with Father Christmas and leprechauns."

We all laugh. I have the distinct feeling this girl is deliberately trying to stir the pot.

We get through a few more people and it comes to me.

"I'm Timothy Ashlock, I'm playing Jacob Marley, and I've actually seen a ghost."

This also gets some murmurs, though mostly it garners scoffing. I do see the girl Sam look over though, and she smiles.

After we have read through the entire play there are various assignments and announcements. We'll be blocking the production at our next meeting, then we break for refreshments; tea and cookies.

We are all naturally too polite (and terrified) to go up and speak with any of the girls. Samantha, however, walks right up to me.

"How old are you?"

"Seventeen," I answer.

"I don't believe in ghosts," she says firmly.

I look at her and up close she is rather pretty. She's uncommonly delicate looking, with a tiny button nose. "No?" I say. "You don't seem to believe in much of anything, do you?"

"So where did you see it?"

I'm not sure how much detail I want to get into regarding Tommy. "He haunts the cottage I live in."

Redgrave has joined us. "It's true," he says, shoving a cookie into his mouth.

She begins to interrogate him. "And have you seen his cottage ghost?"

Billy shakes his head. "No, but I've seen heaps of others. White Oak is ripe with spirits."

"Oh for fuck's sake," she says.

I'm floored. I've never heard a girl curse before. Billy is just staring at her, and that's when Mrs. Logan breaks things up. It's time to whisk the ladies back across the bridge.

***

When I get home to Brigsley I find Jake reading in bed. "So how was it?" he asks me.

"Fine, fine."

"Did you start to feel faint being in a room with teenaged girls?"

"Hilarious," I answer. "What's that you're reading?"

He holds up the book. "Research. Thomas Sweatt, a notorious serial arsonist."

"You thinking of starting some fires?"

"Only in my mind," he says.

I begin to take off my clothes and I watch Jake watching me. When I am down to my knickers I climb in with him.

"Do you mind terribly?"

"I insist, Mr. Ashlock."

"I just don't want to be alone tonight," I admit. He drops the book to the floor and takes me in his arms.

"And why is that?"

"It's the anniversary," I tell him, "of Henry."

He hugs me tight and I begin to relax in his warm embrace.

"I didn't know the date," he whispers. "Did you ring up your mum?"

"I did," I say. "She's spending the night with my aunt. We've both managed to stay pretty busy during the day, keeping occupied. But at night..."

He takes my hand and kisses my palm.

"I miss him, Jake. I truly do."

CHAPTER 41: JACOB

Returning from London this morning I've had Ethan stop so I could pick up all the necessary ingredients for our special dinner.   I never realized how labor-intensive Thanksgiving is to pull off. Where are the servants when you need them?

In any case, I've baked two pumpkin pies by the time I have to go to Fulton's class. On the way there I notice a group of boys queued up in front of the Headmaster's office, and Redgrave is among them.

"So what are you lot waiting for?" I ask.

"It's flogging day," Billy says, staring at his shoes.

"What, all of you?" I'm incredulous, there are eight boys in line.   "What did you do, plot the overthrow of the British Empire?"

"Worse," Redgrave says. "Cannabis violation...and this is my second offense. I stand to get a flogging and expulsion."

"Billy," I grasp his shoulder. "Surely Rothwell won't give you the boot just for smoking a bit of weed. You're the son of an Earl."

"Don't know," he admits.   "Blackie found the whole stash later when he searched my room...nearly half a kilogram hidden in the back of my closet."

I shake my head. That's nearly a pound of weed, what was he thinking?

"Rothwell and my old man go way back, but I doubt their friendship is going to slow the cricket bat down."

***

Tim is already at his desk when I get to class. "How are your preparations coming for tonight?"

"Pies are cooling. I'll put the turkey in as soon as this class is over." I drum on my desk. "It's going to be awesome!"

"I've never had a real American Thanksgiving. It's to celebrate your killing all the native people, right?" He's trying to take the piss out of me.

"We won't be celebrating that," I say. "And don't get me started on British colonization techniques." I lean in close to whisper. "Redgrave and seven other blokes are getting flogged over at the Headmaster's as we speak. Blackmore managed to catch them smoking pot."

"Where were they?" he asks.

"On the roof of St. John's apparently. The jossers. There was so much smoke people thought the place was on fire. You have to wonder where they got all that weed. Someone must have a supplier in London."

He gives me a knowing glance. "I think they have a more local source."

CHAPTER 42: TIMOTHY

Jake is doing six things at once trying to get the dinner prepared on time. I tell him about Guy Fawkes Night and following Paddy and Billy to the shed since it's obviously related to the weed.

"It makes perfect sense," Jake says, mashing a lumpy bowl of boiled potatoes near the sink. "The groundskeeper is cultivating marijuana for a built-in clientele." He sneers. "Talk about a captive audience. It's probably a damn good side-hustle for the old geezer."

"Risky though. One of those lads is bound to rat him out," I say.

Jake disagrees. "Redgrave is probably the only bloke that knows who the actual farmer is, and he won't talk. If Lester gets the sack it will cut off the supply chain."

"So what do we do about it?"

Jake opens the oven and checks on his bird. He's so focused he's barely listening to me. "Excuse me, Julia Child, I asked you what we should do?"

He looks up at me warmly. "Cooking is all about timing, Timothy. Don't let anyone tell you different." He's stirring a pot on the stove; I'm not even sure of its contents, and he's called his butler twice already asking for guidance on the stuffing and cooking of gigantic, wild fowl. "We can't accuse the old boy without evidence," he says, and I know where this is leading. "We'll have to go check it out in person and photograph the premises."

I was afraid he was going to say that.

CHAPTER 43: THANKSGIVING

William Redgrave arrives first, at half past eight, and he's wearing a proper suit and tie.

"Hey," Jake says. "You look dashing."

"I know I'm early," he admits, "I thought I might help out."

"Good man. Help set the table, and all the candles need to be lit...again."

Jacob has wireless bluetooth speakers set strategically around the cottage playing blues music on low volume. It's one of his favorite playlists: Stevie Ray Vaughan, Aretha, Jimi Hendrix, Etta James and others.

Timothy has scrubbed and polished, waxed and shined every surface from floor to ceiling. As he's moving past the kitchen Jacob grabs him.

"Thank you."

Timothy bows. "Just doing my bit, mate."

"No really," Jacob says. "Thank you. Brigsley looks brand spanking new."

Fulton arrives next and he's carrying a bottle of wine. "What's this?" Jacob teases, "breaking more rules, sir?" He takes the bottle, scanning the label. It's a Joseph Phelps (Freestone Vineyard) Pinot Noir.

"Actually students are allowed to drink wine, beer or cider if an adult is present...but it's probably best if we don't mention it beyond these walls."

They laugh. "I was worried you might not have a corkscrew," he says.

"I think we can manage it."

"How many are you expecting?" Timothy asks.

"Two more, and they're coming together." Jacob pats Fulton on the back. "Most people don't know that Pinot Noir is the perfect wine to serve with turkey, and it's from Sonoma. I didn't take you for an oenophile."

"I have a few tricks up my sleeve," he says. "I read your paper this afternoon, by the way."

"Oh?"

"I'm recommending you for a send up."

Jacob looks at his teacher and friend. "That's gracious of you, but not necessary."

"You earned it. I hope that once you graduate from here you'll stay in contact. I'm interested to see what becomes of you."

He removes the turkey from the oven, and it's perfect. He sets it on a large silver platter and places it in the middle of the table. "When I leave White Oak, sir, we will vacation together in Ibiza. We are friends for life."

Ethan comes in with Coach Lir and he is also bearing wine. Two bottles. Jake quickly scoops them up.

"Are these the right ones?" Ethan asks confidentially. Jacob studies the labels. David Duband, Nuits-Saint-Georges. 2013.

"Perfect," he says. "Thanks for stopping for them."

Introductions are made all round while Timothy helps get the food to the table.

"It's going to be crowded," he says.

Redgrave leans over, "If you don't mind, I'd prefer to stand."

Timothy shakes his head in sympathy. "I've been there. How many?"

"Five," he says. "Bloodied my best school trousers on the walk back to St. Johns."

"Jesus."

The Coach is inspecting the cottage. "This place is very posh. When I went to school they had us twenty-five to a room and only two toilets for the lot of us."

"Coach," Jacob says. "No offense, but you went to school in Ireland."

Coach Lir grabs Jacob's ear. "And a damn fine school 'twas, too."

Everyone is gazing at the meal laid out before them. A gigantic roasted turkey with stuffing and vegetables, mashed potatoes, gravy, fresh rolls, corn on the cob, and homemade cranberry sauce.

"You did all this by yourself?" Fulton asks.

"With a little help from our butler and YouTube, but yeah."

Timothy elbows Jacob. "Someone should say grace before we begin, don't you agree?"

Jacob gestures, looking for a volunteer.

"Fine, I'm the oldest one here. It ought to be me," Coach Lir says. Jacob grabs Timothy's hand on one side and Fulton's on the other. When the circle is complete, they bow their heads. Dylan prays: "For food that stays our hunger, for rest that brings us ease, for homes where memories linger...we give our thanks for these. Amen!"

Fulton carves the turkey and Jake pours the Sonoma wine first. Everyone begins to pile their plates with food.

"That was a beautiful prayer," Ethan mentions to the Coach.

"Why thank you, Laddie. Learned it when I was a boy...in *Irish* school." He stares at Jacob, who can only grin.

"How long you been teaching, Fulton?" Dylan asks.

"This is my fifth year. How about you, how long have you been coaching?"

He does the math quickly in his head. "Twenty-six years...longer than these boys have been alive."

Ethan scoops up more stuffing. "I hope you don't mind me asking...but I'm up before dawn driving this little bugger into London twice a week, and he won't tell me how he's progressing. So, how fast is he, Coach?"

Lir gives a sidelong glance in Jacob's direction, and Jacob waves his hand. "Not to puff him up, but he's greased lightning in the water. A dizzying, full-throttled blur. If they held the games tomorrow, he'd medal for certain."

Billy whistles, and Timothy and Fulton look impressed.

"Yeah, yeah...and if my aunt had balls she'd be my uncle," Jacob quips.

"He never speaks about his training," Ethan says.

Dylan slaps him on the back. "You're welcome to come in and watch, instead of sitting in the car for three hours. I would welcome the help."

Fulton has left the table to open the other bottles. "This is an exquisite vintage, Mr. Polley."

"Aye, just picked those up at a wineshop I know in Covent Garden."

Fulton stares directly at Jacob and winks.

"So this holiday," Dylan says, "it's to celebrate your lot kicking Indian jacksy, right?"

"Good God," Jacob mumbles and stands up. "It's a highly mediocre meal that everyone in the United States eats on the same day. Today. It's about family, football and tradition. I've asked you all here tonight to celebrate with me and to hear me give my thanks publicly. Coach, Professor, Ethan, Billy and Timmy. You've made this place my home and you have become my extended family. I'm truly grateful for the kindness each one of you has shown me. Raise your glasses, gents."

They all raise up their wine. "May your neighbors respect you, trouble neglect you, the angels protect you, and heaven accept you."

They gorge themselves for more than an hour and after relaxing by the fire for a bit, Jacob turns to Timothy. "I think it's time we had some live music."

"You're barmy."

"Can't you see that we are five gentlemen in desperate need of cultural enrichment?"

The Coach looks bewildered. "Do one of you lads sing and dance?"

"Timothy here is a violinist," Jacob says.

"Hop to it then, man, we haven't got all night!"

He obediently finds his instrument.

"Can you play something lively?" Dylan asks.

"I've just the thing for you, Coach."

He vaults into the *Swallowtail Jig,* a fast moving Irish folk tune which brings joy to the Coach's eyes as he claps along.

"You could capture the hearts of many a lass with a gift like that, young sir," Dylan says. "Thank you kindly."

Redgrave grins. "He's already stolen the heart of the prettiest bird in our play...he's got that to give thanks for himself."

Jacob smiles and watches Timothy placing the violin back in its case, "Is that a fact?"

"It's an exaggeration," Timothy says.

As the mantle clock strikes midnight, it's time for some to take their leave. Friday is, after all, still a work and school day. The Coach and Ethan depart first, Ethan assuring everyone that he is sober enough to manage the road back.

Jacob whispers to Billy, "I have some aloe ointment that will help with your condition, if you'd like it."

Billy nods. "That would be much appreciated." He follows Jacob into the bathroom. Fulton is admiring the photo of Weston and his mother. He turns to Timothy when they are alone.

"So how are you and Jake getting along as flatmates?" he asks.

"Couldn't be better, Professor."

"You seem extremely close."

Timothy blushes. "He's my best mate."

"Well, don't do anything I wouldn't do."

He chuckles. "A bit late for that."

"Fulton!" Jacob shouts, "could you come to the loo for a moment, please."

Fulton and Timothy both go into the bathroom where Redgrave's pants are down around his ankles. His backside is a flurry of swollen, bloody welts and lurid bruises. Blood has caked into rust-colored gashes where the flesh has been shredded; below the deep cuts his skin has bloomed into an inflamed mix of purple, pink and red.

"My God, boy!" Fulton exclaims as Jacob gingerly applies the healing ointment.

"Our Headmaster," Jacob fumes. "How is this behavior even legal?"

Fulton has turned his face away. "I daresay it isn't. Redgrave you need to see the nurse. Those cuts could become infected, and a report needs to be filed with the Board of Directors. Weston, please photograph his injuries for evidence."

"No," Billy says through clenched teeth. "No way. If I cause any more grief to Rothwell he'll have me expelled for sure. He's letting me stay...so I'll just take my lumps."

"He flogged seven other boys today, and Tim less than a month ago," Jacob says.

"Not as bad as that," Timothy replies.

"So, he's upping his game. How long until someone lands in hospital?"

Redgrave pulls up his trousers. "Please I'm begging, no one else can know."

Fulton puts a hand tenderly on Billy's shoulder. "Someone is going to have to have the courage to come forward and say something so this will end."

"I understand, sir. But it's going to have to be somebody else."

Jacob is deep in thought.

"Billy, please come around tomorrow and for the next few days. I'll get some Epsom salts and you can take warm baths here. It will help your cuts to heal and not get infected. Do you have something for the pain?"

"Just aspirin."

Jacob pulls some pills from the medicine cabinet, then glances at Fulton. "You didn't see this," he mumbles. "These are Vicodin. Take a half tablet before bed, it will help you sleep."

Billy firmly hugs him. "I don't know what I'd do without you."

***

Just before Fulton leaves he pulls Jacob outside to have a private chat. "Your chauffeur has discerning taste in wine; what do those bottles go for, about 200 quid each?"

"You're in the right ballpark. Honestly, I thought your Phelps was every ounce as splendid."

Fulton looks at him in the darkness. "How is your novel coming along?"

Jacob smiles, hair falling into his eyes. "I'm finding my voice."

"I hope you aren't corrupting Ashlock with your charming ways."

He leans on the doorframe. "For the record, he kissed me first."

Fulton scoffs. "That may be true, but you've been seducing him since the moment you met."

Jacob raises a brow. "Yes, since that fateful day when you introduced us. You know, you're a lot more insightful than Dr. Jane. Her observations sound like horrible, inspirational Facebook posts passed along by well-meaning but moronic friends. May I tell you something in confidence though?"

"Yes, of course."

"I believe I'm falling in love. He's different from the usual minions and knuckle-draggers that are the norm for boys my age. I get too easily attached to people...especially the beautiful, brilliant ones."

Fulton nods. "In that case, I advise caution. Love at your age burns with white-hot intensity, but the flames usually die out just as fast, and can be devastating."

Jacob sighs. "When love is not madness, it is not love, and I'm afraid I've gone completely mad."

"What are you going to do about the Headmaster?" Fulton asks.

"What makes you think I'm going to do anything? I'm one of the few boys he hasn't flogged."

"I know you. You have some devious plan in the works."

He turns to go back into the house. "Since you mention it, Professor, I do have an idea or two."

CHAPTER 44: TIMOTHY

It's five-thirty AM and Jake is shaking me awake. He, of course, is used to getting up before dawn while I certainly am not.

"It's time, old chum. Let's not sleep the entire day away!"

I'm trying to force myself awake. He looks fresh as daisies, full of energy and life. How is it possible to be so jovial when it is such a dark, cold and miserable world?

"Sod off, Jake. Honestly."

He looks offended. "I'm postponing my training for this...so up and at 'em."

I climb out of my incredibly warm bed and stumble to the loo. We've decided to wear running gear so that if we happen upon anyone, (not bloody likely at this hour) we will just look like two morons enjoying an early workout.

We start at the Great Lawn so that I can retrace my exact steps from the night in question and it's a good thing too because the trail is nearly invisible.

"You're sure this is the way..."

"Please stop asking," I say, and in truth I'm not certain at all. Guy Fawkes Night was dark, cold and pouring rain. I do know we're heading in the correct direction, generally speaking.

I stop to rest for a moment and Jake looks impatient since he apparently never tires. We watch the sunrise from amid the trees and winter heath.

"I don't understand why this is the perfect hour to accomplish our mission," I say.

Jake massages my shoulders as we stare toward the east. It's a beautiful morning filled with pink and orange streaks across a lavender sky. "Because," he states, "Lester is a nightcrawler. There's no possible way he's awake."

I'm skeptical. "I thought groundsmen thrived in the early morning. That's the common thinking in any case."

"Then he's the exception that proves the rule. I've been monitoring the old boy, and speaking as someone who always greets the sunrise...he's almost never up and about at this hour, unless he's hunting."

"Hunting?" I say with a measure of fear. "You mean with a rifle?"

"Don't worry," he says.

We walk on, and the path does get more conspicuous. It's beginning to look like a game trail.

"This appears right," I say.

We jog, side-by-side. I'm waking up, and even starting to enjoy the break in my routine. "There was a heavy chain and lock on the door of the barn. How do you propose to get in?"

He stares at me like there's drool dripping down my chin. I guess I'd forgotten who I was speaking to for an instant. We come upon the shed five minutes later. As we casually run up toward it, Jake has the audacity to knock on the door.

"No one at home," he says, removing his backpack. I stand next to him, keeping a lookout.

"You can smell it, can't you?" he asks.

I sniff the air, which smells sweet and woodsy. "I can't, to be honest."

Jake has taken out two small metal tools which look like long, thin tweezers. He fiddles with them inside the keyhole of the steel lock and in less than a minute it snaps open.

"Brilliant," I say and we scurry inside.

I'm nearly knocked over by the pungent, sickly sweet smell of all the pot. Dozens upon dozens of the cut plants hang upside down by fishing line attached to the ceiling.

"It's as I thought," Jake says, removing his phone and snapping photos of the interior of the shed. "This is a drying and trimming cabin. He must be growing the plants in one of the greenhouses."

"How much do you think is here?"

He looks around, calculating. "Several pounds at least, once it's all been trimmed." He takes a bag of the merchandise and places it in his pack. I frown.

"Oh, it's not for me," he says grinning. "I get drug-tested every few weeks. But Christmas is only a month away and Redgrave has lost his stash."

"So, what now?"

"I'd burn this little shanty down, if I wasn't concerned about the whole hillside going up in flames. Cannabis is a Class B drug on your little Victorian island. Lester could be looking at fourteen years in prison, which for him would be a life sentence. So..."

"So?"

He zips up his backpack and peeks out the shed door to make sure the coast is clear. He motions me outside and refastens the lock. In moments we are heading back to campus at a leisurely pace.

"Let's not be hasty. We don't want to rush to judgement and ruin an old man's life. He's providing a service, albeit at a hefty profit."

CHAPTER 45: JACOB

I've made two turkey sandwiches and put a couple of slices of leftover pumpkin pie on a plate and I'm off. She's in her garden when I arrive.

"Good morning, Kitty," I say. "I've brought you something."

She's wearing tight-fitting jeans, a denim shirt and a wide-brimmed hat. I believe I've caught her in the middle of planting bulbs for Spring.

"Jake! What a surprise. And what's this?" She pulls off her gardening gloves and takes the plate from me.

"I made Thanksgiving supper last night for a couple of the lads. I would have invited you and the Headmaster, but it was far too cramped in our cottage, and too lowbrow an affair for you to attend."

She slaps my shoulder, "Come inside you scamp."

"I can only stay a moment, I have class in half an hour."

She pours us both a glass of milk, just as the Headmaster enters the room. He's tying his necktie.

"A bit early to be making social calls, isn't it Weston?"

"Apologies sir, this is the only free time I have today."

"Stilly," Kitty says, "Jake made Thanksgiving dinner last night and he's been kind enough to share a bit of it with me!"

She bites into the pie and closes her eyes. "It's divine. I haven't had a good piece of pumpkin pie in years! It brings back memories."

I smile.

"If I didn't know better I'd think you were trying to steal my wife," Rothwell jokes.

"Never, sir," and I wink at him. Kitty has gone positively misty though.

"This is such a kindness," she says, "you have no idea."

"We ex-pats have got to stick together," I say.

"Hmm, it's good to see you can make use of a kitchen, most boys at White Oak would be lost around an oven," Rothwell says.

"I spent a lot of my time with the servants growing up. The kitchen is the best place to hear the latest gossip."

Kitty giggles. "That's so true."

"Shouldn't you be at Ducker this morning?" he asks.

"I'm cross-training. I did a run this morning, and I'll swim tonight."

"Headmaster Fetterman at Eton has already called me this week. I think you have his boys a bit worried..."

"Ha! That's good to know. My coach was over for supper last night, I'll have to tell him when I see him tomorrow."

"Oh," Rothwell says, "I'm sorry I missed Coach Lir. I'd have liked to discuss your progress."

"Apologies again, Headmaster. It was cramped quarters last night at Brigsley. William Redgrave didn't sit down all night..." And I give him a deep, accusing stare.

CHAPTER 46: SAMANTHA

Acting in a play would not ordinarily be my thing, but Mrs. Logan strong-armed a group of us girls so here I am. I'd assumed that the boys White Oak Academy would offer up for its Christmas pageant would be the run-of-the-mill, nerdy, kiss-ass types that I've always been so bored around.

Still, there are a few exceptions in this lot which make the trip into Sausageville worthwhile. The boy who's playing Scrooge has a smashing body, not to be shallow or anything. He's eighteen and his name is Oliver Something and I guess he's God's gift because everyone seems to grovel around him.

The other one that caught my eye is fiendishly clever and shy: Timothy Ashlock. He's my age and may actually be prettier than me with his shiny black hair and blue eyes. He claims he's seen a ghost, which is pure drivel, but it does make me curious.

He's only in the first few scenes of the play, so he spends most of rehearsal off to the side of the stage reading manky paperbacks. I think he memorized all his lines on the first day.

His best friend is a thick chap named William Redgrave who's always clowning around. Lilly did the research on the boys, checking into peerage because, "one never knows." It ends up Redgrave is landed gentry, the son of an Earl. Ashlock doesn't seem to be anybody.

I'm undoubtedly going to be snogging one of them before this play is over...the question is: who to choose?

CHAPTER 47: TIMOTHY

Jake is going to be over the moon when he hears the news. I finally feel like I'm pulling my weight around here.

He comes bustling into the cottage, drops his backpack immediately and collapses onto the couch.

"Rough day at the office, mate?"

He grins at me. "It's exhausting bickering with people who wouldn't know a valid argument if it bit them on the arse."

I put on the kettle. He's always like this after Political Science.

"Fancy a cuppa?"

"Thank you, please," he says. I can't help but smile and he quizzically raises an eyebrow. "Why do you look like the cat that swallowed the canary?"

"Wait for your tea."

He gets up and corners me. Jake's powers of perception are outlandish. I wonder what he will be capable of in five years.

"You rapscallion!" he points at my chest. "What have you discovered?"

I calmly place the teapot on the table and motion for him to sit. "Only the motherlode," I say beaming. He sits forward and blows on his English Breakfast tea.

"Before you begin let me just reiterate that I always had the most profound confidence in your ability..."

"Do shut up," I say, and he laughs. I have a notebook entirely devoted to Tommy, which I consult. "Thomas H. Walker was not the first lad to go missing from White Oak Academy, or from Brigsley Cottage, for that matter. Three months before he disappeared two other boys were kidnapped...and both of them lived here."

"Bloody Hell!"

"Their names were Duncan Greer and Robin Brody, both sixteen."

"Incredible," Jake says, "and were their bodies ever found?"

I gesture toward the laptop. "You might say that. Both of them escaped in March of 1976. They'd be in their fifties today."

Jake's eyes are as big as saucers. "Escaped! And do we know who their abductor was?"

"Indeed we do. A Father David Reeve who was a young chaplain here. He held the boys captive in an unused nuclear bunker that was built for the school in 1959. It was never used and quickly forgotten about. They were imprisoned here at White Oak the whole time."

Jake's head is in his hands. "You just knew there'd be a bent priest somewhere in the mix, didn't you?"

I shrug.

"Anything else?" Jake asks.

"Father Reeve was defrocked and sent to prison after his trial. The Church and the school did a thorough job of burying all this scandal, but I managed to get most of the details. He served twenty-two years at Wandsworth Prison for kidnapping and endangering children. No sexual abuse charges were filed."

Jake glares. "That means he was released in 1998. How old was this bastard when he committed his crimes?"

I look at my notes. "Just a second, he was twenty-four."

Jake has begun to pace. "He's in his sixties now and walking free...and what about Tommy?"

"Yes, that is the quandary. Tommy disappears, then three days later the boys escape and Father Reeve is arrested. Of course, he was the primary suspect, but he denies having anything to do with the Walker abduction. They search the bunker where he held the boys and it's completely empty. No sign of Tommy."

Jake looks at me. "We have more questions than answers. Maybe he killed Tommy, even accidentally, and it scared him. He doesn't want to confess to murder so he does his time for kidnapping the other two and calls it even. Maybe the boys escape but he still can't stop his impulses so he moves Tommy, placing him somewhere else..."

"Then he gets arrested," I mutter.

"And Tommy is left to starve in some new secret hiding place," Jake says. "No matter how you slice it, it sucks for Tommy Walker."

"So what are we going to do now?"

"Only one thing to do," Jake says. "We need to interview them."

"Who?" I ask, but I'm afraid of the answer that I already know is coming.

"The boys: Duncan Greer and Robin Brody...and David Reeve, the ex-priest, naturally. We need some answers."

I stare at him in utter disbelief.

"I don't suppose you see the flaw in your grand plan?"

"What?" he asks.

"You want us, two White Oak boys to go and speak with a man who kidnapped two, or possibly three, White Oak boys?"

He hugs me from behind and whispers in my ear. "Don't worry, I'll protect you, Timothy James."

CHAPTER 48: JACOB

Timothy's a genius. Honestly. I mean I'm as good as the next bloke with keyword searches and database mining, but he was working on something that others had deliberately tried to hide. That's not easy, especially when you are talking about forty-year-old newspaper clippings.

I don't know what I'm going to do to reward him...but it's going to be extravagant. I've got a dozen nagging questions, but I need to clear my mind and see the big picture and there's only one way I can accomplish that.

"What are you up to?" I ask.

He pushes his hair out of his eyes. "I've got to practice a Bach Concerto for St. Andrews Day; it's giving me a bugger of a time."

"Perfect," I say, "grab your gear and follow me."

"Where are we going?"

"I need to think, and you need to play...we should go to Ducker."

"You're daft, it's nearly eleven. The place will be shut tight," he says.

"Not for us. They've given me a key." I take it out of the jar I keep on the mantle near the clock. "You know the acoustics in there are extraordinary. It's like an echo chamber, a concert hall..."

"All right, I'll go," he says throwing his hands up.

***

I open the back office and turn on the underwater lights and half of the arena overheads which slowly sputter to life. The pool has an other-worldly blue glow at night. Thick steam rises from the warm water creating a mini-fog bank.

I change into my jammers and start to do some stretching exercises. Tim seems a bit mesmerized by the whole scene.

"This is so...atmospheric," he says.

"I thought you would appreciate the ambiance. Please make yourself at home."

He sets up a portable stand and a few minutes later the most ethereal sounds are reverberating off the walls. I dive in and as I begin my laps my mind starts to clear.

This is everything... me in the water and Tim making music. We are two virtuosos plying our individual trades. Strength and beauty, art and sport, sound and movement. We stay at it for nearly an hour.

It's funny, when I'm here alone this space gives off an eerie vibe, but being here with Tim makes it romantic.

He stops playing and I can feel him watching me swim, so I go faster. I use the six-beat kick and when I get to the wall I execute a split-second flip-turn and then I stop and pop my head out of the water. I adjust my goggles and flip my hair. I've worn myself out.

"You are truly beautiful," he says.

I smirk at him. "I was showing off a bit there at the end. Your Bach is sounding good though."

He takes a small bow. "I wish the concert was in here instead of Deerfield. You were right about the sound."

He's put the violin back in its case and comes toward the edge of the pool. I watch him as he takes off his shoes and socks and dips his feet in the water. "It's warm."

"At night the water is warmer than the air in here, that's what causes the steam fog. You should get in for a bit...it's so relaxing."

He splashes me with his foot. "I didn't bring a suit or I would."

I pull my Speedos off and toss them to the side of the pool. "We don't need suits," I say. "I prefer skinny-dipping, always have."

He doesn't say another word. He just strips off his clothes and cannonballs into the water. I watch him dive down to the bottom of the deep end and touch the drain and then surface right beside me.

"This is lovely," he says, putting his arms around my shoulders. We stay like that, slowly treading water, gently turning in the fog. When he kisses me it sends a shockwave through my body, a thunderbolt. I've never felt anything like it...and Lord knows, I've kissed my share of boys but this is different. It's become something else, something I can't live without.

It's in that moment when all the lights suddenly go out! It's utterly dark. Tim grabs on to me in a panic. "Tell me these lights are on some kind of timer..."

"They aren't," I whisper. "Take my hand, be silent and I'll get us out of here." I know there are four exits in Ducker, and whoever killed the lights was probably in the office. I grab Tim's violin, our pile of clothes and our shoes. We quietly get dressed and I lead him to the door on the western side. I'm listening as hard as I can, but I don't hear anyone. The pool filter is purring, so I know the power hasn't gone out or been shut off from the main junction box outside.

"Go!" I yell, pushing open the door frantically, and we hook it all the way to Brigsley.

CHAPTER 49: BRIGSLEY COTTAGE

Timothy is out of breath and trembling when they enter the cottage. Jacob made him run in front of him the whole way so he could keep watch. He collapses in a heap just inside the door.

"Who do you think? My God..."

Jacob sits down beside him, rubbing his shoulders and arms. "Hey, no worries. Just someone trying to scare us."

Timothy continues to shudder. "It worked."

"Stay right here," Jacob commands. He searches every room in the cottage; turning on lights, opening closets, peering under beds. He checks and locks every door and window and then goes into the kitchen to retrieve a bottle of brandy and two glasses.

"You're with me in my room tonight."

Timothy reaches for one of the glasses. "You'll hear no complaint from me. Let's get in bed right now, I'm knackered."

When they are safely tucked in, Timothy asks the question: "Man or spirit?"

Jacob traces a pattern on his bare chest and he feels Timothy's heart fluttering like a hummingbird. "If it was a ghost we've nothing to fear. A person is more problematic."

"Who else has a key to Ducker?"

"That is an insightful line of inquiry, Mr. Ashlock. I was told that only three students possess a Ducker key...and I don't know who the other two are. Any member of the staff or faculty might have one. We have to ask ourselves what the person in question was doing, and how long were they there?"

"Do you think we're being stalked?"

Jacob hugs him close, holding him tight in his arms. "I do. I think I've managed to cheese off more than a few people at White Oak who would delight in seeing me humiliated and brought down...but I don't want my actions or words to hurt you in any way."

Timothy turns over and smirks. "We're naked in bed together, I have a feeling I might be implicated."

Jacob frowns. "Are you worried that Chadwick, and the other St. Johnnies... Billy, the beaks and the whole lot of them will think that you are gay because you are so close with me?"

Timothy grins, and reaches over to take another swig of brandy. "I can't be arsed what all those toffs think."

Jacob doubles over laughing. *"Can't be arsed?* My God, that's exquisite."

Timothy smiles. "I've been saving that expression for you."

A moment passes. "But seriously?" he asks again.

Timothy puts his glass down and begins massaging Jacob's broad shoulders. He's quiet and methodical as he works his fingers deep into the muscles of the swimmer's neck and back.

"I was going to wait until your birthday next week to tell you, but since you're so insistent...I've fallen madly in love with you, Jake Weston. Isn't that obvious to a brilliant mind like yours?"

Jacob turns, his eyes beginning to brim with moisture, "What?"

"You heard me. And I'm not saying it again until your birthday. So how do you propose to protect me from all your enemies?"

Jacob fluffs the pillows and pulls the comforter up to their chins. "With wit, and guile and if all else fails I'll use Harold."

Timothy looks confused. "Who the bloody hell is Harold?"

"My pistol," Jacob says. "You didn't think I came to England unarmed, did you? I'm American."

CHAPTER 50: PADDY LESTER

Rich little bastards. I know they broke into my shed. Fucking hell. I'll have to move my whole inventory, maybe even hold up the operation for awhile, and I hate delaying a good harvest. Going to have to put the fear of God into these lads again, maybe make an example of someone.

If I catch any of the boys sneaking around, I'll skin them alive, make no mistake about it, and that includes Redgrave. Heard he got his arse paddled until the blood ran down his legs...Ha! Serves him right.

Of course, it won't be long before he's gagging for more weed. These spoiled little shits couldn't go three days without getting high. Thank God for the upper classes and all their vices.

I'm going to have to have another chat with Stillman soon though... make sure he's living up to his end of the bargain. I don't plan on having any visits from Old Bill. I'm not interested in seeing the inside of a jail cell again, no thank you. One more year, that's all I ask. Just one more year in this ancient hellhole and I can retire someplace warm. I hear Malta is nice.

CHAPTER 51: JACOB

I'm just back from Stratford and it's already been a busy morning, so busy in fact that I've put off worrying about our voyeur at Ducker. If someone is dead-set on watching my every move then today they are watching me shop.

I've kept poor Ethan busy, but I did buy him a beautiful tuxedo and he's on board with all the grand plans. I hope he'll have a little fun too.

Tomorrow is St. Andrew's Day...but more importantly my seventeenth birthday. Hundreds of visitors will descend on White Oak for concerts, speeches and presentations. We have a few sporting exhibitions including waterpolo which I'll take part in. There's both a tea and a luncheon, but I'm really hoping we can start my celebration by three PM.

I put the gift-wrapped box on the table where he's sure to see it as soon as he's back. In the meantime it's sit-ups and more Latin conjugation for me.

Redgrave has come by for his medicinal soak in our tub. It riles me that a sweet soul like Billy has been subjected to such abuse. He comes from a powerful and rich lineage but he told me that all the men in his family were beaten in boarding school. It's how proper English Lords are made.

Tim dashes in, violin case and backpack in hand, but he looks frustrated.

"Final practice went well, I see."

"It was a train-wreck," he says, moving to the kitchen to find something to drown his sorrows with. He notices the package. "I see your presents are already starting to arrive..."

"Oh that," I say. "That's not for me, it's for you."

"What?" he opens the card. "What are you doing buying me a gift for your birthday? Are you a hobbit?"

I smile. "A charming and very obscure reference. This isn't so much a gift as it is a necessity."

He opens the box to find the Stefano Ricci blue silk patterned dinner jacket I've picked out for him. He immediately puts it on.

"This is fabulous!" he gushes. He hurries to see himself in the full-length mirror in the upstairs loo. "Billy!" I hear him shout. "How's the water?"

"Soothing. Looking good, mate." I overhear Redgrave say.

"I'm never taking this off," he calls out.

"So you like it then?"

He walks down the stairs, striking a pose every few steps. "Wait until my mum sees me in this!"

"Speaking of your mum...she's five-foot-two and 135 pounds, right?"

"Oh who knows with your weird American weights and measures. She's less than ten stone, and about 157 centimeters. Why? Did you buy her a fur coat?" he jests.

"Yes," I say.

"You didn't!"

"It would be impolite to buy a woman I've never met a frock...and she's being kind enough to chaperone my birthday dinner. Everyone knows a mink coat makes everything else a woman is wearing irrelevant."

Tim hugs me. "She'll faint dead away when she sees it."

"Perfect, I'm trying to make a good impression. How is she planning to get here?"

"There's a coach that runs from Hackney Central to Greenknoll. She'll be here by ten."

"That won't do," I say. "Call her and tell her that a car will be by to collect her at nine AM and bring her to our doorstep. I'll text the address to Ethan right away."

"Really?"

"Of course, she's your mother."

Billy comes out of the bath wearing only a towel. "How is your arse, m'lord?"

"Healing nicely, thank you," he says, "I want you to meet my family tomorrow too, Jake. I've told them all about you."

"I'd be honored."

"Will your father be coming over from America?"

I look at my two young friends.   "Sadly, he has a previous engagement," I say. "I'll just have to make do with you lot."

CHAPTER 52: TIMOTHY

Jake's birthday. A concert, a waterpolo match, an afternoon tea and my mum is coming to White Oak. I'm nervous as a whore in church. We are celebrating tonight at some mysterious restaurant so who can guess what the boy has in store? I know him well enough to be certain it will be extravagant. Jacob Weston loves excess.

He's sleeping in because he's not going to Stratford and we have no classes today. I'm cooking breakfast-in-bed...my specialty is french toast. I've also cooked bacon and squeezed fresh oranges for juice. I hope he's duly impressed.

At seven-fifteen I carry the tray upstairs and he's already sitting up awake and beaming. "I like this!" he says, immediately grabbing for the food.

"Don't become accustomed..." I warn.

"Do I get a birthday kiss?"

I oblige him and I can taste salty bacon on his lips. "I love you, Jacob Weston."

"Why is that, sir?"

I watch him eating his breakfast. "Because you treat me like I walk on water. My mother says you should never love anybody who treats you like you're ordinary, therefore..."

"I love you too, Timothy James. Now let's talk about your mother before she arrives."

I sit down next to him on the bed. "Okay, what do you want to know?"

"Is she aware of this? I mean, does she think I'm just a friend...or..."

"I told her you are more than a friend."

"Did you now?"

He's exasperating. "I didn't tell her we were getting married or anything. I didn't even say *boyfriend* because that word is just so *gay*. I don't even know what this is yet, to be honest. I do still like girls, you know."

He's laughing at me. "You like girls but you *love* me."

"Jesus Christ," I mutter.

"So I shouldn't expect any PDA in front of her?"

"Let's play it by ear, shall we?"

He's getting up and I can tell he's going to enjoy taking the Mickey out of me all day. "I would think your mum would prefer you to be with an extremely wealthy, clever young man than some average girl..."

I raise a brow. "Hmm, first of all, what makes you think I would settle for an *average girl*? Secondly, my mum isn't that shallow. I think she just wants me to be happy...with whomever."

He grins. "Bravo, Timmy. One of the things I so admire about you is that you don't allow me to get away with any of my pretentious bullshit...just like another great man in my life."

"Who's that?"

"Blake Abbot."

"So, I remind you of your butler?"

"That's high praise. But let me ask you this, and you must be perfectly honest...are you?"

I look into his twinkling eyes. "Am I what?"

"Happy, mate. Are you?"

"Deliriously," I say. "Now please take a shower before she gets here."

While Jake is cleaning up, I practice the Bach again. The cottage is spotless. He hired a crew to come in two days ago and professionally clean. He's bought dozens of gardenias and primrose which sit in vases and pots all around Brigsley, and he insisted on purchasing an entire cord of yew wood for the fire which is slow-burning and pleasant smelling. His favorite candles are a soy-wax French lavender and lemongrass which are alight everywhere. It's like he's expecting *Architectural Digest* to be stopping by for a photoshoot.

When he comes downstairs he's perfect too. His hair is lightly slicked back and shiny. He's wearing a turquoise cashmere v-neck which brings out his eyes, and simple cotton trousers. He hasn't put on a single piece of jewelry; no rings, watch or necklace. No artifice that would signal his wealth.

"Is this okay?" he asks, holding out his arms.

"Beautiful," I say, and there's a knock at the door.

CHAPTER 53: JACOB

She's here.

I let Timothy open the door, and Ethan is standing beside a comely dark-haired woman in a simple print dress. Her face is care-worn but kind, and she has those same eyes. Tim has his mother's clear blue eyes.

"Mum!" he shouts, embracing her. I can see her sizing me up as she gives her son a big hug. "Timmy," she says, holding his face in both her hands. "I've missed you so."

Ethan begins carrying in some parcels, patting me on the back as he makes his way out. "She's a corker," he whispers.

"And you must be Jacob Weston," she says. "Don't just stand there staring, give us a smooch!"

I bend down to kiss this stout, happy woman and she pulls me into a warm embrace. I kiss both her cheeks, European-style. "Happy birthday, child." She hands me a small gift-wrapped package.

"It's so nice to meet you, Mrs. Ashlock. I've been looking forward to this day..."

"Call me Bea, for God's sake. Bea for Betty. And what shall I be calling you?"

"I guess you should call me Jay. Jay for Jacob."

"What?" Tim says. "No one calls you Jay!"

"Your mother does."

"Yes I do, easy to remember. Now Jay, I want to thank you for sending out young E in that shiny new car. What a magnificent thing to do, I could get used to being squired around like the Queen herself."

"Think nothing of it." I open the present; homemade strawberry jam. "Bea, this is so kind. My favorite. Thank you."

"Many happy returns of the day...made it myself."

She grabs her son and gives him a good looking over.

"It seems my Timmy is finally putting on a bit of weight. I'll have you to thank for that too. You're an angel, Jay, to be looking out for my boy."

"He eats like a bird, but I do what I can."

Ethan comes in with two bottles of Champagne. "Still cold, Jake," he says taking them into the kitchen.

"Excellent!" I say. "Do you like Champagne, Bea?"

"Who doesn't?"

I pop open the Salon Brut Blanc de Blancs Le Mesnil. Tim has already brought out glasses. "This 2006 is something rather special," I say while pouring.

"I do have a growing appreciation for Jake's hidden liquor cabinet," Tim says.

"Happy birthday, Jay!"

We all touch glasses and sip. "Oh that hits the spot," Bea says. "I didn't want to have to face all these posh tossers without a bit of a buzz going."

God, I think, what a tremendous night this is going to be.

CHAPTER 54: TIMOTHY

Mum and Jake trading bants, that's one for the record books. I watch them sitting front and center for the string quartet, two peas in a pod, grinning like Cheshire cats. The four of us aren't half bad with the Bach; a few missed cues, Ferguson grinding away at the cello like he's trying to churn butter, but it came off all right. We're all wearing our maroon waistcoats with our tails. We look smart.

Father Hodgson gets up and speaks about Saint Andrew introducing his brother Saint Peter to Jesus the Messiah. It is indeed a day for meaningful introductions.

It's while the ancient priest is speaking that the idea comes to me. The chap has got to be in his eighties. He surely knew David Reeve and must have been in the eye of the storm during the whole White Oak scandal. He might even remember Tommy.

Next mum and I attend the waterpolo match. The game is incomprehensible. Jake and Ollie Morgan are the only two boys who ever seem to have the yellow ball for any length of time. Jake's team ends up losing, but it was close...two to one.

He says most of the game takes place underwater and out of the view of the referees or the spectators. I guess it can get brutal below deck. After Jake is dressed we head down to the Great Lawn where a massive white tent has been erected for tea.

"It's a shame your parents couldn't be here, Jay. I mean it's your birthday!" Mum says.

He puts one arm around her and the other around me. "Thank God I have you lot or I'd feel like an orphan."

"That's the first waterpolo game I've ever watched," I say.

"Boring as hell, yeah?" Jake asks.

"I rather enjoyed all you buff boys splashing about," Mum says. Here it comes, I think, she's winding him up.

"You know, I'd have scored that last goal but Ollie reached under and gave my John Thomas a grab."

"He didn't!" Mum says.

"I paid him back in kind," Jake states.

"Good on ya'."

"If you two don't mind, we are supposed to be attending a high tea."

"Ollie Morgan is the school's Head-Boy. He thinks he's God's gift."

"I know the type."

"Still, I'm glad I played today," Jake states. "I finally got to see him nude in the locker room."

"Oh for the love of God," I mutter but Mum is laughing.

"Did you know that he has the White Oak crest tattooed on his bum?"

It's odd, but I actually did hear that rumor awhile back. I guess it's true. Jake pours us each some black tea. "Don't get me wrong," he says, "I'm all for loyalty and devotion to school...but what will he do when he's off to Oxford next year?"

"Turn the other cheek, I suppose," Mum says and the two of them are in stitches. Naturally, this is when Headmaster Rothwell chooses to greet us.

He inclines his head, "Gentlemen. I understand it's your birthday, Weston. Many happy returns."

"Thank you, sir."

"Do you remember my mother, Headmaster?"

"Certainly," he says, "so nice of you to join us today, Mrs. Ashlock." She takes his hand. "I received your note," he says, glancing toward Jake.

"Oh, good," Mum says.

"We don't usually allow boys to leave the country, even if it is their birthday. But it's exceedingly kind of you to offer to chaperone in the elder Weston's stead."

Mum smiles. "Ah, it's a special occasion, isn't it? And Jay's parent's promised him a memorable event."

Jake is just standing there with a petrified smile plastered on his mug. "I'm sure it will be. Splendid concert today Ashlock, keep up the good work." Rothwell slowly meanders away.

"What the devil?" I ask.

Jake has turned to Mum, "I could kiss you."

"Please do."

He pecks her cheek and I'm lost. "I didn't know you sent Rothwell a note," I say to her.

"I didn't."

Jake has a guilty expression. "Oops," he says.

"And who's leaving the country?" I ask.

"I believe we are," Mum says.

"Jacob?"

He just shrugs. "It was supposed to be a surprise."

CHAPTER 55: PARIS

Ethan Polley arrives at Brigsley Cottage at exactly three PM and he's wearing the beautiful black tuxedo recently purchased for him in London.

Jake runs out to meet him. "You look very posh!" he says.

"I feel like James Bond."

Jake grabs the box and they hurry inside where Timothy has already cracked open the second bottle of Champagne.

"Bea," Jake says, "this just arrived and it's addressed to you."

She looks confused. Jake drapes an arm over Tim's shoulder. "Get ready for some serious waterworks," he whispers.

She opens the box and can't believe her eyes. "No," she says, running her fingers through the silky fur. "It can't be. Jay, what have you done? I can't accept this." Her chin is quivering.

"Stuff and nonsense," Jake says, grabbing up the coat and helping her put it on. "Every great woman deserves a fantastic coat."

"It's a perfect fit, Mum," Tim remarks, handing her a handkerchief as her tears begin to fall.

"But all I brought him for his birthday is strawberry jam," she sniffles and they laugh together.

"Homemade strawberry jam which I will cherish every morning, Madam. Now we really must be going."

"Where?" Tim asks.

"Paris, of course. You can't find a decent restaurant on this side of the English Channel."

Ethan drives to RAF Northolt where they are to board one of the Weston's Gulfstream V jets.

"I'm gobsmacked!" Mrs. Ashlock says to her son. "Every day must be an adventure with this one."

"Mum, you have no idea."

Ethan parks the Rolls right off the tarmac. "Are you sure you want me to come along?"

"Not afraid of flying, are you?" Jacob asks.

"No," he says, "it isn't that, but..."

"Then climb aboard the jet. I'm not going to be calling for Ubers in Paris, Sport."

Inside the cabin it's all creamy leather and inlaid Hawaiian Koa wood. Patrick Commons, the head steward hugs Jacob tightly. "Happy birthday, little guy. We've missed you."

The rest of the crew, including the pilots come out to greet him. Janice Parker, a stunning black woman who has known Jake all his life, kisses him on both cheeks. "Hey handsome," she says.

"Janice! I didn't know you'd be here!"

"I switched to the European routes...less hassle. Hey, I brought some of that scotch you like, and those chocolate-raspberry truffles."

"I love you."

Patrick puts an arm around Janice. "Seventeen-years-old, where does the time go?"

Janice dabs her eyes. "Your mom would be so proud."

Jacob introduces his passengers to the crew then says, "Let's all go to Paris, shall we?"

It's a thirty-five minute flight to the small Paris Le Bourget airfield, seven kilometers outside the capital.

Patrick hands Jake an envelope from home. He immediately recognizes the formal stationary. Sitting down next to Tim he silently reads the letter, penned in its familiar, precise hand, and then he begins to sob.

"I'm so sorry," he tells the others, folding the letter and placing it inside the Tom Ford Jacquard dinner jacket he's changed into. "I guess I'm getting emotional in my old age."

"Abbot?" Tim asks holding Jacob's hand.

"He's coming to watch me swim against Eton."

Mrs. Ashlock absently pets the sleeve of her coat. "Tell me Jay, will we be able to see the Eiffel Tower from the restaurant? I'd like to take a photo of it to show the ladies back home."

"Bea, I promise you'll get a good look at the famous tower."

She shakes her finger at Ethan, "I guess this explains that cock-and-bull story you gave me about White Oak needing to photocopy my passport."

"Sorry, Ma'am. Orders from the top."

Timothy turns to Jacob. "What about my passport?"

"Oh, I pinched it."

Jacob faces Ethan. "So the car will be waiting for us on the tarmac, it's another Phantom VIII, but you do know the steering wheel will be on the other side, right?"

Ethan just sits with his arms tightly folded across his chest. "I've been to bloody France before. Can we please go to New York for your eighteenth birthday?"

Jacob considers it. "That's a bit more than an afternoon excursion, and we may have to contend with my parents...but whatever you want, Ethan. Next year, New York it is."

"What's the name of this famed restaurant?" Tim asks.

"I don't want you looking it up on your phone and spoiling the rest of the surprise. But it's one of Alain Ducasse's establishments, and it's Michelin starred."

CHAPTER 56: JACOB

Le Jules Verne Restaurant isn't near the Eiffel Tower, it's *in* the Eiffel tower. It's one staircase up from the second level with its own private elevator, and I've been coming here since I was a child.

Bea is tearing up again. "Mum," Tim says, "what is it this time?"

She's wiping her eyes with my handkerchief. "I just can't believe I'm wearing a mink coat and riding an elevator in the Eiffel Tower."

It's a clear night and the city is beautifully laid out before us. I watch the lighted tour boats slowly making their way down the Seine. This was a good idea.

The staff treats me like a returning hero, and then the old chef, Pascal, comes out to see how much I've grown. They seat us at Alain's private table.

"No menus?" Tim asks.

I shake my head. "Frederic, the new chef, will just prepare a seven or eight course tasting menu. It's French nouveau cuisine so the portions will be small." I order a Montrachet Grand Cru for the white and my favorite Petrus for the red.

"When was the first time you ate here?" Bea asks and I try to remember back. "This was my mother's favorite place. I think they still have the wooden highchair they used to sit me in when I was a toddler."

I hold my glass up. "To Bea, and also to Ethan. We wouldn't be here without you both."

The waiters bring out an amuse-bouche of marinated sea bream and then plates begin to arrive in a flurry. Foie gras, salmon and caviar salad, roasted asparagus. Escargots with watercress. The famous cookpot of seasonal vegetables. Course after course arrives with champagne sorbet between each one. Duckling fillet cooked in a cocotte with cider, apples and turnips. Souffléd potatoes, poached blue lobster, quail cooked with green cabbage. Each plate a work of art and a taste sensation.

Ethan, despite his disdain for the French, loves all the food. "This is a proper nosh up, it must be costing you a fortune," he mutters.

I smile. "Gentlemen don't discuss such things, but it is occasionally nice to be a Weston." I pour a bit more wine.

"I have a question. Since your parents couldn't be here for your big day...did they send you a gift? I'm dying to know what that might be."

I grin. "Driving age in the UK is seventeen...so my father bought me a Mercedes. A black AMG E63 S. It should be at Brigsley by the time we return."

"Wonderful," Ethan says. "I suppose I'll be out of a job."

I look at him and scoff. "Don't be ridiculous. I'm not going to be driving myself to London at five in the morning... I'd end up in the Thames. I still need you, brother."

They totally embarrass me when the whole staff sings "Happy Birthday" in their French accents, while seventeen petite candlelit deserts are placed before us.

"My coach will kill me if I even attempt to taste seventeen deserts."

Tim has his hand on my thigh and he gives me a squeeze. "You know this whole evening is off-the-charts, right? I mean, even for you."

"It is," I admit. "I'll tell you something though, when you have a mountain of money, the things you can buy aren't important. The only things that matter aren't things at all. It's people and experiences. Long after the moths have eaten Bea's fabulous coat, and my new car is sold for scrap metal...we'll remember this night, this meal, this conversation. I'll always cherish how happy we are together, right this instant. That's what life is truly about."

CHAPTER 57: TIMOTHY

We're home by eleven. Ethan is driving Mum back to Hackney, and Jake is brewing us tea. His new car is parked in front of Brigsley and it is phenomenal. A black sedan that looks a bit like the Batmobile.

"Ah, that was a memorable time," he sighs. We've changed into warm flannel pajamas.

"You've completely won her over."

He holds my hand. "That was always the plan. I had no idea she'd be so fun though."

"When can we take the Mercedes for a spin?" I ask.

"Tomorrow, I guess. Driving from the other side will be challenging."

I stand up, "I have a birthday present for you too."

He grins his evil grin. "You mean besides the shagging, right?"

"Yes," I whisper, "besides the sex."

"Oh, good. Because I was looking forward to that later."

I take out the small package from where I've hidden it in a drawer.

"You didn't have to," he says while ripping open the wrapping. "I do enjoy getting presents though." He examines the pendant. "It's jade?"

"*Pounamu*," I say. "Greenstone, from New Zealand. It was my father's...he was a Kiwi."

Jake holds it in his closed hand. "You never talk about him."

"Because I didn't know him. He was in a car crash on the M25 a month before I was born. He gave this to Henry when he was just a wee lad...and Henry gave it to me before he went off to Afghanistan."

He shakes his head and tries to give it back. "It's far too precious, Timmy, it's a family heirloom."

"The Maori believe greenstone has a soul. These can only be given as gifts, you can never buy one for yourself because that would anger the spirit within. This one is in the shape of a *hei matau*, a fish hook. It honors Tangaroa, the God of the sea. Who better to wear it than the fastest boy in the water?"

Jake's face is wet with tears as he puts it on and tucks it under his pajama top.

"For once I don't know what to say."

I lay back against his chest. "It's not easy to shop for a guy who can buy anything he wants. I don't know what the fuck to do about Christmas."

CHAPTER 58: JACOB

Another mammoth winter storm is heading our way so I decide to get outside a take a nice long run before I'm trapped indoors. I jog back to see the ghost tree, still standing sentinel and marking the seasons.

I'm taking a circular route, trying to see if these walking paths form a course around the entire campus and grounds. To the north I see the old conservatory, which is much more grand than a greenhouse. It's a beautiful Victorian structure of stone, iron and glass.

I can see Lester working and I decide to rattle the old hermit's cage. The rusty door squeals a complaint as I pull on it to enter, and I'm immediately hit by the thickness of the warm, oppressive air. The close, dense foliage and humidity make it a tropical wonderland. I can hear the sound of water dripping all around.

"Who's there?" he calls out.

"Me, sir," I say, not able to see him through the tall fronds and thick greenery.

"Me who?" I hear him shout. I find him hauling a wheelbarrow of dead leaves and old blooms toward the back.

"Jacob Weston. I was just on a run and saw you working in here. Do you need a hand?"

"The American. Aren't you the chap in Brigsley?"

"I am indeed."

"Is that your posh German car?"

"It was a gift."

"God damn Germans."

His face is deeply wrinkled but his eyes are clear and sharp. Here's a man who has labored his whole life and although he must be in his seventies he still looks fit.

"No need to *sir* me, just call me *Paddy*. All these windows need to be shut and locked tight. There's a storm coming and I don't want any loose panes giving way in the wind."

I begin making my way around the edge of the chamber. There are clever pulleys and ropes that help to move the glass vents near the top which is at least two stories above us. I need to wedge myself between long bedding tables to reach the lower locks. Every one is tight and rusty.

"So, how long have you been the groundsman, Paddy?"

He scoffs. "All me bleeding life. My Pa was the caretaker before me, and his father used to run the stables back when there were horses here."

I stop and turn on a garden hose to have a drink, and then spray cool water over my head. He walks over and washes his dirty hands before closing the spigot.

"Did you know a boy named Thomas Walker? Back in the seventies?"

He smiles and I can see that several of his teeth are missing. "He been visiting you, has he? Up at the cottage?"

I nod.

"I knew that boy, same as I know all of ya. Seen thousands of toffs go through this place in my time. He looked a bit like you, towheaded and fair, but he was a slip of a boy, and scared of his own shadow. Used to catch him hiding all over the grounds. Caught him once in here, not ten feet from where you're standing."

"Any idea who killed him?" I ask. He turns away but I can see him grinning.

"Walker was a bum boy. Looked like the runt of the litter too, he was never going to be long for this world. The other lads were rough on him, never giving him a moment's rest. The fag-masters. None of my business what you boys do to one another though, I got my own concerns. You best be on your way, Jacob Weston."

I press closer. "Let me ask you about Father Reeve then. You certainly knew him, didn't you?"

His eyes narrow. "Don't know what your game is, but that is all donkey's years. There are those around here who might not want you poking your posh hooter where it doesn't belong."

I bend down to retie the laces on one of my trainers. "Yeah, so, I guess that's just hard cheese."

The groundskeeper turns away and starts walking toward the back of the conservatory. I gather he's done talking with me.

"Hey Paddy," I call. "Don't know where I might buy some dank White Widow, do you?"

I watch his shadow moving swiftly as I leave the giant glass house.

CHAPTER 59: TIMOTHY

Wardrobe fittings for the pageant today and my costume is much more ridiculous than I had envisioned. They basically have me in a long blue nightshirt, which was the nineteenth century equivalent of pajamas, and a nightcap (did grown men actually wear these to bed?) I also have hundreds and hundreds of grey plastic-linked chains which are draped over and around me.

Samantha, who is playing Scrooge's long lost love, is in a fetching red velvet dress. She runs over.

"Help zip me, will you? I can't reach." She turns around exposing her bare back and shoulders. I can see she's wearing a lacy black bra. I quickly zip her up.

"There you go."

"Thanks love," and she is off to show the dress to the others. I see her flirting with Ollie, her paramour in the play. She takes his hand and he gives her a little twirl on the stage.

It's difficult to know if she's flirting with Oliver to make me jealous or if it's the other way around. I do know that he is being a right slick git about it though. What a wanker. *Show her your tattoo*, I think, and chuckle.

Unfortunately, he's fairly good at playing the lead... a born ham. I can see Oliver Morgan going on to becoming some kind of actor or public speaker in the real world. He could even be an MP. Meanwhile I'm dragging a bunch of plastic chains around like an idiot. If she could hear me play a little music the tables would surely turn.

They're also doing tests with the lights, so they have us all in full make-up. Blackmore is running around like it's the Broadway production of *Hamilton*. A lot more kids from both schools are here...there must be thirty or forty of us all told.

Some of the boys are hammering canvas onto long panels which will then be painted for backdrops. This rehearsal is mayhem. We've yet to speak a single word of dialog from the play itself.

I go sit backstage where I can have some privacy. My paper for Fulton's class is on the Beat Generation which Jake is absolutely keen on. He immediately got me reading Ginsberg and Burroughs and exploring the ideas of free love and sexual liberation. It's all fairly enlightening, especially when you consider this was happening fifty years ago. I'm reading a paperback edition of *Naked Lunch* which originally had to be published in France because of US obscenity laws at the time.

A good book can make me forget where I am. I get immersed in the world of whatever I'm reading, so I don't hear Sam until she's practically on top of me.

"Always backstage reading your smutty, little books," she says. "How do I look?"

Theatrical make-up is always overdone when you see it up close. "Hmm..." I begin.

She pouts. "I think they've made me look like a tart."

"It's meant to be seen from a distance," I mention.

"Do you think I'm pretty?"

I dog-ear the page in my book and put it to the side. "I'm sure Ollie thinks you're gorgeous."

Sam grabs me and kisses me, her tongue goes so deep she's nearly cutting off my air. (She smells like vanilla and flowers though). When I'm finally let loose she smiles and gets up, brushing the dust from her skirts.

"I've been wanting to do that for weeks," she admits and runs off to tell her friends.

If you want to get a girl interested in you nothing seems to work as favorably as ignoring her for awhile. Redgrave walks up moments later. He has a long black robe on and he's carrying a sickle.

"Why is the Ghost of Things Yet to Be dressed like Death?" I ask him and he shrugs in response.

"What I want to know is why I don't have any frigging lines. Is the Spirit of the Future a mute or something?"

"Going to have to ask Dickens that one," I say. He sits down beside me.

"I saw Samantha come back here...what did she want?"

"To give me a tonsillectomy apparently."

He doubles over laughing. "I knew she was snogging you, you lucky bastard. There's red lipstick all over your mouth. Did you grab her tits?"

"Billy," I say, "why don't you tell her how much land your family owns, and that your father is an Earl."

"Do you think that will help my chances?"

"It couldn't hurt."

CHAPTER 60: JACOB

I'm back at Brigsley just before the storm kicks in. I've made sure all my devices are charged because knowing White Oak the power will soon be out. The Doppler weather radar for the UK isn't pretty tonight.

Coach Lir put me on a raw diet going into the competition in three weeks. I've stocked up on every fruit and vegetable available at the Queen's Park Farmer's Market and I am starting to feel leaner and meaner...but I'm craving a juicy steak. Ethan now comes to my workouts and helps run me through my paces. He enjoys yelling even more than Coach Lir does.

Tim hurries in. "Storm's gonna be a whopper," he says, dropping his backpack off near the table. I can hear him in the loo brushing his teeth and cleaning up.

"How was your day?"

"Dreadful. Dickens is turning over in his grave. I really need to do some preps before we are left in the dark."

He's already seated at the table and working on the laptop. "Do I still have make-up on my face?"

"No," I say, "perfect, as usual."

He looks up. "Hey, come here."

I scoot my chair next to his. "Closer," he says, and I lean in near enough to smell his minty toothpaste. He kisses me, slowly putting his hand on the back of my neck.

"Okay," he says, glancing back to the screen.

"What was that for?"

He grins. "Just doing some comparison shopping. You're a really good kisser."

"Practice makes perfect."

A howling wind rattles the cottage and the electricity immediately flickers and then blinks out. We hear the rush of hail hitting Brigsley and the roar of a fierce wind. I can feel the air pressure dropping.

Timothy is up and lighting candles, when the front door bursts open. I struggle against the wind to close and bolt it shut as two of the heavy front windows dash open and then collapse loudly down on themselves.

"What's happening?" Tim yells over the sound of wind and rain. We hear the windows upstairs banging open and shut. The salty smell of the ocean surrounds us.

All the candles have gone out. The rush of wind is so strong down the chimney that it's extinguished the fire and blows thick, white smoke into the room. We can taste the darkness.

I'm holding Tim tight and in his ear I say, "This isn't just the weather."

The door slams open a second time and Tommy Walker is standing at our threshold, and he appears to be screaming. Tim cries, "Make him stop! Please, Jake, make him stop!"

"Enough!" I shout, staring directly at our wet, little wraith. "Thomas H. Walker you stop this shit right now!"

And surprisingly, he does. The fire in the hearth even flickers slowly back to life. We re-latch all the windows and I re-bolt the door. I sprint upstairs to secure those windows too.

"Can we start drinking now?" Tim asks.

"Splendid idea," I say. I recently acquired a bottle of Patron Lalique that I've been waiting to try. I gather some of the limes from the market and some salt and we sit on the floor doing shots.

"I could smell the ocean this time, it was like a storm at sea, and Tommy seemed a lot angrier. Why do you think that is?" Tim asks.

I nod. "I believe he's jealous."

"Of us?"

"I've been working it out in my head. If Tommy was scared, bullied, beaten and gay...then what goes on in Brigsley these days might make him envious and upset."

Tim takes another shot.

"Be careful with that," I warn, "this stuff will knock you on your arse."

"He listened to you," Tim says. "He can hear us."

I nod again. "We need a way to return the favor. If we can establish a line of communication, maybe he call tell us who the killer is."

Tim rests his head against my shoulder, "how do you propose we do that?"

"Ouija board?"

"That's an incredibly bad plan," Tim says. "Have you ever read a novel or seen a film where someone used the Ouija Board and it ended up being a good thing?"

I laugh. "You make a valid point." We look out the windows at the turbulent night. "If we're going to do it we should do it tonight. He seems to be at his strongest during a storm."

"Do what?"

I grab a candle and hold it up. "Tommy, we are trying to help you, but we need you to help us too. If you can understand me knock on wood!"

Tim's eyes widen and suddenly all around us we hear a dozen hands knocking on wood everywhere. Tim springs up and grabs ahold of me. "This is such a horrible idea."

"Okay, Tommy, okay. Knock once for yes and twice for no. Do you understand me?"

We hear one very loud knock. Tim buries his head in my neck.

"Tommy, do you know who killed you?"

Another single, really loud knock which seems to surround us. "I'm seriously going to piss my trousers," Tim whispers.

"Tommy," I announce loudly, "Can you tell us his name?"

There is a pause and we wait while the storm rages. Then two loud knocks, and he has abandoned us.

"Little blighter," I mutter.

"Can we do something else now?" Tim pleads.

I take his hand and lead him up the stairs. "What did you have in mind?"

He reaches to the table and grabs my laptop. "Let's lay in bed and watch funny videos on YouTube."

"That wasn't my first choice, but all right."

CHAPTER 61: FULTON

Weston is sitting in the corner when I arrive.

"Good morning, Professor."

"Did you break into my office?"

He bashfully looks at the door. "I picked that sad little lock. There was nowhere to sit in the hall, and it isn't exactly Fort Knox around here."

I'm rifling through my briefcase and flipping on my computer. "It's a shame you're so rich, you'd make an excellent criminal."

"That's my fallback if things go tits up."

I reach into my bottom drawer and pull out a wrapped package. "I was going to give this to you at the end of term, but I heard it was your birthday last week, so, two birds and all that..."

Jake smiles. "I adore presents!"

He begins tearing the wrapping paper off. "So what did you end up doing for your birthday?"

He glances up at me. "Tim and I went to Paris for dinner."

"You and I lead extremely different lives."

He's holding the leather binder. "What is this?"

"Salinger published a lot of short stories that were never collected in any books. This is a 207-page trove of twenty-two out-of-print pieces I've collected, most were from magazines. Frankly, you remind me of a gay Holden Caufield, but without the silly hat."

"Ha!" he says, thumbing through the binder. "This is really special."

"I thought it might give you some insight into his development as a writer. His publishers say they may be releasing several unpublished books in the coming years; One is called, *The Family Glass.*"

He nods. "I heard something about that. Blimey, Salinger was an odd duck. All that amazing writing sitting unread in a box somewhere in New Hampshire because he was too reclusive to be bothered by people who admired him. Yet, now that he's dead, out come all his unpublished manuscripts. I find that sad."

"Maybe that work discloses more about him than he wanted his public to know."

Jacob smiles. "Nobody ever writes anything that isn't autobiographical...They say Salinger only had one testicle and may have married a Gestapo informer."

"How on earth do you know and remember such things?" I ask, and he just shrugs.

"Are you still working on your novel?"

He beams. "It's going well. I hope you'll read the first few chapters."

"I'd be honored. So why are you breaking and entering this morning?"

"I wanted your advice. The ghost of a former student is haunting my cottage."

"I don't believe in such things."

He's gotten up and is perusing my bookcase. "Hmm, then you should spend the night at Brigsley the next time we have a big thunderstorm."

"How much had you been drinking when you saw this poltergeist?"

He gives me a pejorative glance. "I only drink enough to keep my sanity around here."

"And how much is that?"

He shrugs again. "The dosage increases as this place becomes more absurd."

"I don't know what to say. Your classwork is exemplary, at the top of the rolls and you came to us mid-term...but you're still a seventeen-year-old man. Are drugs a factor in your lifestyle?"

"Absolutely not. I get tested every month, and I am old enough to remember that photo of Michael Phelps and the bong."

"Has Ashlock seen this apparition?"

He puts the stories into his backpack and zips it closed. "You should ask him sometime," he says. "Thanks for the Salinger, sir."

CHAPTER 62: TIMOTHY

It's been awhile since I've been to see her. She was one of the few people who took an interest in my welfare before Jake arrived. I head into Kyler with a vase of gardenias from the cottage.

As soon as I come near she is reaching her arms out for a hug. "It's funny you come by today, I've just been thinking about you," she says. "How are you, Timmy-Tim?"

I think my mum must have enlisted Mrs. Jessup long ago to keep an eye on me at school. "Never better, Mrs. J. These are for you."

She places the vase on the edge of her desk. "I love gardenias! So kind of you, poppet. Do you fancy a cuppa? I could use one..."

"That sounds wonderful," I say and we head back to her office. She fiddles with her ancient kettle and I sit on a small leather couch in the corner. There were many days when I would come here and help Mrs. Jessup repair old books that were losing their bindings, or needed a new cover.

Her office is enormous with windows looking out toward the lawn, giving her loads of natural light. Two long tables crowd the center where they are always stacked with old books requiring special care. A row of ancient wooden filing cabinets line the back wall, God only knows what treasures she's hidden away in all those drawers. She has paintings of churches, cities and old maps hanging on the walls...all the fascinating places she has traveled to as a younger woman.

"How's Mr. Jessup doing?"

"Ah," she sighs, "my old goat is doing as well as can be expected. He has good days and bad. His mind is often adrift, but he always seems to find his way back to me."

I wonder how it must be to love someone for fifty-five years only to have them fall into dementia and occasionally not know who you are. She smiles at me.

"What brings you to Kyler today, Sweet?"

"I was downstairs trying to locate some old yearbooks the other day...and several from the 1970's seem to be missing."

She scowls. "Vandals and thieves! People these days have such little regard for books."

"Wasn't that about the time you started working here?"

I can see her remembering back. "Clay had been offered a teaching post here, so I applied to the library. It was 1973 and I was all of nineteen-years-old. After he retired I just felt I couldn't give it up."

"Did you know the boys who were kidnapped back then?"

I see a cloud cross her face. "I didn't, not really. That was a terrible time."

"What about Tommy Walker?"

She takes a sip of her tea. "Poor, dear Tommy. I did know him because he was always hiding here. He knew this old library better than me. He was such a troubled soul."

"Why do you say that?"

"The other boys teased him mercilessly...he was different. Sensitive."

"He was gay."

She looks away. "Oh, who knows? He was sixteen, a year younger than you. Why are you asking all these questions?"

"I've seen him twice now."

She looks startled. "What?"

"His spirit haunts my cottage."

She moves to one of the tables and starts fiddling with a glue-gun. "I heard you were living at Brigsley with that new chap."

I nod. "Yes, Jacob Weston."

"Be careful poppet, there are rumors going 'round."
"What rumors?"

She looks at me through her thick librarian glasses as she smooths a few wayward strands of grey hair back into place.

"Just gossip about a rich toff corrupting a beautiful poor boy. Taking him on trips, buying him things...getting him tipsy."

"You shouldn't believe everything you hear, Mrs. J."

"I know you better than that. I know you're a good lad."

"I'm happier than I've ever been. He's my best mate."

She touches my shoulder. "Then I'm jolly-well happy for you, Timmy. See as much of this world as you can, soak up the sunshine and make heaps of happy memories, because our time here is far too short."

I hug her. "You're a wise old gal, you know that?"

She scoffs. "Yeah, yeah. Enough of your blarney, leave me be...I've got work to do."

CHAPTER 63: JACOB

We've searched the obituaries and unfortunately found one of the boys. Robin Brody died in 1988 of a heroin overdose; he was twenty-eight years old and homeless. You have to wonder if what he went through as a boy at White Oak was a contributing factor.

Duncan Greer took over his family's business. A bookstore in Westminster called, The Spiral Staircase. We'll try to visit him over the weekend. We haven't been able to locate the slippery David Reeve, but Tim thinks he's still in London. We're going to talk to Father Hodgson and see what he remembers.

"You're deep in thought today," Ethan says as we make our way back to the school. I look over at him.

"Sorry," I say. "I'm not good company this morning. I've got a lot on my plate."

"Your practices are going fine, mate. I can't wait for the Eton Swim. You are going to kick some toff arses."

I grin. "You know, you've been a big help and I want to thank you. I know Lir appreciates the time you put in too."

"I'm enjoying it. I like the coaching and I'm learning tons. My nephew is wild about footy, you know, what your people call soccer."

Yes, I've heard that game is popular here," I say sarcastically.

"Anyway, I was a good footballer, so I'm going to try my hand at coaching the lad's team. My sister is chuffed that I've taken an interest."

I playfully punch his shoulder. "You're a natural."

"Do you think so?"

"No one has ever screamed louder at me from the edge of the pool."

"I just want you to know when you're in the water, I'm on the sideline pulling for you."

"I do know that. You'll be awesome."

I've made a decision on what to do next. I text Tim so he'll be ready to go when I'm back. It's high time we saw the bunker.

CHAPTER 64: FULTON

"Jane," I say, "I'm just concerned about him."

She's sitting up in bed. All she has on is one of my old Magdalen college tee-shirts. "That demented little bastard can take care of himself," she says.

"Seriously Dove, you're supposed to be a councilor. He drinks too much for a boy his age, and he thinks he's seeing ghosts in his cottage."

She stares at me. "Trust me, he's just fucking with you."

I fold my arms across my chest. "He is keeping our little secret safe."

"And what would you have me do, TJ? He hates my guts."

I hold her hand. "He doesn't hate anyone. Visit him at Brigsley Cottage for a friendly chat, you know, just to see how he's getting on."

"If you really want me to, I'll go. But I'm telling you right now...he's queer as a clockwork orange, and not just because he's a sausage-jockey. We've got plenty of limp-wristed teens in the venerable houses of White Oak Academy. Jacob Weston has a mean streak that he's adept at hiding, and with his kind of intelligence...if he goes off the rails it could be dangerous."

I bend down to kiss her. "All the more reason you should re-evaluate him."

CHAPTER 65: TIMOTHY

We have a little more than two hours before class and he wants to crawl around exploring underground. I'm not even positive I can find it, but there's honestly no stopping Jacob Weston once he gets a notion into his head.

I hear the car pull up. He comes in and gives me his expectant look. "You're ready?"

"I suppose," I say, "but this may not be a wise course of action."

He's grabbing some fruit, a water bottle and a flashlight and shoving them in his backpack. "I can't do this without your help. You know every nook and cranny of this whole damn campus."

"All right," I say. "White Oak Chapel then. The entrance is beneath it."

***

The old stone church was actually built atop Roman ruins more than four centuries ago. I found early schematics for the bomb shelter in the archives, along with some receipts from the contractors who built it. Construction began in 1958 and had some connection with similar buildings at Eton and Cambridge. Unfortunately, the blueprints don't give an exact location.

I have a feeling, just by examining the documents, that they used the existing catacombs under the church as a kind of framework to support the new structure. That's probably why they picked the site in the first place.

A chapel service is just ending as we enter. I'm wearing the school uniform but Jake is in a blue tracksuit. We immediately sit down in one of the back pews and attempt to be less conspicuous.

"Which way do you reckon?" he asks.

"We have to go behind the altar, and into the back rooms. There are stairs that lead down to the catacombs."

We watch the people file out of the chapel. "Have you explored here?"

"Once," I answer. "It freaked me out back then, and that was before my first ghostly encounter."

We make our way up the side aisle and then quick as a wink Jake darts into the back. It's a trick just to keep up with him.

The stairway is as I remembered it, crowded with metal candleholders, music stands and other church paraphernalia. No one is around to stop us.

"Don't they have storage closets?" he says. I just shrug as we push past all the junk and step deeper underground.

When we get to the bottom there are three stone passageways all filled with cobwebs. Jake shines his flashlight around looking for any kind of switch.

"If they put a nuclear bomb shelter down here they must have set up electric lighting."

"They did," I say. "And they also had some sort of elaborate ventilation system that required it."

He locates the switch and miraculously, some of the lights are still working. "Which passage?"

"This one," he says confidently, pointing to the middle tunnel.

"You can't possibly know that's right."

"Look up. There are several thin cords bundled up with the lighting cord in the middle route." He's so observant. I take his hand as we push through the thick cob webs.

"Just so you're aware, I am not fond of spiders," I mention. We work our way deeper and further in. There are stone cubbies which are where the caskets are supposed to be entombed, but we really haven't seen that many occupied spots. I did see a rat scurrying about... I'm not overly fond of them either.

We can hear water dripping from somewhere, and overall the place has a damp, mildewy smell. "I think we're on the right track," he says. "It appears they have relocated all the residents to other locales."

We come to a fork. "Left, I think," he announces.

I gaze up, but the electrical cords look identical down both avenues. "How do you know this time?"

"Just a guess. It feels more menacing this way."

Grand, I think. He ends up being correct again, because around the very next turn is a wide steel door. On one side is an ancient keypad. He wont be picking this lock with his little set of tweezers.

"Interesting," he says examining the old device closely. "Hewlett-Packard. It was fifty years ago, so we can probably assume no more than a four digit code." He presses his nose extremely close to the mechanism.

"Still 10,000 combinations," I calculate.

He grins. "Let's narrow them down, shall we?" He digs through his backpack and finds what looks to be a pen, but is actually another small light. He flips it on and it casts a purple glare.

"Is that a blacklight?"

"Cheers, Ashlock. UV light can pick up a lot of evidence...even old evidence." He shines it close to the keypad. I can see that four of the buttons seem to lightly glow. "Why does the *end* key gleam?"

He's smiling, "It was like *enter* back then, or the *return* key."

The numbers that are fluorescing are: one, five and nine. He puts an arm around my shoulders. "If I guess it on the first try, I get brekky in bed again this weekend."

"What if you're wrong?"

He just chuckles. "That seems implausible, but I'll be your slave all week."

"You have a flutter, mate."

He reaches down and types in *1-9-5-9* then *end,* and the door mechanically thumps and swings open. "I like my bacon extra crispy."

***

The shelter is set up much like a dormitory. Rows and rows of steel-framed bunks stretching down either side. Fluorescent lights buzz erratically to life. There are huge storage areas, presumably for food and supplies. The air smells stale and dusty. Toward the back is an entryway containing a lavatory with a complicated septic tank system; ancient machines which seem to have something to do with air purification, and a lot of boxes still unopened. It's like some weird apocalyptic time-capsule.

Jake inspects everything. "You know, if the Russians had actually dropped a bomb and people managed to get down here...they wouldn't have lasted long."

"I counted the beds. Seventy-eight bunks. They weren't planning on saving everyone," I say.

"Why doesn't that surprise me," he scoffs. "Look, I found something."

He's pointing down near one of the furthest bunks. Someone has scratched a phrase into the plaster of the wall. *Nemo Sine Vitio Est.*

"Shall I test your Latin, Timothy?"

"I happen to know this," I say proudly. "No one is without fault."

"Hmm," Jake says, "some folks certainly have more fault than others in this scenario. Can you imagine being trapped down here for three months?"

"They must have thought they were going to die...that the priest would eventually kill them. How horrible," I say. It really is ghastly.

While we are staring down at the bunks, the shelter door slams shut and locks. "Jake!" I shout.

He starts sprinting for it when the lights all flash out. We're in utter darkness yet again. You'd think I'd be getting used to this kind of thing, but I'm terrified. He shines his flashlight so I can make my way to him, and I grab on to his waist.

"Ghost?"

"Almost certainly," Jake answers. He's punched the code into the keypad on this side, to no avail. We're locked inside a bomb shelter, under a church where they will find our skeletons grasping each other in a starved embrace someday. "Did I tell you I have a fear of being trapped underground?" I say.

"Um hmm, that's called cleithrophobia," he pulls away and is inspecting the mechanism. "My guess is Robin Brody." He sits down against the wall and pulls a couple bananas out of his backpack. "Want one?"

I take the fruit and start to peel it. "You seem exceptionally calm for someone who's going to die deep underground."

I sit down between his legs and he holds me. "He'll let us leave once he sees that we aren't scared."

Jake turns off the flashlight and we sit together in the dark. We hear the beds creaking, then footsteps and laughter. The smell of chimney smoke and roses fills the underground air.

"But I'm very much afraid," I whisper.

"No you aren't," he says, and he pulls me down and starts kissing me. He's the bravest person I've ever met.

After about fifteen minutes of snogging, Jake gets up and types in the code again. The door swings open for us, but before we go back out into the stone passageway he turns toward the depths of the bomb shelter.

"Thank you Robin. I just want you to know that we're going to find Father David...and we're going to fuck with him."

CHAPTER 66:   FULTON

Weston and Ashlock both arrive late to class, and Weston is completely out of uniform.   "Why are you two gentlemen late?"

"Trapped underground, sir. It won't happen again."

I sigh.   "See that it doesn't." I turn toward the entire group. "Now I hope you are all studying for exams. Ours will cover the ten novels we've read this term and ask for analysis and comparison. For those of you who have not yet turned in your term papers, you have two weeks left."

This is my favorite class. They understand the process and seem to actually apply themselves. Our discussions even make me look at the material in new ways, and I know to some degree I have Weston to thank for that. I can see him becoming a don at Oxford, his potential is unlimited.   His writing is brilliant.   He's working on his first novel which I'm sure will find a publisher.

When the bell rings and they are dismissed I ask Ashlock to stay behind.

"Sir," Jacob says, "his tardiness was my fault entirely..."

"Thank you, Weston. He isn't in trouble. Please leave now so we can talk about you behind your back."

He whispers something to Timothy and makes his way out.

***

"I'm not going to ask where you were before class."

He brushes his jacket sleeve. "Probably best you don't."

"I'll get right to the point. Have you seen any ghosts at White Oak?"

He bites his lip. "Of course, we live with one after all."

"Jacob hasn't coached you to tell me this?"

"No Professor."

"Do you have any proof?"

I watch him thinking. "Nothing concrete. There surely are a lot of references to ghosts and spirits in literature though, wouldn't you say? I'm even playing one in our *Christmas Pageant*...and that's Charles Dickens."

"That's fiction, Mr. Ashlock, and you know it."

"I think all writers draw from experience and reality. When there's a whole genre of work devoted to these kinds of strange encounters..."

"Okay, okay," I say, holding my hand up. "How much are you boys drinking in that cottage?"

He looks toward the window. "I'd rather not comment."

"Fine, let me ask it in a roundabout way...do you think Jacob has an issue with alcohol?"

He laughs. "No, Professor Fulton, not at all. I'd tell you if I thought otherwise. He likes to take the edge off, that's all, but he'd never jeopardize his training. Swimming is his true religion."

I sigh and sit down. "It's a relief to hear you say that. Just one more thing, and it's really none of my business..."

"Sir?"

"Do you love him?"

Ashlock, who's a naturally pale chap, deeply blushes. "Is it that obvious?"

"No," I say, pointing toward the door. "Just take care of each other."

CHAPTER 67: JACOB

I've got to run back to Brigsley and put on proper clothes. Fulton is one thing, but Blair will make me do lines if I show up in a tracksuit. Chadwick stops me on the way out.

"Listen, Weston, don't know if you've heard, but Blackie is going to be out of the house tonight."

"Yeah?" I say, "where's he off to?"

"Wales, something to do with his family. So, I'm in charge until he returns tomorrow night."

I smile. "What about Nanny?"

"Nah," he says, "she'd never do bed checks or rolls. Just so long as we're not too rambunctious Matron Finlay will leave us be. I already told her I'd run a tight ship."

He's followed me nearly to the cottage. "So, what's up?"

He looks around. "I know you can occasionally get a bit of strong drink. I wonder if you and Ashlock might like to meet me and a few of the Sixth Forms in my room. Just the lads shooting the breeze and unwinding."

I take his shoulder. "Count us in. I appreciate the invitation...oh, and I might have some tequila to offer the group."

***

After Poly Sci I head to the Chapel. I wanted Tim to come with me, but he's rehearsing the play over at Hoisington Place, so I'm flying solo.

The rectory sits right behind the old stone church. It's a stately little parsonage that's a natural brick extension of the chapel itself. Hodgson has lived there for more than half a century. I've heard that he has a sweet tooth so I've come bearing gifts.

My knock is answered by a nun who also serves as his nurse. "He's feeling good today," she says, "but don't tucker him out."

I promise to go easy on the old boy as I head into the back room where he is sitting next to the hearth. He has a blanket wrapped around his shoulders.

"Hello, Father," I say. "I hope I'm not disturbing you."

He waves me over. "No, no, my boy. I'm happy for the company. Mary-Katherine isn't much of a conversationalist, I'm afraid."

I hand him the present. "I brought these for you. Champagne truffles from La Maison Du Chocolat in Paris."

He's opening the box and grinning. "Bless you! Chocolate is my weakness." He's already starting to eat them. "These are divine."

I smile. "You've been at White Oak a long time, haven't you?"

"I'm on my fifth Headmaster," he says. "My roots go as deep as that twisted old ghost tree."

"Seen a lot of changes in all those years?"

"Yes and no," he pats my knee. "I look out from my little perch during services and still see bright-eyed lads singing the same hymns that I sang when I was a boy. You still learn Latin and wear tailcoats, but now you all have cell phones."

I nod. "There's someone I wanted to ask you about, but I know it might be unpleasant to remember him..."

"Who would that be?"

"David Reeve," I say, looking for his reaction. He just looks rather sad.

"David is always in my prayers," he says. "Some people start down the right path but lose their way so profoundly that it defies reason."

"Did you have contact with him while he was incarcerated?"

He nods. "He writes to me often. I think he is looking for a way back into the fold. God may have forgiven him, but White Oak Academy never will."

"Do you think he was responsible for the disappearance of Thomas Walker?"

"I do. Mores the pity. I performed the memorial for that poor lad. His parents were beside themselves with grief. There's nothing sadder than an empty coffin. It's the darkest time I've known here."

The priest pulls a scrapbook from a crowded bookshelf. He turns the brittle pages, searching for something while I look over his shoulder.

"Here we are," he says, pointing to a faded image. It's a much younger Hodgson standing next to another priest. So this is who David Reeve once was, I think to myself. "I never would have imagined back then that he was capable of such evil deeds."

"Do you know where he is living now?"

He looks into my eyes. "Why, child? What interest is he of yours?"

"Father," I begin, "I know you may not believe this, but Tommy Walker is not at rest. I mean Mr. Reeve no harm, but I'd like to see the lad cross over and be at peace."

He closes the album and takes another chocolate. "I'm an old priest, and I believe in spirits...Holy and otherwise. Our faith confirms that our souls are eternal. Be careful though, especially if you are planning on speaking to David. I don't want any other boys to go missing."

"I promise I'll take every precaution."

He goes to a small desk near the back of the room. "He's in Brixton. He tends bar at a pub called, The Wolf & Fiddle."

"He's a bartender?"

Hodgson nods. "It's really not that different from being a priest..."

I grin. This old guy is astute. "May I visit you again?"

"Please do, my boy, please do. I need to keep making young friends, nearly everyone I've ever known is dead."

CHAPTER 68: PETER CHADWICK

We managed to find some Irish Red Ale and a few bottles of Porter & Stout between us. I've invited a couple of the Head-Boys from the other houses in addition to a few of the older St. Johnnies.

Chase Hampton, the Head over at Farrington, promised some whiskey but he didn't come through with it.

"Pathetic," Ollie Morgan says. "We're never going to get trollied off of these odds and sods."

"If Jake shows up he won't disappoint," Redgrave says with encouragement.

Hampton looks at me with eyebrows raised. "Why did you go and invite that shirt-lifter?"

"He's a decent bloke," I say. Honestly Jake makes me a shade uncomfortable with his open homosexuality. I'm almost certain he's pulled Ashlock into his life of sin. The penniless boys are always the most susceptible to such things.

Jake did get a fantastic car for his birthday though, an awesome black Mercedes. I'm hoping he'll let me take it for a spin.

Ollie says, "Caught him looking at my twig-n-berries after the waterpolo match on St. Andrew's Day. I mean, it's one thing to cop a feel from the laddies now and then, it's quite another to fashion it into a lifestyle."

"Says the Head-Boy who's copped a feel from every lad at White Oak," I say, half-joking. But I must have struck a bit too close to home because Ollie pushes me on the chest and nearly lands me on my arse.

"Shut your laughing gear, Chadwick. You're the one inviting the flamer to a sleep-over."

Just then Weston and Ashlock enter. "Speak of the Devil," Hampton says.

"And the Devil appears," Weston answers. "Did I hear you mention a sleep-over, because I didn't bring my pajamas."

Ashlock elbows him, "Please behave."

He's holding a backpack, so that's a promising sign.

"What's in the knapsack, Weston?"

He pulls it from his shoulder. "Oh this? Nothing much, just my Latin preps for Silver...I thought we might have a study group."

"You're barmy," Ollie says.

"He's kidding," Billy scoffs, shaking his head.

"I've forgotten more Latin than you lot will ever learn," he says as he pulls a bottle of tequila and a bottle of whiskey out of the pack.

Ollie's eyes widen. "Nicely done, Weston, nicely done indeed."

"Do you have any glasses or cups?" Ashlock asks me, so I'm scrounging around trying to find a few.

"This is a thirty-year-old Laphroaig, so let's show her some respect. We can't be drinking from the bottle like a pack of hobos," Jake remarks.

Soon all of us are doing shots and feeling no pain, though I'm sure Redgrave will be in tatters tomorrow. He can't hold his liquor.

"I hear you're sweet on one of those Bentley Wood girls," I say to him.

He looks over at me. "Nah, Sam only has eyes for Timmy here." Ashlock scoffs.

"I think that Lilly has looked once or twice in your direction," he says.

"I'd need a lot more whiskey to go there," Billy remarks. "Her face looks like a blind cobbler's thumb."

"Ha, Redgrave," I say. "One and your anyone's, two and you're everyone's."

Jake lifts his cup. "To the poetic couple of Billy and Lilly."

"Truth or dare," Ollie says to me. I watch Ashlock whisper something to Weston.

"Dare," I say back.

Morgan looks up to the ceiling trying to find a sufficiently humiliating task for me to perform. "I dare you to wave your willy at Mr. Weston."

Jake looks at me and smirks. "Oh, I think I like this game."

"Fair enough," I say. I pull Weston to the hall and drop my trousers. "Take a good look, but no touching." I'm already starting to laugh. We come back to the group in stitches.

"What's so funny?" Timothy asks.

"I've yet to see a circumcised penis in England," Jake says.

Ollie interjects, "Come over to our House, we have a couple Jewish lads." We laugh again. It's my turn so I turn to Hampton. "Truth or dare?"

"Truth."

"Have you ever gotten to third base with a girl, and if so, who?"

He shrugs, but he's also gone red. "I've been half way to third with Shelly Barton, a girl from home." I find this extremely funny, but we are all steaming drunk.

Hampton turns to Weston, "Truth or dare?"

"Dare."

There's something not altogether right about Chase Hampton. It's one thing to take the piss out of someone, but it's another to cross the line. A gentleman should know the difference. Of course, Weston knows no shame so it's going to get interesting.

"I dare you to French kiss the handsomest boy in this room."

I see Ashlock close his eyes and shake his head, but Weston stands and slowly makes his way around the room, looking carefully, if drunkenly, at each of us. I'm half-afraid I'll win this boyish beauty contest.

"Since it's impossible for me to kiss myself," he says and we chuckle. He moves over to Timothy, who's sitting beside me.

"Shock and awe, Ashlock," he whispers and takes him in his arms. They snog like they are in a movie. It's a long, passionate, deep kiss, utterly embarrassing to witness up close.

"Save a bit for your girlfriend," Redgrave says to Timothy, but they just keep snogging. I finally reach over and pull them apart.

"Enough, gentlemen," I say quickly. "We don't want to set off the fire alarm."

"That was truly disgusting," Hampton announces.

"You're lucky I didn't pick you, Chase. Maybe next time."

CHAPTER 69:   JACOB

Between the Coach and Ethan I'm getting an earful of colorful Irish and English profanity heaped upon me this morning. Admittedly, I'm thoroughly hungover.

"Go home!" Lir finally shouts. "I can't stand the sight of you. If one of those braying toffs at Eton beats you I'll hang up my whistle for good and all. I swear to Christ Almighty..."

It goes on and on like that, so part of me just wants to dive to the bottom of the pool and deeply inhale. I climb out and look at Ethan.

"I suppose you don't want to drive me back."

He looks away.

"Fine," I say loudly.   "Both of you get out your goddamn stopwatches. I'm going to do a 200 meter sprint."

I shake out my wrists and give my neck a quick crack.

I can feel them both watching me as I get into the starting position. "Someone has to blow the fucking whistle," I mutter.

When I hit the water I can feel it.   The pure speed. Sometimes it isn't even a part of me. I become some kind of robot and all my muscles simply remember what to do. But I always sense when the water is resisting me and when I'm cruising with it, not against it. It gives me a weird euphoria.

The first shouts I can hear are Ethan's, but soon the both of them are yapping like a couple of wild dogs. We've been working on the flip-turns and they're flawless. I kick into a whole other level for the final lap.

My mind clears. I can't even feel the water. I'm not counting, I'm not even sure my eyes are open...I just see blue.

When I hit the last wall I expect to hear them both screaming but it's absolute silence. I peel off my goggles and look over to the Coach. He and Ethan are comparing their watches.

"How fast?" I ask. I know it was pretty fast.

Dylan has come to the side of the pool, and he bends down. "You bastard," he says. "One-fifty-eight and change. You bloody bastard."

It's not a world record or anything...but I would've won a gold medal in the 1960 Rome Olympics, and the 200 isn't even my race.

Ethan is just staring at me. "How the fuck?"

I motion to my head and tell him, "Mind over matter." Then I bolt to the locker room to vomit, because Jesus I'm hung-over and that swim nearly killed me.

***

I'm excited to see Tim when I get back to Brigsley. I open the door all smiles only to find him having tea with Dr. Rowland.

"As I live and breathe," I say, wondering how long she's been interrogating my lover. I study Timothy's face, but it's difficult to read.

"This is a surprise, Jane."

She stands to shake my hand. "I took your advice," she says, "and I dropped by to see where you live. I hope you don't mind."

"Not at all," I say. Tim has gotten up to leave us alone but I grab him. "I see you've met my boyfriend, Timmy."

"Is that what you are?" She's asking Tim as if I'm not even present.

"I prefer not to define it," he says quietly.

"You're an interesting couple," she admits.

"We're not the only ones," I mutter under my breath.

She came without all the makeup this morning, and she's hidden the twins behind two layers of cotton and wool. She's even wearing black-rimmed glasses which appear more theatrical than prescriptive.

"Tim was telling me about your ghost."

I sigh.

"Was he now?" I look over at him as if he's been airing our manky knickers.

"She already knew," he whispers. Of course, I reason, Fulton has been using my neurosis as pillow talk.

"I'd love to see a real phantom."

Tim is pouring tea, which I immediately gulp down. What a day this is shaping up to be, and we haven't even gone to classes yet.

"Well," I tell her, "he only shows himself in the rain."

"Pity," she says, nearly pouting.

"We could show her the thing with the candles," Tim offers. I stare at him because he's obviously lost his bloody mind. I guess Dr. Jane's siren's song actually does have an effect on some young males of the species.

"Oh, why not," I finally say. I light a candle and hold it up. "Tommy Walker," I call, "if you can hear me blow this out."

And nothing happens. I just stand there like a mental patient holding an open flame.

"Hmmm," Jane says.

"Maybe the knocking," Tim suggests.

Seriously, Timothy?

"Yeah," I mumble sarcastically, "I'm sure that will work much better."

Still, if you're going to get up to sing you might as well dance. "Okay, Tommy, if you can hear me, please knock on wood."

Dead silence, no pun intended.

"Perhaps he's off haunting someone else this morning," she says with a mocking tone.

"It's a lot easier to dismiss a ghost in the daylight, Jane."

"Let's talk about your mother," she says, holding the photo from the mantle.

"Smooth segue, Doc."

"She died rather suddenly, didn't she? How old were you then?"

My head is pounding. I need a little hair of the dog. "I was twelve, and yes, brain aneurysms have a reputation of being rather unexpected." (I feel like I'm having one now).

"You must miss her terribly."

"I *must* get ready for my first class but this has been delightful." I start to walk up the stairs to my room.

"Drop by if you need to talk," I hear her whisper to Tim as she is leaving. I was raised as a gentleman, but I'd really like to give her one good slap.

As soon as she's gone the knocking begins. The doors slam and the windows rattle. "Everyone's a comedian," I say to myself.

CHAPTER 70: TIMOTHY

It's been a week and Kendel has yet to speak a single word to me. He doesn't look my way or call on me anymore, so Chemistry is still oddly uncomfortable.

When class is finished I run to the cottage to pick up my violin before meeting Jake at the Buttery. I text my mom about coming to the Eton swim competition and surprising him. He needs our support since his family isn't going to be there, and she immediately agrees to attend.

I'm late so I decide to take the path down by the river. It's a quicker, if muddier route but it's down there that he corners me...Chase Hampton, the Farrington boy from the party.

"If it isn't Timothy Ashlock," he says. "What you doing down by the river?"

"Hampton," I say. "Nice to see you. I'm just on my way to lunch."

I try to appear casual, but I'm scared shitless. This bloke is twice my size and we are literally off the beaten path.

He grabs my arm. "Hey," I say, "that hurts. What do you think you're doing?"

His face is inches from mine and I can smell that he's been drinking again (or still). I try to break free but he clamps down tighter.

"Why don't you give us a kiss the way you kissed your boyfriend last night," he whispers.

"Sod off," I say, and he wrenches my arm tighter. It feels like he's going to snap the bone like a twig. He roughly turns me around and tries to undo my belt with his free hand, but he's not having much luck with the buckle.

He locks my arm behind my back and hisses in my ear, "Pull down your trousers Timmy, or I'll break your fucking arm."

185

He gives it a quick jerk to underline his point and I yelp. I drop my violin case into the mud and I'm nauseous with pain.

"Let him go, asshole!" I hear Jake shout. He's standing above us on the hill about forty feet away.

"Stay where you are, Weston, or I'll break your lover's scrawny arm."

I look up at him and he is calmly smiling at me while pointing a gun directly at us.

"Hampton, I'm going to give you one last chance to let him go. If you don't I'm going to put a bullet between your eyes."

"Ha! Is that a revolver you've got, you mad bastard? You're all piss and wind, there's no way that's loaded."

He immediately shoots the tree right beside us. As soon as the bullet explodes into the bark Hampton throws me down into the mud.

"I'm going to kill you," he yells, staggering away. "I'm going to kill the both of you knob-jockeys. Wait and see." Jake is down the hill and holding me in seconds.

"Are you all right? Do you need to go to the infirmary?"

I'm sobbing uncontrollably and hugging him close. "I dropped my violin."

"Clumsy," he says.

"I'm a magnet for closeted perverts," My whole body is shaking.

"I'd take offense to that statement...if I was closeted. It's probably your cologne."

We grin at each other. My life would be empty without him.

"Would you really have shot him?" I ask, and I look into those piercing blue eyes of his.

"If he had seriously harmed you...I'd have put a bullet into his brain without a second thought."

I reach out to touch his hair, which is getting so long. "Where were you hiding the gun?"

He winks and lifts his trouser leg. "In a small holster on my lower calf."

"Can I hold it?"

He gets up and inspects the tree. He pulls a Swiss Army knife out of his pocket and starts digging into the trunk.

"I'll show it to you back at Brigsley. We need to leave the scene of the crime before the town cryer tells his tale." He holds the spent bullet in his hand. "Evidence," he says. "I'm probably going to need some plausible deniability for this incident."

He notices me rubbing my arm, which still hurts, and quickly comes over and starts touching and probing me.

"It's sprained," he says. "You'll have to ice it down."

We start walking back toward home.

"I don't think I could ever shoot anyone," I say.

He drapes an arm around me. "Well I hope you never have to, but you are braver then you imagine."

CHAPTER 71: JACOB

When classes finally conclude for the day Tim and I are off to London. He loves my fancy black car more than I do, he calls it the Batmobile, but I'm not letting him drive today with his sore arm. I input our destinations into the navigation system. First stop is The Spiral Staircase, the bookstore in Westminster.

It's a quaint shop, dusty and overcrowded with old tomes stacked up to the ceiling. The brass bells over the door announce our arrival. Duncan Greer quickly recognizes our uniforms which is one of the reasons I insisted we wear them.

"You boys from White Oak?" he asks. He's a middle-aged balding chap with a slight paunch.

"We are," Tim replies.

I can see his mind drift back to the halls and passageways of his boyhood. I wonder if his lasting memories are always of the bomb shelter and his imprisonment.

"I went there," he says quietly. "I don't suppose it's changed that much in all these years."

"Haven't you ever come back for an Old Boy's Day?" I ask.

"Nah," he admits. "I'm too busy with this shop to spend my free time strolling down memory lane. So what can I help you lads with?"

"I'm looking for a Christmas gift," I say. "Something special; an old edition of Lewis Carroll or A.A. Milne."

"Hmmm," Greer says, beginning to hunt around, "I might have just the thing." He fiddles with a ring of keys and opens assorted glass cases where he keeps the valuable editions. Tim has started to wander about the shop, idly browsing. We both have a fondness for places like this.

"Ah," Greer says, "here it is!" He comes down the staircase holding a leather-bound volume which he hands proudly to me. It's a beautiful edition of *The Hunting of the Snark.* "That's from 1925, a real gem."

"It's lovely," I say. "How much?"

"Suppose I could let that go for...125 pounds, seeing as you're a White Oak boy."

I smile and place the book gently on the counter. "Your name is Duncan Greer, isn't it?"

He looks surprised. "It is indeed."

"Mr. Greer," I say, "I'll give you 200 pounds for this book and the answers to a few questions."

He looks suspicious, but I can see he wants the money. "What sort of questions?"

"We know what happened to you," I say, "back at White Oak when you were a boy."

He quickly looks away. "I can barely remember any of that...time. It wasn't pleasant."

"Do you remember a third boy? A little blond bloke?" I press.

He looks at me as he is carefully wrapping my purchase. "Tommy Walker? Are you speaking about him?"

"Yes," I say. Tim comes up to the counter holding a cloth-bound book. We look expectantly at Greer.

"I knew Tommy, we all did. He was in St. Johnnies, but Robin and I were both in Exeter."

"Did you see him down in the...in the bunker?"

"Nah, but that poor little fag-boy was getting tortured by all the fag-masters. The basement might have seemed like a vacation for that chap. Boarding school, what a fucking joke. The three B's we used to say."

"What are those?" Tim asks.

"Ah, can't believe you don't know that old boarding school adage. The three B's are: *Bullying, Beatings and Buggery.* I assume they are all going strong."

The boys exchange glances. "Do you think that Father Reeve..."

Greer flares up. "Don't say that pervert's name inside my shop!"

"I'm sorry, sir, I do apologize. Do you think he, the priest, took him too?"

"Of course I do! And so did Scotland Yard at the time. He should have hung from the gallows for what he did to Robin and me, let alone whatever black hole he buried Tommy Walker in...and now that nonce is walking free. There's no justice in the world. What's all this to you boys, though? It's ancient history."

I look at Tim's book, it's a biography of Niccolo Paganini. I push it toward Greer. "This too," I say.

"A fiver more." I hand him the cash.

"Tommy's ghost, and Robin's too I think, are haunting the school. We're just trying to bring them a little peace."

He hands me the package and walks us to the door.

"Then I wish you blokes luck, but none of us will have any rest until that priest is in hell where he belongs."

***

We're driving out toward Brixton to see Reeve next. Timothy looks anxious. "You don't have to go in if you don't want to," I tell him.

"I'll be just as nervous sitting in the car. You have Harold, don't you?"

I tap the inside of my leg. The pistol is a Glock 19, one of the best compact 9mm handguns on the market.

"I just don't know what you expect him to say...Oh, yes, that Walker lad? I buried him under the rosebushes in the chapel's garden."

"I don't expect him to say anything. I just want to see his face when I bring up the name," I explain.

"How is that supposed to help Tommy?"

I touch his leg as I'm driving. "I think we're supposed to find his body and give him a proper burial. That's the closure he needs."

"Reeve is never going to give that up. He's kept his mouth shut for decades. He doesn't want to be implicated again."

Tim is making good points, even if he is doubting my powers of persuasion and deduction. "Then we will have had a nice drive and done some Christmas shopping."

CHAPTER 72:   THE WOLF & FIDDLE

It's mid-afternoon in Brixton, one of the poorest areas of London. There aren't any power brokers having impromptu meetings on this side of town.

Jacob and Timothy walk down into the subterranean pub where it takes a moment for their eyes to adjust to the darkness. The Bee Gees are playing from a jukebox somewhere in the back and the whole place smells like stale beer and despair. There's an ancient television set showing a rugby match with the sound turned down, as well as a sagging dartboard on the wall.

Reeve is there behind the bar, staring at his new customers like a fat spider waiting in its web. He wears a white apron which only exaggerates his obesity. David Reeve is a triple-chinned man in his sixties who appears pasty and unwell, peering at the boys through thick-lensed glasses.

"Hello lads," he says as they approach the bar, "have you lost your way?"

Jacob exudes schoolboy charm, "What makes you ask that, sir?"

"You're miles from White Oak Academy...unless you came all this way just to see me," Reeve says. He isn't buying whatever Jake is selling.

"May we have two soda waters with lemon?" Timothy asks politely.

Jacob and Reeve continue staring at one another, sizing each other up.   He momentarily turns his attention onto Timothy and smiles wickedly.

"Don't tease me, Handsome. You're in a pub, have a beer."

"Two Guinness," Jacob orders. Reeve turns and looks at his own reflection in the mirror as he draws the pints and frowns slightly. He's let himself go. Putting the mugs down, he adjusts his comb-over.

"So," he says under his breath, "how did you two shits find me and what the fuck do you want?"

Jacob takes a long pull on his beer before answering. "It was easy to find you, David. You're not exactly in the Witness Protection Program, are you? Not to mention you blatantly sending feeble little postcards to our parish priest."

His eyes narrow and then he chuckles, his jowls wobbling from side to side. "Hodgson? Christ, what ever happened to clergy-penitent privilege?"

Timothy is moving from foot to foot like he needs to piss. He won't even sit down.

"I don't think he thought that your communications were privileged."

Reeve is watching Timothy dance about. "Do I give you the collywobbles?"

"Leave him be," Jacob commands, and Reeve's focus shifts back.

"Oh, I see what the story is...You two are together, eh? Personally I always liked a good three-way...just ask Duncan."

"Let's go," Timothy whispers.

"In a minute," Jacob says calmly. "Drink your beer, while I ask the defrocked bartender here a few questions."

Reeve tightly purses his lips. "Do you two gorgeous boys feel guilty for what you've been doing to each other? Did you come to Brixton to confess your sins?" He giggles. "I'm afraid I can't absolve anyone anymore."

"We'd rather hear you confess a few of your transgressions," Jacob counters. "Why don't you tell us what happened to Tommy Walker?"

Reeve pounds on the bar and cackles. "Is that why you're here? You pathetic dolts. It's like I told everyone years ago...I never had anything to do with him. Didn't hardly know the little bugger because he wasn't an altar boy, you see. Robin and Duncan were the most beautiful lads to ever work a Sunday Mass. You boys wouldn't happen to be altar boys, eh?"

"Sod off," Tim says under his breath.

"Hmmm, not the spiritual types, huh? What's your name?" he asks Timothy but Jacob shakes his head.

"Never mind what our names are. Robin is dead, you know. Why did you torture those boys?"

Reeve wipes his hands on a dirty bar towel. "Torture is such a harsh word. I never hurt anyone, not permanently...just tied them up and had a bit of naughty fun, and for what it's worth, I think everyone enjoyed it, I truly do. I paid the price with the law for what I did, twenty-two long years, and I made my pact with Almighty God to boot. I'm just a harmless lag these days." Looking toward the ceiling, he sighs loudly. "Sad about Robin though, he was such a beautiful lad, I heard he developed a drug problem."

"I wonder what drove him to that?" Timothy says accusingly. Jacob picks up a matchbook with the Wolf & Fiddle logo on it and slips it into his pocket.

Reeve rubs the dark stubble on his chin. "It's been months since I've been back to church at White Oak...how are all my old friends?"

Jacob drops some money on the bar and gets up to leave but Reeve grasps his wrist tightly and pulls him closer. "I'll tell you one thing, boy," he says with dead seriousness. "If I was back in business you'd be just my type." He releases Jacob and then vulgarly grabs his crotch under his apron pantomiming sex.

Jacob leans across the bar and bats his eyes. "You disgusting old queen...I'm everyone's type."

The boys can still hear him wheezing and cackling as they exit the pub.

"That was insanely creepy," Timothy says as they're getting into the car. "I'm going to have night terrors for months. He was looking at us like we were two suckling pigs."

Jacob pulls quickly into traffic. "Yeah, if he's out of business then I'm the Queen of Sheba."

CHAPTER 73: JACOB

I'm halfway to Hackney before Tim realizes where we are going next. "Hey," he says, "where are we headed?"

"Brixton is only six miles from Hackney. I thought we'd pay a visit to Bea."

He's horrified. "I don't think that's a good idea."

"Why? Don't you want to say hello to your mum?"

He's giving me daggers with his eyes. "Listen, I told you, we are extremely poor. She might be embarrassed."

I grab his knee. "She might, or you might?"

He turns and stares out the window. "Must you always find new ways to humiliate me?"

"Yes, I must," I joke. "I'm trying to keep you humble."

"This should do the trick then."

"Ethan has already told me the conditions. He came to collect your mum for my birthday, and you know what a gossip he is. Also, I Google-Earthed your address."

"Oh brother."

"I texted and told her we are on our way. She's making tea."

"I hate you," he says, and I grab his leg firmly.

"No, you don't. And don't ever say that again, not even in jest."

We pull up to the apartment and it is as advertised. A sad, dilapidated tenement. The paint is peeling and the garden is an overgrown disaster. Bea is already outside waving both hands, overjoyed to see us.

"She certainly looks embarrassed," I say.

Tim leans over just as he's opening his door, "I'm not speaking to you."

"Bea!" I shout.

"My handsome lads! This is a surprise." She embraces us both. "I missed you Timmy."

"Mum," he says, "you saw me a week ago."

"Still, I think you've grown," she beams. "Hurry now, come inside so my neighbors can get a good peek at your car."

"We'll be lucky if it's still out here when we've finished our tea," Tim says.

Inside it's sparse, but meticulously clean. The parlor isn't much bigger than the turret Tim used to live in. Bea serves us from her family's antique china service.

"What brings you boys out this way?"

"We had to see someone over in Brixton, and with you being so close..."

"Aye," Bea says, "decided to see how the other half lives."

"Not at all," I say. "I did want to discuss something with you though."

She's opening a box of Hobnobs. "Jake loves those," Tim tells her.

"What can I do for you? Need me to write another note to the Headmaster?" She gives me a good-natured shove.

"No Bea. It's just, uh, I was thinking. In another year Tim and I will be off to Oxford..."

"If we get accepted."

"Oh please," I say and wave my hand in the air to make my point. "In any case, that's sixty miles from here."

"A bit of a hike," she agrees.

"I was talking to my associate, Mr. Abbot, back home..."

Tim leans over to his mum and whispers, "The butler."

I clear my throat. "He helps me make all my business decisions. We are going to be purchasing a home in Oxfordshire where we can be comfortable during our time there. Who knows, I may want to teach someday so..."

"That seems sensible," Bea says.

"A place came on the market that I fancy. A five-bedroom Edwardian with lovely walled gardens. We expect to have the deed by New Year's Day."

Tim is stunned. "You never told me about this!"

I shrug. "I didn't want to get your hopes up in case the deal fell through. Anyway, Bea, I know how attached you are to your home here...but I wonder if you wouldn't consider moving into our new place. I'd hate for it to be empty until we move, and there are so many things to do between now and then."

Tears are already streaking down her face, Tim holds her hand. "What do you think, Mum. Won't you miss your friends here?"

She scoffs. "That's why they invented the telephone...and I'll make new friends. When can I move in?"

"In January. Bea, I'm going to trust you to hire us a gardener and a maid. And of course, to get all the furnishings that you think are missing."

She hugs me tightly. "And what about next year when you boys move in?"

I look over at Tim. "You'll stay with us, of course. You'll be our Matron, and make sure we don't step too far out of line."

The three of us all start sobbing.

***

I'm driving back to White Oak fast because we've been gone half the day. We both have preps to do and trials and exams to study for. Tim holds my hand during the entire drive.

"I thought it was one of my better ideas," I tell him.

"This is a kindness I can never repay," he says, squeezing me. "I worry about her, old and alone in Hackney. You've saved us, both of us."

"Pish-posh," I say to him. "Timmy, you are one of the lucky ones because boarding school has been a grand opportunity for you. It was your chance to rise above the circumstances you were born into...and you have proven yourself worthy of the task. But Bea loves you regardless...most of us have parents who sent us away for convenience, or notions of status, or just because they did not love us enough. In some ways you are richer than me."

"So what is this house like?"

"It's perfect," I tell him. "Wait til you see it."

CHAPTER 74: DUBAI

Paul Weston has flown halfway around the world to watch a horserace. His prized three-year-old filly, Theresa's Torment will be running, and she hasn't lost a race yet.

He spends nearly an hour in the paddock talking to his trainer, and discussing the race strategy with their young jockey. The plan is to stay just off the pace until the final stretch and then let her loose; hopefully by that time the early speed will have burned itself out of the competition.

"I'm counting on you," he tells his trainer Art Beckman. "I flew halfway around the world to have my picture taken in that Winner's Circle."

"No worries, Mr. W., she won't let us down."

In the plush owner's box he sips a gin and tonic, which is a rather rare commodity in this Muslim country.

Andrew Levin, an investment banker (and occasional rival) comes by to wish him luck.

"Do you have a horse in this race, Andy?" Weston asks.

"No, no. We're all betting on your filly. The Arabs are all going to be pissed off when she wins."

They both laugh and clink glasses. "To the Sport of Kings."

"You should be happy this race is in December, it's only ninety-degrees today," Levin remarks.

"Tell me about it. I can't wait to get back on my plane, get drunk and go home."

Levin sits down. "Say, speaking of fast horses...I heard your boy is swimming in the UK."

Paul smiles and nods. "Indeed he is. We hired a fine coach in London. He's going to be a star in the next Summer Olympics."

"Why do you have him enrolled at White Oak Academy? That's a bit of a backwater for a future Olympian, isn't it? Our Andy Jr. has been at Eton for two years...that's a proper school."

Weston frowns. "Oh, Eton wanted him, but they couldn't admit Jacob until mid-January and he was eager to get back to the grindstone."

Levin is gesturing. "You should talk to the Headmaster... Fetterman is his name. If Jacob wins at the Trials he'll probably offer your boy a full ride...and it's a far superior institution."

Weston contemplates the idea, and a full scholarship would be icing on the cake. "Maybe moving him over would be the best arrangement for everyone."

Levin agrees, "Our Andy can show him the ropes and help him get settled. Both Princes, William and Harry, went to Eton...It's where royalty belongs."

Paul is nodding as the starting bell rings and the gates spring open. The race is a mile on the turf and the jockey sticks to the intended plan. Theresa's Torment wins easily by three-lengths. While he and his friends are laughing and posing for the winning photo, Paul Weston decides to transfer his son to Eton.

CHAPTER 75: TIMOTHY

A mandatory assembly has been called in Deerfield for the entire school. It's unusual for something off the schedule to pop up this close to exams and Christmas break. Jake is barely back from London before we have to go.

"Jesus!" he shouts, "must they ring the bells incessantly?"

He's right, they've been tolling for a good long while. He grabs an apple as we head out. "This is odd," I tell him. "We've all got exams to study for and the winter break coming up. It must be something important."

He grins his lopsided evil grin. "Maybe Rothwell is dead," he whispers conspiratorially.

"That hypothesis is in poor taste, Mr. Weston," I tease.

"Still, Kitty is young... she can find another Headmaster to give head to."

We both start laughing just as Billy comes running up next to us.

"Redgrave," Jake says. "Who died?"

"Dunno," he answers. "My dad would have called me if it was someone in the gentry."

He's the son of an Earl so they keep up with which Lords and Ladies are still above ground. We all settle into our seats and Rothwell takes the podium in his black robe. He looks somber.

I elbow Jake. "Your powers have failed you today."

He shrugs, but he does look concerned. He stands up and is searching the dais and then he starts to visibly go to spare.

"My God," he whispers to me. "I think Father Hodgson is dead."

***

We walk back to Brigsley hardly speaking a word to one another. I touch Jake's back as we go inside.

"I just saw him last Friday. Don't you think it's strange that I spoke to him about David Reeve's whereabouts and he perishes three days later?"

I take my violin and place it gently on the table. I've got some tools and some wood glue at the ready. The neck started to crack when I dropped it in the mud. "Jake," I say, "he was a hundred and fifty years old."

He is carefully watching my repair operation. "In fact he was eighty-eight and in relatively good health."

"So you think someone snuck into the rectory and smothered an old priest in his bed?"

"I'm just saying... but you're right, of course," he combs through his hair with his hands, a mannerism I've seen him perform when he's distracted.

"I'm being paranoid," he says. "Still a former White Oak priest would know his way around the pastorate. What I'm wondering is if David Reeve has the goolies to show up for his mentor's funeral." He sits down next to me and drinks a fruit smoothie while I attempt to fix my broken instrument.

"Are you using *Elmer's* glue on your violin?"

"It works extremely well," I answer, "and it dries completely clear."

CHAPTER 76:   THE BELL TOWER

"Wouldn't it be simpler," Timothy says, "to just attend the service with everyone else?"

"Probably," Jacob agrees, packing his backpack and zipping it up. "But I hate funerals."

"What? You're obsessed with death, you never shut up about it. I would think funerals would be one of your favorite pastimes."

They leave the cottage and hike up the hill toward Kyler Library. "Then you would be wrong. I'm fascinated by death and suicide...but funerals aren't about the dearly departed. They're a public display. A dog-and-pony show where people can exhibit fake sympathy and say nice things about someone they may not have even liked. A funeral is all about the living...and I find them in rather poor taste. If you love me, please tell me while I'm still breathing."

Timothy leads them down a flight a steps and through the labyrinth stacks of books to an alcove tucked far to one side. They have reached the wall that adjoins the tower. A small oak door sits in front of them, securely bolted, chained and double locked.

"I told you," Timothy said, pointing to the security measures.

Jacob shakes his head. "It looks more imposing than it is." He opens his backpack, takes out his tools and immediately begins fiddling with the locks.

"A boy climbed up two years ago and jumped to his death. I remember it vividly. Finn Williams was his name. He was a good lad; quiet, studious...he played the guitar."

Jacob opens one lock and moves on to the second. "Did he leave a note?"

"A suicide note?" Timothy thinks back. "I don't know, I don't think so. What percentage of people do?"

The second lock pops open and Jacob replaces his tools. "Thirty to fifty percent. A note, a video, or some kind of message to friends and family. One mystery at a time though, Sport."

Once inside the tower Jacob finds a small electronic switchboard. He examines it with his flashlight.

"The controller for the bells," he explains. "I'm going to disconnect it so we aren't accidentally deafened up there."

"Good idea," Timothy says.

They climb to the top via an extremely rickety staircase and open the trapdoor, scaring away a group of pigeons. The ancient bells hover right above their heads. The view of White Oak Academy and the surrounding countryside is spectacular from this perch.

"Wow!" Timothy exclaims. "This is amazing!"

They sit with a perfect vantage of the chapel so they can watch the mourners arriving. Jacob pulls out a bottle of Viognier and opens it.

"To Hodgson," he says. "May the old boy rest in peace." They touch glasses and take a drink.

"You really think that bastard will show up?" Timothy asks.

"I haven't the faintest," Jacob answers. "He is certainly crazy enough. You know, I sent a matchbook from The Wolf & Fiddle to our friend, Greer at The Spiral Staircase."

"Was that wise?"

"I think it was necessary."

Timothy leans against Jacob and holds his hand, their fingers interlacing. "What is your greatest fear?"

Jacob blinks his eyes, thinking. "I've only ever had one. I'm afraid of being a lonesome, old man. I would hate to end up all by myself in this world."

Timothy scoffs. "I hardly think that's a possibility."

"Anything is possible."

They watch the people arrive and shuffle into the chapel. "It would be hard to miss Reeve's fat ass waddling in here," Timothy says, making Jake laugh.

"Can I ask you something else?"

Jacob pours more wine. "Timmy, my love, you can ask me anything."

"Do you hate your father?"

He considers the question. "I don't hate him...I hardly know him. He's never shown any interest in finding out who I am as a person."

"Really? But he pays for everything..."

"That isn't love, Tim. Let me give you the perfect example: No one in my family calls me: *Jake*. Doesn't that seem odd? I mean, isn't it disrespectful not to call someone by the name that they prefer? Even Abbot will occasionally call me Jake, though he considers it against the Butler Code. You don't hear anyone calling Billy Redgrave, *Guillaume*."

"I didn't even know Billy had a French heritage. So why doesn't your family call you Jake?"

He shakes his head. "Who knows? Maybe my step-mother and father think it's too familiar or somehow beneath them...but more likely they just don't notice or care. It's very hurtful."

They wait until everyone is inside and the chapel doors have closed.

"I don't think he's coming," Timothy says.

"I guess Reeve is a chicken shit after all," Jacob says. "Let's finish this bottle of wine and I'll turn the bells back on."

CHAPTER 77: JACOB

Exams have gone well for Timothy and me, and my swim competition at Eton is only ten days away. There's a Christmas Faire in Greenknoll Village this week, and of course, the White Oak Pageant.

I need to call Abbot again regarding several matters, financial and otherwise, so I go out and sit in my car. I can't risk Tim earwigging these conversations... but before I can ring him up, Blackmore is pounding on the tinted window.

"Weston!" he shouts, "Please come with me."

I get out of the car. "Where are we going?"

"Headmaster Rothwell has asked to see you immediately."

'Marvelous,' I think.

***

He's sitting behind his big oak desk when I walk in. "Ah, Weston, please have a seat. Mr. Blackmore, I expect you back in twenty minutes."

He leaves giving me a sorrowful gaze. I sense the inquisition coming.

"I'm afraid we've had a disturbing report from one of our prefects regarding you."

I try to look shocked. "Headmaster, I don't know what anyone would have to report about me. I'm the model inmate."

Rothwell gives me one of his patented contemptuous stares.

"I must ask, do you own a gun?"

I laugh offhandedly. "Of course I own a gun, I'm an American...they issue us revolvers with our passports."

He doesn't laugh, or even smile.

"But do you currently possess a gun?"

I feign surprise. "Here? In England? Don't be daft, sir."

"Mr. Hampton has reported that you shot at him."

"Chase Hampton is as bent as a nine-bob note. He's obviously playing you, Headmaster. Perhaps you should ask him again."

"Yes, perhaps I will."

I stand and look out the window toward the church. The back of the parsonage directly faces Rothwell's office...that's interesting.

"If you still don't believe me, you're welcome to search Brigsley Cottage."

Rothwell smiles, baring his teeth. "What a grand idea...that's exactly what I have Mr. Blackmore and Matron Finlay doing... I assure you if they locate a firearm you will be expelled post haste."

Blackmore returns carrying the monogrammed silver flask I left conspicuously on the mantlepiece.

"Did you find a weapon?"

Blackmore shakes his head, "No Headmaster, but we did find this." He hands it to Rothwell who takes a whiff.

"Scotch?"

"That's not just scotch, it's a thirty-year-old Laphroaig. You're welcome to have a swig."

"At least you have good taste...but I'm afraid contraband of this sort merits a flogging. We usually wait until Friday to dole out punishment, but in your case I'll make an exception. Mr. Blackmore, please give us some privacy."

Blackie looks distraught but I give him a wink as he exits. The headmaster pulls his cricket bat from the wall.

"Three hits should make a lasting impression," he says. "Please assume the position."

I bend over his desk.

"Drop your trousers, boy."

I comply.

"And those colorful undergarments," he commands. I'm wearing *A Christmas Story* boxers. (I love a good pair of novelty knickers).

"Are you kidding?"

"I assure you we take our flogging at White Oak seriously...and bare buttocks is the way we've been doing it for the last 400 years."

I pull them down. "Merry Christmas, sir."

I'm silent and stone-faced during the sadistic beating. I wouldn't even give him the satisfaction of an audible grunt. I pull back up my trousers and he extends his hand to shake mine like the proper gentlemen we are pretending to be. It's a barbaric custom sheathed in aristocratic tradition.

"Will that be all, Headmaster?"

He sits back down behind his desk. "I understand you were one of the last people to speak with Father Hodgson."

I smile. "He was a fine man with a wonderful sense of humor."

"Is there a reason you did not attend his funeral?"

My arse feels like it's on fire. "I prefer to honor people in my own way when they pass. Memorial services repulse me."

Rothwell looks like he'd enjoy giving me another beating. "He told me you were his fifth Headmaster."

"Is that so? What else did you discuss?"

I stare at him, pausing. "The idiocy of corporal punishment in British boarding schools."

"Very amusing...you may go."

"Enjoy the scotch, sir."

CHAPTER 78:   LONG DISTANCE

"I can't wait to see you!"

"The feeling is mutual," Abbot replies.

"Were you able to secure it?"

His butler pauses. "It's at Sotheby's, I can pick it up in London before the Eton Trials, but the insurance will be an issue since this is a private transaction and not a Weston Industries acquisition."

Jacob is fidgeting with the controls on the dashboard of the Mercedes. "Do whatever needs to be done. Did you liquidate ten percent of the Alphabet stock?"

"Last week, just as you asked. I've also funded the Swiss account but you'll need to set up the passcodes via secure link."

Jacob smiles. "What would I do without you?"

Abbot looks out over the grounds from the terrace of the estate. "Endure the service of lesser mortals, I assume. I'm looking forward to watching you compete, Jake; are you wholly ready for it?"

"I believe so, and speaking of enduring lesser mortals, I was flogged today by the Headmaster...so my last few practices may sting a tad."

"What did you do to deserve a caning?"

"Sir, I believe the point is that no one ever does anything that merits a beating, it's inhumane and savage...and he doesn't use a cane, he prefers a cricket bat."

Abbot straightens his tie.   "How sporting of him...obviously, change will come slowly, if at all."

"Spoken like a true Welshman. Is my father flying over to watch me swim?"

Abbot hesitates. "Unfortunately no, he sends his regrets. He has a prior commitment in Asia, so I will be the only spectator from the household attending."

"What about the holiday? Will I be going back to New York?"

"Your father has asked for you to join your stepmother and him for Christmas in Bali...because nothing says *joyeux noel* like an Asian monsoon."

Jacob is crushed. "What am I going to do?"

Abbot turns his back to see if anyone is near enough to hear him, but no one is. "You're going to skive off this trip by coming down with a nasty bout of the flu which will require me to stay in England to care for you."

"Am I?"

"Yes. Your parents will not want to be exposed to your hideous germs in Bali and jeopardize their own health and holiday. We can depend on their selfishness in your time of need. There's an extra bedroom in your cottage, is there not?"

"I'll have it ready for your arrival," Jacob says excitedly. "Listen, as long as we're going to be staying in Britain...I'd like to invite Timothy and his mother to have Christmas with us."

"Splendid," Abbot agrees. "I'd also like to ask my sister to join us for dinner on Christmas Eve. It's been a long while since we've had a traditional English holiday."

"I guess I have a lot of decorating to do..." Jacob says.

"Please Master Jacob, leave all of that to me."

"Are you sure?"

"Of course. After all, I am the butler."

CHAPTER 79: TIMOTHY

Jacob is soaking in the upstairs tub because of his flogging. "Are all these bubbles supposed to be medicinal?" I ask.

"They're fun. I would think you'd have more sympathy for me. I've been horse-whipped."

"Hmmm, the way that silver JPW flask was left out, one might think you had planned for it to be discovered."

He flips some bubbles my way. "It might have been a part of my calculus. My arse should be sufficiently bruised for the swim meet. It would be scandalous if news leaks that White Oak's star swimmer has been viciously beaten by the Headmaster only days before the competition."

"So your plan is to scuttle the grand tradition of boarding school beatings?"

He's now given himself bubbly horns. "I'm just trying to shine a light on the subject."

"You know I was here when they came storming in for the search. I nearly had a heart attack when they opened the pantry."

He adds more hot water to the tub. "I told you no one would ever be able to find the false bottom we built to hide the liquor cabinet."

"You are a genius," I admit.

"I did have a tense moment myself when Rothwell told me to drop my trousers. I was going berserk thinking he would see the holster laced to my shin...but he was so distracted staring at my shapely ass, he missed it."

"Jake, seriously," I tell him. "Rothwell is married with three adult children."

"Listen, I know when someone is drooling over my goods. You Englishmen are all so depraved...God Bless you."

I just have to laugh. "What are you going to do about Hampton?"

Jake's given himself a bubbly white beard. "He's going to tell Rothwell he was mistaken, and that he must have simply heard a firecracker going off."

"How did you manage that?"

"I promised him a thousand quid and a hand-job to lie about it all."

"What?" I say, rather shocked.

"Don't worry...I'll certainly fork out the money, but not the other."

"By the way, a boy dropped off an envelope for you this afternoon while you were out; I put it on your desk."

"Oh thanks, that must have been Kyle."

"Who the bloody blazes is Kyle?"

"Dr. Jane's assistant. I paid him 500 pounds to make a copy of my confidential psychological profile."

I shake my head. "Really spreading the holiday cheer around, eh?"

"I try." He stands up in the tub and turns his back to me. "How does my arse look?"

I whistle. "Still lovely, but it is going to be badly bruised."

"I'll need my valet to apply some ointment to my injuries." I nod my agreement.

"I have a surprise," he says, putting on his robe.

"Is it better than getting to rub *Neosporin* on your bum?"

He musses my hair. "People would buy tickets and stand in line for that honor...every exhibitionist needs his voyeur. It's about the break...I'm staying here! I want you and your mum to come for Christmas at Brigsley."

"Really?"

"I promise it will be amazing. Abbot will have the room by the kitchen, your mum can have your room and you can stay with me upstairs. It will be cozy."

"That actually sounds kind of nice, but you mustn't spend a fortune. Christmas is supposed to be about peace and love, not presents and money."

He scoffs. "You've obviously never spent the holidays in America. Besides, I crave excess. I want to share my wealth, surely you can understand that *Mr. Marley.*"

***

It's half past eleven and Jake is lying face down on the bed. He's naked and I'm gently applying the medication. He winces dramatically at every touch so I know he just wants sympathy and tenderness.

"You did invite Bea to the Eton Trials, didn't you?"

I sigh.

"As a matter of fact I did. Must you spoil every surprise?"

"It's just that Ethan will be busy with his coaching duties so I wanted to arrange another car for her."

"That's both kind and generous, but you do realize that we Ashlocks have been navigating the United Kingdom by ourselves for generations..."

He looks back at me pouting. "Timothy, it's over twenty miles and I want her to be comfortable...can I at least hire an Uber?"

"I suppose," I say. Suddenly we hear breaking glass as a huge stone comes flying through the window right above our heads. Shards of glass rain down everywhere.

"Get down!" Jake yells, and I roll to the floor as he covers me protectively with his naked body. We lay frozen there at the foot of the bed, waiting to see if the onslaught will continue. "That was no ghost," he whispers. He grabs his robe and his gun and runs downstairs.

I reach across the floor to examine the projectile. Someone has thrown a large red brick through the window. In crude black felt-tip the vandal has scrawled the words: *'He that is without sin among you, let him first cast a stone...'*

CHAPTER 80: JACOB

"Did you see anyone?" Tim asks.

"Not a soul," I mutter. I'm looking at the brick as he is working to clean up all the shattered glass. *"King James Version,"* I say, reading the quote.

"Very old school," Tim agrees.

"...Let him first cast a stone? Sounds like Yoda was transcribing from the Greek. There are far more accurate translations available."

"You're not seriously making value judgements on the thug's choice of reference material, are you?"

I turn the brick over in my hands. "What kind of a moron writes this particular Bible verse on a stone that they then intend to cast at someone? I doubt it was our blameless Lord and Savior who was outside Brigsley chucking bricks..."

Tim is shaking his head. "I think it's meant as a warning aimed at our lifestyle; since we are sinners we should not be implicating others for their transgressions. Who do you think is responsible?"

I'm mentally counting up the suspects. "Paddy Lester, Chase Hampton, Wayne Kendel...certainly David Reeve...even the nutter Doctor Jane or Peter Chadwick. But if it's just someone going off on my sexual orientation it could be any one of a dozen or so other people."

I cut some cardboard to fit the missing pane and together we duct tape it into place. "Does the handwriting match the homophobe who defaced your desk in Blair's classroom?"

"An insightful question, however it's difficult to compare penmanship when one sample was created by wielding a knife. The only thing we can say for certain is that someone isn't fond of me."

After doing several nerve-calming shots of whiskey, we climb back into bed and I hold him until his breathing is deep and regular. Fortunately Timothy sleeps like the dead. I stealthily reach for my phone and open the app.

I'm extremely careful not to wake him as I take his right hand and place each finger in turn on the screen. In about two minutes I've scanned all his fingerprints into my iPhone.

CHAPTER 81: TIMOTHY

Tonight is the White Oak Christmas Pageant, so I'm fairly excited to finally perform the play. Everyone has pulled together and I think we've done a decent job.

Jake and I are headed into Greenknoll for the Christmas Faire beforehand. I'm hoping to pick up a few odds and sods for stocking stuffers. He doesn't realize it, but I've been composing an original piece of music for him as part of his present, as well as doing my special art project. It's impossible to buy a rich person anything when you're skint...so gifts have to come from the heart or not at all.

The Faire is a collection of booths set up on the main boulevard near the village square. Artisans of every stripe have brought out their wares. Candlemakers and painters, woodworkers and gardeners...everyone has some homemade good to sell.

Jake is enthralled by the music and exotic smells of spices and roasting meats. He loves all the personal touches as the townspeople beckon to show their offerings.

"You're going to have to hold me back or I'll buy out the entire village."

We stop to watch a few musicians playing Christmas carols. "Maybe I should do that next year to earn some extra income," I say.

We sample some cheese from one of the local farmers, and Jake buys a basketful. By the time we are halfway down the aisle he has bought flowers, candles, cheese, a hand-carved chess-set and a clock.

"I need to call Ethan to bring the car down," he says.

I put my hands on my waist. "I thought you weren't going to buy everything," I scold. "Leave some things for others, Mr. Weston, it's only proper."

He waves his hand at me while he samples some fresh pies. I know it's a lost cause so I sit down by the side of the road and watch two gypsy women telling fortunes near a small tent.

"These pies are amazing, you should try one," Jake says, handing me a large basket full of purchases.

"I thought you had an important competition to trim down for this week..."

"Don't spoil my fun during the holidays."

"Tell your fortune, young sir?" One of the gypsies has her eye focused on Jake and can see by all the packages that he's an easy mark. He moves toward their caravan and tent.

The pikey women are both swarthy and plump and seem to be true eastern-European immigrants festooned in glittering silver jewelry and long colorful silks. Their make-up is comically overdone, bordering on clownish.

"Give me your hand," one of the women reaches for him but he dodges her advance. "I already know my future," he states. "What I need is someone who can talk to my ghost."

The women exchange a few words in a strange tongue I don't recognize...possibly Romanian. "For this you need Miranda. She has the gift of speaking to the dead."

Jake perks up. "Does she? So, where is this mystical woman?"

"Weston," I say. "These types are known to run all sorts of scams and..."

"Don't be a snob," he says.

One of the women has gone into the tent and when she emerges moments later, she is holding on to a small girl wearing a Mickey Mouse tee-shirt.

Jake raises a brow. "Are you the great and powerful Miranda?" he asks, bowing deeply.

"I am," she says, looking us both over while playing with her long, braided hair. "You chaps have a problem with a spirit?"

He winks at me, then he bends down to meet the child eye-to-eye. "How old are you?"

"I'm not that much younger than you," she says quickly. "I'm ten."

Jake sighs. "Trust me, Love. There is a universe between ten and seventeen."

"You two are from White Oak," she states. (It wasn't a question).

"We are."

She considers us both. "Your ghost is at White Oak too. A former student?"

She's insightful, that is apparent. The best charlatans in this racket have an uncanny knack at ferreting out little details and weaving them into their 'predictions.' I can see Jake is completely entranced.

"It will cost you twenty-five quid for me to go up there and speak with him," she says. "Do you want him to leave? Because it's an extra twenty for me to cast a banishment spell."

"Jake..." I whisper, "please don't waste your money on this...performance art."

"Hold on," he says motioning to me. Ethan has arrived with the car and is at the end of the lane waving. "I hate to come off as a Doubting Thomas, but how do we know you're on the up and up, little one? How can we be sure our ghost will speak to you?"

She's already putting on a sweater and whispering her plans to the two women. When she finally looks our way again she says, "He won't have any choice but to speak with me...the dead find me irresistible."

"I don't know," Jake says. Perhaps he's coming to his senses.

"You need proof?"

"That would be..."

She grabs both my hand and Jake's at the same time and then closes her eyes. We stand like that for a full ten seconds and then she opens her eyes and stares at us.

"You've both lost people before their time...people you were extremely close to. Family members."

Jake whistles. "Not bad," he says, "but that is as vague as a horoscope."

She shrugs. "Henry and Janett. They miss you."

Jake and I are shocked into silence. "Is Janett?" I ask finally, but he is already shaking his head.

"That was my mother's name." I feel the gooseflesh rise on my neck and arms.

"Fair enough," I say. "Let's go talk to the dead boy."

Jake is looking into Miranda's big hazel eyes. "We're trying to find out who killed the chap who haunts our cottage...to bring him some peace, if possible. I'll give you fifty quid if you can help."

"Let's go," she says. "I don't have all day."

***

We climb into the car after loading all of Jake's purchases into the trunk.

"Who's this then?" Ethan asks brightly.

"Miranda," Jake says, "this is my dear friend, Ethan."

She takes his hand firmly.

"Hello," he says, wondering when his hand will be returned.

"You should go back to her," she says to Ethan.

"What's that?"

"Your wife," Miranda says, "she's waiting for you to come back home."

Ethan looks bewildered. "Who the devil?"

"Apparently our small medium is good with both the thoughts of the living and the dead," Jake says.

She is playing with her braids. "This is the nicest car I've ever been in," she says openly.

"Thank you," Jake answers.

When we've pulled up to Brigsley she opens her own door and goes skipping up to the porch. I unlock the house and she immediately walks to the center of the living room and plops down cross-legged in front of the fireplace.

Jake and Ethan carry in the packages and then we three stare at the ten-year-old sitting silently with her eyes closed, trance-like. The scent of jasmine and smoke is everywhere.

Ethan looks a bit freaked out as he always does when we mention ghosts. "Umm," he says, "I hate to interrupt the seance...but I'm off to pick up your mum in Hackney for tonight."

"Thank you," I say, patting him on the back. Jake is sitting on the couch transfixed by our guest.

"Right, cheers then," Ethan says and quickly makes his getaway. I go into the kitchen to make tea. Oda Mae Brown is immobile for a full five minutes. Finally she gets up and sits down next to Jake.

"He's chatty," she tells him.

"Did you ask him who the murderer is?"

"I did," she answers. "Like heaps of spirits he won't discuss his own death, in fact he refuses to even admit that he's gone. It's common, especially with those who leave this world very young. He's confused. That's one of the main reasons he hasn't crossed over."

Jake seems to accept this. "Are there other reasons? And what about the cottage? Why is he stuck here?"

I bring us all tea and biscuits. Miranda tucks in as though she's famished.

"Thank you," she says. "I've barely had a bite today..." Then with her mouth full of biscuits she says, "Oh, he isn't stuck here. He's waiting for someone."

"Who?"

"Another boy. Someone he was close to...a relationship similar to..." She points at the two of us with a knowing look.

"Something bad did happen in this cottage though, right in this room. Unkind words, angry voices. Some terrible argument that left a scar...that is a pain that still survives. Places take time to heal, just like people. Back then there were eight boys living in this cottage. They were all so mean to him, except the one. Tommy loved him...still loves him."

Jake looks warmly toward me. "It's perfectly romantic. He's waiting for a lost love."

Miranda tilts her head.   "Hmm, yes and no.   He was betrayed by this lad. Stabbed in the back...not literally, but he is still smarting from that slight. It's a terrible loneliness he feels. Love can be horribly cruel."

"Why does he only appear in the rain?" I ask.

Miranda shrugs.   "Fire and water.   He can only draw close when they are present."

Jake holds her hand.   "Can you sense, I mean, do you know...is he buried somewhere near Brigsley?"

She shakes her head.   "His bones are far from here, I'm certain of that."

"How do you do it?" he asks.   "I mean, how does it work, this gift you possess?"

She takes both his hands. "I shut my eyes and empty my mind." I watch as he closes his eyes and waits. Suddenly Jake releases her as if touching a hot stove. His eyes are wide and he has lost all the color in his cheeks.

"I saw something..."

Miranda crosses herself.   "That wasn't a departed soul. You have a touch of clairvoyance, Mr. Weston, a lot like my Aunt."

"The future?" he asks. "It was so vivid."

She stands and takes an apple from the table which she immediately bites. "Maybe," she says. "Don't trust it though. The future is always moving around...just seeing a peek of it can change what finally comes to pass. It's a frustrating talent."

"Thank you," Jake says. He's up and going to the pantry where he selects a bottle of wine. "This is for the women you live with," he says. "A Christmas gift."

She smiles broadly.   "My aunt and grandmother will appreciate it."   She takes the bottle.   "I can banish him, you know. He won't like it, but he wouldn't be able to return."

Jake looks at me and I frown.

"No," he says.   "We're used to him, and this was his home long before it was ours. Let him cross over in his own good time."

"Then you should find his friend...Tyler, and bring him here."

"Tyler? That was the name of the boy he was in love with?"

"Yes," she answers.

"Our next challenge," I whisper.

He is handing the girl an unidentifiable amount of money, but I'm fairly sure it far exceeds the agreed upon price of her mystic services. Then she hugs him, so I'm certain of it.

"I know what you saw. Don't take it to heart. You might be able to side-step it. Knowledge is power." He thanks her again.

"One more thing," she says, "you should go speak to his mother. She lives in Botany Bay."

CHAPTER 82: JACOB

A Christmas Carol is not my favorite Dickens tale simply because it's so damned predictable. Of course that mean bastard Scrooge turns out to be an old softy deep down. In my experience rich assholes stay firmly entrenched in their assholery despite any ghostly intervention. Still, it's theater.

Hoisington Place looks altogether grand and festive this evening. Poinsettias and holly are everywhere, along with twinkling lights and other joyous Christmas decorations. The English have a way with the yuletide season. There's magic in the air.

Bea is wearing her fur and I've put on a tux so we get our fair share of looks among the posh crowd as we make our way to our seats.

"Jay," she says, "you always know how to show a girl a good time."

I squeeze her hand. "You're a corker. But you've seen your son perform dozens of times."

"True enough," she says. "But never without his violin. He must feel naked."

The lights dim and the play begins. It's not half bad, to be honest. I feel a surge of pride when Tim takes the stage dressed in his nightshirt and chains. They've given him hollowed black eyes and ghostly white makeup. He looks to be reveling in it.

My favorite bit is when he turns toward Ollie Morgan, the prat who's playing Scrooge, with his arms extended wide, jangling his plastic shackles and saying, "I wear the chains I forged in life..." Classic.

A few scenes later Ollie is visiting his past and we get a chance to watch the girl I've heard so much about, Samantha. She's pretty enough, no Meryl Streep when it comes to the stage, but Dickens wrote her part pretty thin to begin with.

Bea gives my ribs a nudge with her elbow. "Is that the competition?"

"Mrs. Ashlock," I murmur, "I don't know what you could possibly be referring to."

When it ends we all give it a dutiful standing ovation. Professor Blackmore is in the wings beaming and it's then that my gifts arrive. Long-stemmed roses, one for every member of the cast and crew, being handed out by Matron Finlay. I did this in careful anonymity, and I swore our Matron to secrecy, but Tim catches my eye when he receives his rose and bows his head slightly.

Afterwards we rush backstage to congratulate everyone. It's chaos with the cast jumping about hugging each other and basically anyone who is standing nearby. I shake Ollie's hand and he pulls me in and kisses my cheek... maybe I should have tried out for this thing. There's always next year.

Tim introduces Samantha to his mother and me.

"What a lovely fur," she says.

"Oh thank you dear, it was a gift from my son-in-law..."

Samantha turns to Tim, "You have brothers and sisters?"

Tim is rushing her along, "It's a long story."

"And you must be Jacob Weston," she says pointing her chin up at me. "I know all about you."

She looks as though she might have guessed quite a bit concerning me and been fairly accurate. "Honey," I tell her, "no one knows *all* about me."

Thankfully Billy interrupts us and saves me from more scrutiny. "Redgrave!" I say, "You were phenomenal!"

He scoffs. "Oh yeah, I can point a sickle with the best of 'em. Come along Jake, my parents want to say hello to you..." He tugs at my sleeve.

"Excuse me," I say directly to Samantha, "I have to go chat with an Earl."

While I am bowing and exchanging pleasantries with Lord and Lady Redgrave I see Samantha kissing Timothy and pulling him somewhere backstage.

***

There's going to be a big cast party that Blackmore has arranged and so I invite Bea to walk down to Greenknoll with me to drown my sorrows.

"It's so kind of you to keep me company while he's out with all the drama nerds," I sigh.

She takes my arm in hers as we stroll down the hill toward the lights of town. It's a clear, crisp night and every shop is decorated brightly.

"You have no cause to be jealous."

"Hmmm," I reply. "That's an extremely pretty girl, and worse yet, I think she's smart."

"You boys are young, you'll figure things out."

We enter into my favorite pub. I pay the owner here a few quid on the sly so I can always get served, and tonight I need it. I order us double Irish Coffees and we move to a booth in the back.

"Bea," I say, "I don't have any grand illusions about my future with your boy. We're both just kids and I'm sure our lives will be turned upside down in the next few years...it's just that..." I look up to the ceiling. I should try to be less of a blubbering idiot in front of Tim's mother.

"Then why are you upset?"

It feels like my heart is in my throat.

"I suppose it boils down to me being a spoiled little shit that's used to getting everything he wants..."

She sips her coffee and licks whipped cream from off the straw. "I'll tell you a secret ...no one ever gets everything they want, and you usually get a nice heaping spoonful of pain to go along with the joy. Life is funny that way, the bitter with the sweet."

She's a wise woman who has endured a lot of hardship and come out the other side shaking her fist at God and smiling.

"You are spending Christmas with me, aren't you?"

"I am indeed, it was kind of you to ask. Can't wait to see what a Weston Christmas looks like."

I pat her small hand. "Then I'll try to pull out all the stops for you, Betty, I truly will. Ah, I wish..."

We get up and make our way out into the chilly night air. Ethan should be along to drive her back to Hackney soon.

"What do you wish?"

"I guess I just wish things were easier."

She shakes her head. "Ah, if wishes were fishes, we all would cast nets. But life isn't supposed to be easy, or simple. It's meant to be difficult so we will grow stronger, and hard so we will be tougher. Don't ever expect it to be fair, even or equal."

"And when it makes no sense at all?"

"That's just God giving you a chance to find wisdom."

CHAPTER 83: TIMOTHY

It's half past midnight when I get home and Brigsley is dark and silent as the grave. He didn't wait up for me and it feels like the darkness is meant as a rebuke. Even the dying embers in the fireplace seem to be accusing me of cheating.

I place my rose in a vase and put it on the mantle, then I decide to take a long, hot shower. Standing under the steaming water I scrub the smell of her perfume off my skin but the guilt doesn't wash away so easily.

My mother never allowed my brother and I to go to sleep angry, and I think that rule applies for unresolved issues between intimates. I'm sure I won't get a good night's rest thinking that Jake is upset, so I wander naked into his room and climb into bed with him.

He doesn't stir, but it's obvious he's not asleep because he's doing his fake snore.

"I know you're awake," I say to his back.

"How could you be so sure?"

"Intuition," I whisper, reaching for him under the covers. "Thank you for the rose."

"I can still smell her perfume on you."

I sniff around my own hands and arms and all I can smell is Jake's expensive body wash, Aesop. "That hardly seems possible," I say.

He turns over and gently moves the hair out of my eyes.

"It's Black Opium by YSL," he states.

"Are you furious with me?"

"No," he says. "Your mum talked me off the ledge. Did you have sex with her?"

"No."

"But you wanted to..."

I touch my hand to his bare chest and feel the slow, steady beat of his heart. "Honestly, yes I did."

He sighs.

"Then I suppose you should."

"I don't think you mean that," I say.

"Oh Timothy, what's the good of temptations if you don't yield to them now and then? It just surprises me because I always assumed that I'd be the first one to stray off the reservation..."

"You mean you haven't?" I ask, surprised.

"I've been as faithful as a Labrador retriever, not that I haven't looked at a few of the lads passing by."

There's an awkward pause that hangs in the space between us. "You know, she tried to grab my knob tonight, over my costume, but still. It made me feel a bit ashamed..."

"That little tart," Jake says. "Seriously though, we haven't pledged undying fidelity and monogamy to one another. Sweet Fanny Adams, we're only seventeen."

"Even so, I want you to know something..."

He kisses me deeply and pulls me on top of him. He is always so warm to the touch.

"I already know, Timmy, I already know."

***

It's before first light when I hear the sounds. Someone is downstairs, in the cottage. I hear drawers opening and closing.

"Jake!" I urgently whisper.

He sits up and cocks his head to listen, then he hurries to his dresser and pulls out two pairs of pajamas. "Quick, put these on."

"Aren't you going to get your gun? Or go down and see who's broken in?"

"It's Abbot," he says.

"How do you know?"

He gives me his lopsided grin, "Those footfalls are like a familiar song."

"How did he get in?" I ask. "I'm sure I bolted the door last night."

"Who do you think taught me to pick locks?"

We are both sitting up in bed, bright-eyed and in anticipation as we hear him climb the stairs. He knocks twice quickly and enters holding a tray.

"Good morning, Master Jacob," he says and looks over to me. "And you must be Master Timothy, a pleasure to make your acquaintance. I took the liberty of bringing up two espressos."

I'm not sure how the hell he knew we were both in this room together.

"Extremely kind of you, sir. You're looking robust."

"Thank you," he says and places the tray down at the foot of the bed. Two perfect demitasse cups sit neatly waiting. Jake immediately takes one and inhales the aroma of strong coffee and sighs contentedly.

"I wasn't aware that we owned an espresso machine," he says.

"Hmm," the butler replies, "you do now. The British are brilliant when it comes to tea, but only the Italians understand the nuances of coffee."

"What about the Turks?" Jake asks.

"Oh please, we are still gentlemen here, after all."

"It's an honor to meet you, Mr. Abbot," I say. "I've heard so much about you."

"Likewise," he says, inclining his head. I can sense he's evaluating my demeanor, making some mental calculations in his head. He reminds me of an older version of Jake.

"Can this new machine make a bunch of funny flavored coffees?" I ask.

"Only if you think a *macchiato* is funny," he deadpans. Jake starts to quietly chuckle.

"Unless you have other plans, Master Timothy, I thought the three of us would venture to Stratford together this morning. I'd like a few words with Coach Lir and then perhaps we could do some shopping and have a light lunch."

I look over at Jake who is already getting ready to go. "Trust me, save your breath. If the old boy has made a plan there's no use arguing...he always wins."

"All right," I say. "Let's go to London."

CHAPTER 84: LONDON

Abbot makes a thorough inspection of the London Aquatics Centre while Jacob puts on his suit and begins his warm-up exercises with Ethan.

"So, what do you think, Mr. Abbot?"

He silently looks up to the black painted ceiling and then turns his gaze to the coach. "Impressive. The seating capacity for the event?"

"Just under 3000," Lir says. "But we don't expect the Eton Trials to draw a full house."

"Five schools will be competing?"

Lir nods, "That's my understanding...including the best boys from Eton and Harrow."

Timothy stares up into the stands. It's an intimidating venue simply because it is so professional and immense.

"What do you think, Timmy?" the Coach asks.

"It's like a concert hall."

"You boys were only ten when the Olympics were held here."

Abbot considers the fifty-meter competition pool. "The depth is three meters?"

Lir shakes his head. "Just like the one in Beijing. This is the fastest pool in the United Kingdom...and our advantage is that this is like a second home to Jake. He knows this water better than any of the other boys he'll be up against."

Ethan is helping Jake stretch and whispering some private joke to him. They both laugh.

"I thought he was only going to compete in the 400, but I understand that you've also entered him in the 200?"

Lir sighs. "You've done your homework. He'll swim the 400 first, then we'll see how he feels. He posted some remarkable times in the 200 but that is not our focus. He wants to compete in both, and you know how stubborn he can be."

They all watch as he jumps into the clear water. Ethan blows his whistle twice.

"All right you bloody toff, let's do some warm-up laps!" Lir yells. "No showing off, save all that for tomorrow."

***

"I'm so peckish, where are we going to eat?" Jake asks.

Ethan is behind the wheel and Abbot is next to him giving directions. "You can't have any liquor until after the meet," Abbot says.

"And you need to stick to your diet so you will be in top racing form," Ethan adds.

Jake turns to Timothy sitting next to him in the backseat. "Now I've got two old women watching me like hawks," he whispers.

"I can hear every word," Abbot says. "I wanted to dine at the Ledbury, but in deference to your requirements Master Jacob, we will be dining at Quo Vadis in Soho."

"The sacrifices one makes," Jake mutters.

They acquire a table in the private members area where Jake is allowed to have fennel and lemon cured cod with olive oil mashed potatoes.

"Is it your intention to starve me?"

"It won't kill you to eat like a normal human being for one day," Ethan says.

Timothy orders peppered venison which makes Jake fold his arms across his chest and loudly sigh. "I'm eating whatever you don't finish."

"Don't be a baby," Abbot says. "If you behave we will order you a smoked eel sandwich that you can have as a snack later."

"Smoked eel?" Timothy makes a face.

"It's a specialty here," Ethan says.

Jake puts aside the menu. "May I at least have a glass of the Chateau Moulin?"

Abbot and Ethan exchange glances. "If you must," Abbot concedes.

Timothy chuckles.

"What's so funny?" Jake says.

"I rather enjoy watching the butler and the chauffeur ordering you around. The world seems more balanced somehow."

"Sir," Timothy says to Abbot when they are midway through their meal. "I wonder if I might have a private word with you later regarding a project I'm working on."

Abbot inclines his head. "Of course."

"What project?" Jake asks.

Timothy looks smug, "None of your business."

"So it's a secret project?" He prods.

"Must you turn over every stone?" Abbot asks.

"Yes."

Tim places his hand on Jake's thigh under the table. "It's a Christmas project, if you must know. So please stop asking about it."

Ethan rests back and admires the intricate stained glass. "I've never been to the private part of this place...it's nice."

"Did you know this establishment was formerly a brothel?"

Ethan grins. "Is that a fact?"

"It was also the home of Karl Marx," Jacob states.

Abbot sighs. "I have missed London and you, Jake. It's good to be back."

CHAPTER 85: JACOB

At precisely six AM there are two quick knocks and he enters just as he has thousands of times in my life. He carries a tray with espresso, orange juice, scrambled eggs and an assortment of fresh fruit.

"Good morning Master Jacob. I trust you slept soundly?"

I sit up and stretch widely. "I'm well rested, thank you. How did you fare downstairs?"

"Quite comfortably. Mr. Polley is en route to collect you. Is there anything that I can do to assist in the meantime?"

I look at this fine gentleman that has guided me through my entire existence. "Please sit," I say. "I wanted to thank you for traveling the distance to watch me swim. I do not intend to disappoint you."

He sits on the edge of the bed as I devour my light breakfast. "You could never disappoint me...but please remember to wear your bathing suit."

"I'll put that on my To Do list. Speaking of which, I'm making a few adjustments to my legal affairs which will need your signature."

"This involves JP Weston Inc. and Mr. Ashlock?"

"You are perceptive, my friend. My own secret Christmas project. I want to insure that Tim and his mother are farting through silk for the rest of their lives."

Abbot shakes his head. "What a charming picture you paint. The paperwork is easy enough to draw up, and it is an extremely kindhearted gesture. We'll make him a VP. I assume this also involves the Swiss account we just opened."

"Yes. I want this all kept separate from my father and Weston Industries."

"Consider it done."

I grin. "You are the closest thing to real family I have in this world."

He is at my wardrobe selecting my outfits for the day and evening. "That is not entirely true, although I appreciate the sentiment. As a matter of fact, your father sends his love."

"Does he?" I ask, doing some sit-ups beside the bed.

"Indeed."

"Talk is cheap," I quip. "When will you and Tim be arriving at the Centre?"

"One hour before the meet. I don't want you to be overly distracted."

"Don't be late or I will be distracted." I hand him my car keys. "I'd prefer if you drove today, don't let Timothy talk you into giving him the keys...he loves that car."

"He has excellent taste."

***

I take a shower, load my gear and head downstairs where Tim is having breakfast with Ethan. I can feel them watching me while attempting to avert their eyes.

"As you were, gentlemen. I feel strong as an ox, I slept fine, and I'm more than ready to kick some toff arses today. They won't even know what hit them."

Ethan practically explodes out of his chair. "That's the spirit!" Tim also gets up and motions me back into his room. I close the door behind us.

"What?" I ask.

He puts his arms around my neck and kisses me. "I love you Jake Weston."

"Is this the pep talk?"

He grins. "No, this is: Stay focused, swim fast and be humble."

We kiss again. "Would you settle for two out of three?"

He laughs. "I'm so proud of you. Show them all how extraordinary you are."

***

Coach Lir is already pacing around when I arrive at the Aquatic Centre. He's jumpy as a cat.

"The boys from Eton and Harrow are just arriving," he says.

"How do they look?"

"Fat and lazy," he jokes.

"Then why are you so nervous?" I ask. "Coach, I'm ready. You've done all you could hope to do with me."

"Jump in the warm-up pool and do some sloppy laps. I want the numpties from Eton to think you're no damn threat."

I chuckle because that is ridiculous. They've been talking about me for weeks, even having their spies out to watch my workouts...but I do exactly what the coach asks because he's the boss.

The stands are already starting to fill up and the first familiar face I see is Bea's. She has saved seats for Tim and Abbot and is smiling and waving. What a treasure she is in my life. I wink at her.

I sit down in a folding chair near the wall and put in my EarPods. I listen to Timothy playing the violin before all my workouts. It's relaxing. I don't look at the other swimmers, and I don't talk to anyone, not even Ethan. I take the time to focus my energy inward. This is my home turf, my pool. I don't see or hear the massive crowd. I'm alone. The race isn't about Eton or Harrow or White Oak...it's just about the clock, the water and me.

I don't even watch any of the early races. I can't avoid the huge flashing scoreboard and Eton is, naturally, outdistancing all the other schools in points. Who cares?

My hair is under a tight red swim cap. *Weston* is stenciled across it in black. When it's time for me to go out to the main arena Ethan taps my shoulder. I've put just a touch of baby oil on so I shine like a polished Greek statue walking around.

I hear the cheers from the White Oak section but I don't look. I stare into the crystal blue water. When they call for positions I take one quick glance and see Tim and Abbot leaning forward, watching me intently. I'm ready. I splash my face with water before I take my mark. It's my tradition.

One of the Eton boys is in the lane next to mine. He looks over and says, "Good luck," which catches me off guard because he's cute.

"And to you," I say and give him a smile before the starting gun goes off.

***

I could say it felt different, but it didn't, not really. The water was fast and inviting. I slip through it like a machine. I've never felt stronger in my life. My breathing is perfect, the flip-turns are spot-on.

On the fifth lap I sense the gorgeous Etonian is near and that makes me fly into a supersonic gear. Maybe they are trying to burn me out midway through the race but I know I have plenty left in the tank.

On the seventh lap I explode, using my special six-stroke kick and that puts it to bed. No one can catch me... it's just about the clock. Faster and faster! All I can hear is my heart pounding until I touch the wall and hear people screaming my name.

My goal has always been to do the 400 meter in under four minutes. I look up at the huge digital clock and it flashes 3:41:32. I don't believe it. That can't be right, I think. That's Ian Thorpe territory. My God, I realize I might actually make it to the Olympics.

The rest is a bit of a blur. I remember standing on the podium as they play our horrible school song. The Etonian came in second. He hugs me and tells me his name is *Cotton*.

"Cotton?" I say thinking there is still water in my ears.

"It's Matthew Colton actually, but everyone calls me Cotton."

"Jake."

He pulls me in and whispers in my ear, "You belong at Eton."

***

We have about an hour before they run the 200 Meter Freestyle. Coach Lir drags me to the sauna so I can loosen my muscles back up. I consider having Abbot get both Lir and Ethan some Xanax.

"Listen to me, boy," he says. "You were one second away from the world record. One bloody second. I can get you that by the time you turn eighteen. I fucking guarantee it. You are going to win gold in the Olympics."

I'm laughing and Ethan is jumping up and down like a four-year-old. "Okay boys," I say. "Let's just calm down. One race at a time."

"We should leave right now," Coach says.

I stare right through him. "No way. I'm swimming the 200 in less than an hour."

"It's a gamble," he says. "What if we lose?"

I wave my hand. "So what? This isn't an international meet... it's a boarding school pissing contest... and I'm not going to lose. The water loves me today."

"Use the kick at the end of the second lap." He grabs my hand. "Your left paw was sloppy going into the water, extend that elbow and let your hand pull you through."

I nod. It's always something, always some minuscule refinement which is why Dylan Lir is the king of coaches.

"Ethan, get him some drinking water if he's going to sit in this goddamn sauna. Your whole fucking school is out there. They brought in two busloads of White Oak wankers. The Headmaster wants a word with you."

"Tell him to sod off. I'm preparing for my next race."

***

I'm much more relaxed for the 200. I smile and wave to the White Oak crowd. I've put on my hot pink Speedo jammers. Cotton is in the lane next to mine.

"Jesus, you again?" he laughs.

I splash my face. "Don't worry, Gorgeous. This one is just for shits and giggles."

But when the race starts I fly. I don't pace myself at all. I decide to just throw caution to the wind and if I flame out...so be it. Except I don't. It's a blur. This is a genuinely fun race. Maybe *this* is my best distance.

I leave everything in the pool, every ounce of energy I've got left. I can feel all my muscles burning. My chest is heaving and my heart is about to burst. I slay the race.

When it's all said and done the clock flashes 1:49:20. Not close to the world record but fast enough to beat the shit out of all these posh tossers.

I'm knackered.

Holding my arms over my head with the medal around my neck I look over to Timmy who is both laughing and crying. Then right in the middle of our bloody awful *Boys of White Oak* anthem I jump off the podium and run into the stands to hug him. I take the medal from around my neck and put it around his. "Shock and awe?" he asks me.

"Are you sure?" I say over the cheering crowd and music.

He smiles...and we kiss. I'm in a pink Speedo dripping pool water onto Blake Abbot with everyone watching: His mother, our school and God Almighty.

***

It did throw a bit of a wrench into my plan. Every reporter wanted to talk about my overt gayness and my Olympic dreams. I made sure the guy from the Sun tabloid was nearby when I pulled down my Speedo to change though. Every exhibitionist needs his voyeur. He got a good showing of my bruised bum.

He didn't ask the question, but I shrugged and said, "Our Headmaster likes his cricket bat."

He wrote down the quote and my heart glowed. The Sun may just be a cheap penny-dreadful but an article about my flogging will surely get Rothwell's fucking goat.

CHAPTER 86: TIMOTHY

The kiss.

There's no walking that back. It's even a meme because loads of people had their phones out and ready. The first person to text: *WTF?* to me was Sam.

I don't know what to say to her, but it feels like we'll be putting off the heavy petting for awhile.

Today Jake became a celebrity and everyone and his brother wants a selfie with him and to pat him on the back. He is gracious to all, but he's a sensation. When he climbed out of the pool and pulled his cap off, letting his long blond hair shake out as the crowd cheered, everything shifted. I knew he didn't just belong to me anymore, not that he ever really did. He has fans. He's a gay heartthrob, an icon and an example. More than a million people follow his Instagram.

The Headmaster and his wife walk up to him filled with pride. "Well done, my boy. Well done indeed."

"I guess you won the bet this year, sir."

He winks at Jake.

"We are just so proud of you," Mrs. Rothwell says.

Jake motions to Abbot who comes over and shakes the Headmaster's hand.

"I've got something for you," Jake tells him. He opens up his duffle and pulls out the other gold medal and hands it to the Headmaster, who, I swear, starts to get emotional. "I couldn't possibly accept this, Weston."

"Please," he says.

"But why?"

Jake grins. "You gave me the key to Ducker...I think we both know those late night workouts have made all the difference." He pauses and I can sense there's something weird transpiring. "Besides," he says, "it means more to you than it does to me."

"I will hang it in my office with pride for all to see. Thank you."

When we finally get out he's made promises to see about a dozen people, including one of the swimmers from Eton.

Abbot very kindly offers to drive my mum home in Jake's car. Ethan is taking us back to White Oak where we need to swing by St. John's for more congratulations. Professor Fulton waves as he and Jane get into his red Fiat.

"See that?" Jake asks. "Red sports car, as inevitable as his mustache."

I grin. He does have insights.

"You know you could have given me one of those medals..." Ethan says.

Jake scoffs. "You don't want one of these crappy pieces of junk," he says and then looks at me. "Just kidding," he whispers. I notice a bottle of Champagne that has been left chilling in our car.

"Besides, there will be tons of medals...better ones, Ethan. I did leave you a little something in the glovebox though. A thank-you gift. But you mustn't peek until we're home and I'm out of the car."

I can't imagine what's he's left in there, but I'm betting it's extravagant.

"Open the Champagne, love," he says to me.

I clumsily fiddle with the little steel cage holding back the cork of Veuve Clicquot while Jake gleefully watches me struggle.

"I only drink Champagne on two occasions..." he quotes, pausing dramatically. "When I am in love and when I am not."

The cork explodes from the bottle with a loud 'pop!' narrowly missing Ethan's head in the front seat.

"Bloody hell, you two," he shouts.

We laugh and drink half the bottle before Jake passes out in my lap exhausted.

CHAPTER 87: ROTHWELL

I'm turning the medal over in my hand. He's an extraordinary boy, perhaps the best athlete we've ever had at White Oak Academy. Eton's Headmaster comes over to congratulate me.

"That boy is truly a find, Stillman."

"He is indeed."

"You win our bet this year, even though Eton scored more points, Weston's two performances were, frankly, remarkable."

It's rare for Heath Fetterman to be so forthcoming with a compliment about a rival, so I'm suspicious. I slip the medal into my pocket.

"What are you playing at?"

He pulls at his collar. "I'm afraid there's no delicate way to broach the subject, old man. The simple truth is that we're taking him. Weston will be at Eton for the Lent Half in January."

I can feel the bile rising in the back of my throat.

"What? That's impossible." I shout. I see Barbara getting concerned.

"His father called me more than a week ago to see what we would offer. I told him if his son beats our boys, Eton would extend a full scholarship."

I look around the Centre but Weston, his butler and entourage have left the building. There's no possible way Jacob is on board with this transfer unless his boyfriend is part of the package. It's not as if the Westons need the charity.

"I suppose Eton's giving a full ride to Ashlock then as well..."

"Who?" Fetterman asks.

"Never mind."

I still have a few cards to play...not many, but a few.

CHAPTER 88: ABBOT

I've agreed to drive Mrs. Ashlock to Hackney and I can see that I'm in for an interesting ride.

"You've known Jay his entire life then," she says patting my leg.

"I have indeed, and I've never heard anyone refer to him as *Jay*."

"Live and learn," she mumbles. "And why aren't you married, Blake?"

I glance over at her in her fur coat, an amused expression on her face. "Madam, that's a rather personal question."

"You like the ladies, though?"

I clear my throat. "Another very inappropriate question, but if you must know I do enjoy the company of women."

"Hmm," she says. "It makes no sense to me why a man as handsome and refined as you hasn't found someone to settle down with."

There was a compliment weaved in there so I continue the conversation. "I suppose I'm too old and set in my bachelor ways. Most people find me rather tedious to be around."

"I think you just need to let your hair down every once and awhile. You obviously did a superb job raising that boy."

Yet another compliment. "I would say the same for what you've accomplished with Master Timothy. He's a fine young man."

"Wait until you hear him play the violin. He's a wonder to behold. I don't know where he gets that talent..."

"Actually I've heard several recordings of his playing. He has a rare gift."

We pull up to her tired little apartment. "May I walk you up?"

"No need," she says. "I'll just be a moment, wait here for me."

"Are you coming back to Brigsley then?"

"I was invited," she answers. "And this will save E the trip tomorrow. Back in a flash."

I watch her scurry into her home and come out carrying two small suitcases. I jump out of the car to retrieve them.

"Let me help," I offer.

"Shoo," she says. "You aren't my butler. Just open the damn trunk."

In moments we are back on the road traveling toward the school. "I must say I'm looking forward to a proper English Christmas."

"I completely agree, Madam."

"Can't you at least call me Bea or Betty when we're alone?"

"Which do you prefer?"

"I don't care, but every time you call me *Madam* I feel like a brothel owner."

I chuckle.

"Saints preserve us, did you just laugh? You're human after all."

"Please don't tell anyone, Betty."

"So what do you think about our boys sleeping together?"

She doesn't mince words and I find that refreshing. "Um," I say. "I suppose none of us can control who we fall in love with. Jake has always been a handful in that area...but he has a warm and gentle heart. I think Timothy is a good influence on him."

"They're young, of course," she comments. "A lot can happen at their age."

"Indeed."

"I suppose it's our job to keep them together," she declares.

"I believe we should leave that matter to the boys."

She laughs heartily. "Oh you men! You never know what's good for you."

"I beg your pardon?"

"Blake, if you had a lick of sense about such things you'd have fathered five kids by now. But even you aren't a totally lost cause."

I believe she just winked at me.

CHAPTER 89: TIMOTHY

St. John's House is decorated all in gold when we arrive. A large banner proclaiming: *Weston Wins!* is above the entryway. Nanny has even baked a chocolate sheet cake.

"Wow," Jake says as we make our way inside. "This would have been a lot of wasted effort if I'd lost."

"Little chance of that," Pete says. He managed to take silver in the Hundred-Meter Butterfly, which Jake vigorously congratulates him on.

He has made me wear the silly gold medal into the common room, which is embarrassing, but soon we are passing it around for the younger Johnnies to admire.

Blackmore comes running over with a box. "For you, Weston. We are all so very proud."

Jake opens the gift to find a grey flannel waistcoat and black tie signifying his athletic prowess.

"Thank you, sir," he says. "I'm honored."

Billy hugs us both. "So when are the two of you tying the knot?" he teases.

"We haven't set a date yet," Jake deadpans.

"I always knew you two were doing it."

"Nothing gets past you, m'lord."

I stare at Billy. "You don't look like a Guillaume."

He shakes his head. "No one calls me that. My mum is half-French but we don't speak of it..."

"Your secret is safe."

Blackmore has even managed some cheap sparkling wine for all the lads. Corks start popping and in a flash we are raising our plastic cups to toast the greatest athlete in the house's long history.

I excuse myself to go to the loo, but while I'm upstairs I can't help myself. I climb the steps and open the door to my old turret room to have a nostalgic peek. It's being used as a storage closet, which is what it should have been all along. How far I've traveled since I was sleeping here.

Jake is thoroughly knackered so we say our good-byes and head down the trail to Brigsley.

"That was the worst Champagne I've ever tasted," I say once we are walking down the path.

Jake wraps an arm around my backside. "I've turned you into a wine snob...my work here is done."

We both have a laugh. "You're right though," he says, "that stuff tasted like piss."

CHAPTER 90: JACOB

"Are you sure you don't want us to stay and help?" I ask.

"You would just be in my way."

We've been banished to London so Abbot can decorate. Ethan already has the car idling in the drive. Bea finishes washing dishes and tidying up the kitchen. "Let the boys go shopping and I'll stay and lend a hand."

"Madam, you are a guest here, not the housekeeper. Stop cleaning this cottage and go and enjoy the capital. We have an account at Harrods so feel free to buy anything you want and have it charged to the Westons."

Tim pulls me aside. "I don't think mum and I are comfortable wasting your father's money."

"But you're buying gifts, not spending it on yourself! And we have cash to burn."

"Jake, please."

"Bea," I call out. "Do you have a problem running through a bit of my family fortune?"

She's putting on red lipstick. "How much money do you Weston's have?"

I look toward Abbot. "Six billion?"

The butler leans over, "It varies, but closer to eight, I'd say."

Bea smiles. "I'm fine with a shopping spree...it sounds fun. What can I bring back for you, Blake?"

"A box of macaroons from Ladurée would be lovely."

He puts a hand on my shoulder and whispers, "Please speak to Rene in the Harrods jewelry department. I've had my eye on a pair of yellow diamond cufflinks that I'm certain your father would want me to have for my years of dedicated service."

"That's the spirit," I say. "When should we be back?"

Abbot looks at the clock. "Not before sunset, if you please. Now get a move on, I'm expecting the first delivery truck any moment."

CHAPTER 91: CHRISTMAS EVE

It's eight o'clock by the time the car has returned to Brigsley and the transformation is complete. The outside of the cottage is covered in hundreds of champagne-colored lights twinkling brightly and a holly wreath has been placed on the door.

"It's beautiful," Tim says.

Jake takes his hand. "Let's go inside and see what he's managed to accomplish. Ethan, you too."

The Christmas tree is an eight-foot noble fir covered in antique crystal ornaments sparkling near the front windows. A dozen neatly-wrapped presents sit beneath it.

A holly and ivy garland with dozens of red bows winds its way up the banister to where a gramophone plays Christmas carols which echo down through the cottage. "This is unbelievable," Tim whispers.

Dozens of fat red and green candles are lit, giving off the scents of cinnamon and vanilla. Potted red and white poinsettias have been placed on every step of the stairs while evergreen boughs have been cut and arranged on the bookshelves and counters.

Jake giggles and points above their heads. He and Tim are under a sprig of mistletoe. Tim kisses him willingly.

Two wooden nutcracker soldiers sit next to the mantle clock and below a fire rages in the hearth. Jake hugs the old gentleman, "Beautifully done, sir."

The table is set in fine china on a tablecloth of red and green silk. White roses and long taper candles in hurricane lamps form the centerpiece.

Jake stops to play with a small model train that's been set up beside the espresso machine. Ethan says, "It's like a dream."

The smell of roasted turkey and other delicacies waft from the kitchen where Abbot is checking on the Christmas pudding.

Bea is holding back tears as she walks around marveling at the details. There are even stockings with all their names hanging on the chimney.

"It's as if Christmas fairies came in and used magic to transform this whole cottage."

Jake whispers, "Did I miss the Christmas fairies?" Timothy pokes him.

"These particular fairies were paid double to accomplish this miracle so quickly," Abbot notes.

Jake is searching under the tree until he finds a small package which he gives to Ethan. "This is since we won't see you tomorrow. Happy Christmas, my friend."

Ethan smiles and gives Jake a hug. "You didn't need to after what you've already..."

Jake holds up a hand to stop him. "I wanted to, so please open it up."

He rips the red wrapping paper off and opens the box. "Oh my God!" he shouts.

"What is it, E?" Bea asks.

Tears begin streaming down Ethan's cheeks, and he's not usually one for emotional displays. "Season tickets to Man United...Oh Jake..."

He gives him another hug.

"Two seats right behind the coaches, close enough to smell them, so you can pick up a few tips for your lads. Old Trafford will be like a second home."

"I don't know what to say."

"In that case help me unload the Harrods packages from the car."

"What have you got cooking in there?" Bea asks.

"A proper feast, Madam."

"Better let me have a look," she says. "Get me an apron...and stop calling me Madam."

Abbot attempts to chase her off, "I assure you Mrs. Ashlock everything is perfectly..."

She looks at him sternly. "You've done a lovely job with Brigsley, but now you need to change into some regular clothes."

Abbot looks down at his tailored black suit. "These are my regular..."

"You look like an undertaker. Put on a soft sweater and some comfortable shoes, unless you're expecting the Prince of Wales and Camilla to be stopping by."

He looks pleadingly at Jacob who has entered laden with packages. "Do what she asks, old chap."

"Oh, very well," he says. "Someone please relight the candles, they keep blowing out."

"Really?" Tim asks, grabbing a lighter.

There's a knock which Jake turns to answer. A statuesque and very elegant woman in a white evening gown is holding two pies.

"Jacob? My heavens, is that you?"

Abbot hears her voice and comes out from the back wearing a dark green sweater and slacks.

"Sister," he says, "right on time." He takes the pies from her and she immediately hugs Jacob.

"Do you remember me? It's been ages."

"Of course I do," he says. "Everyone this is Abbot's sister Rachel."

They greet her warmly. "She makes the best mince pies in England," Abbot brags.

Bea looks at her. "Does she now?"

"Is it Casual Friday, Blakes? I thought we'd be dressing for dinner."

Abbot looks down at his outfit and sighs. "Times are changing."

They kiss each other on both cheeks. "Still, you look wonderful, brother."

***

At nine PM sharp dinner is served. Places have been carefully arranged with Jacob at the head of the table, Timothy to his right and Abbot to his left. Surprisingly Bea is seated next to the Butler and not next to her own son.

"Interesting," Jacob whispers.

"What's that?" Timothy asks back.

"The seating arrangement."

Abbot clears his throat. "Mrs. Ashlock, will you be kind enough to give the blessing?"

"It would be my honor, Mr. Abbot."

Jacob lifts an eyebrow. "Curiouser and curiouser."

As they hold hands Bea prays: "Walls for the wind and a roof for the rain. And drinks beside the fire, laughter to cheer you, and those you love near you, and all that your heart may desire."

Rachel squeezes Bea's hand. "How lovely."

Timothy taps on his wine glass lightly. "Before we begin I'd like to raise a toast."

Jacob is astounded because Timothy is rarely so bold.

"To Mr. Blake Abbot, the closest thing to Father Christmas that I have ever known."

Abbot blushes as the group touches glasses and voices their approval. Bea is the first to pull one of the Christmas Crackers. It makes a wonderful pop and she is awarded a paper crown which she immediately places on her head. Soon everyone is opening a cracker.

"It's odd that this tradition never made it to America," Jacob observes.

Timothy loudly sighs.

"What?" Jacob asks.

"Maybe it's a nice thing that the United States hasn't usurped everything from Britain...yet."

Jacob puts his hand on Timothy's arm. "Easy Sport," he says. "I agree. It's just unusual that such a lovely tradition didn't cross the Atlantic. Do you know it's origin, Abbot?"

"I do," he says. "It's a wholly British invention dating from the late nineteenth century. It was the idea of a London sweet maker named Tom Smith."

"So, it began as a marketing ploy," Jacob says.

Abbot swats him on the shoulder. "That's a fairly accurate, but rather cynical observation. I think we can safely say that the tradition has survived so many years because it is innocent and joyful."

Jacob has never been more proud of his friend and butler... every detail is perfect. From the Yorkshire pudding to the Christmas ham wrapped in puff pastry, it's a dinner to remember.

When the plates are cleared Timothy excuses himself to his room to work on his 'project.'

"The suspense is killing me. What is that boy up to?" Jacob asks.

"Maybe it isn't about you," Abbot says lightly.

Jacob pours them all some Louis XIII Cognac as they sit by the fireplace. "Pull the other leg, it plays "Jingle Bells." You might at least give me a hint, Abbot."

"I'd sooner face the rack."

"Well, while we're discussing secret surprises...how are we going to make the switch?"

Abbot moves closer to him so that Bea, who is gossiping with Rachel, can't overhear. "It's hidden in my suitcase, inside the wardrobe. I would switch it at the last possible moment since he's been playing every evening."

***

Rachel leans conspiratorially toward Bea. "He's fifty-eight, it's well past time for him to start thinking about his own happiness. He's worked like a slave for that family for twenty years."

"But I'm asking you," Bea whispers, "if you think he'll be happy away from it. They live high on the hog with the private jets and such. I can't compete with that."

Rachel smiles and takes her hand. "He's wearing a sweater you bought for him today and drinking with the heir by the fire. I think you've already won that competition."

Both women laugh. "Well, he's unlike anyone I've ever known...once you dig past the stuffiness."

"Oh, that's always been an air he's put on. All he's ever really wanted to do is paint...although cooking is also a passion."

Bea looks shocked and then laughs out loud. "Paint?! You mean like Picasso?"

Rachel is giggling. "More like Turner, but yes."

"My, my," Bea exclaims. "He's got more layers than a bloody onion."

CHAPTER 92: JACOB

"What a day," he says as we pull back the comforter. Tim and I are wearing matching flannel reindeer pajamas as he jumps into bed.

"Admit it," I say. "You had fun shopping."

He throws a pillow at my head. "I confess."

I climb in after him and we wrestle until his arms are pinned above his head. "Say *Uncle,*" I demand.

He's laughing hysterically. "Bugger off."

I lower my face down and kiss him.

"This is the best Christmas I've ever had," he finally whispers to me, still a bit breathless.

"And it's only Christmas Eve!" I say. "By the way, Mr. Ashlock, I believe my butler fancies your mother."

He rolls over and begins massages my shoulders until I moan with satisfaction. "Talk about opposites attracting," he says. "My mum has dated but never been serious about anyone. She said no one could hold a candle to my dad."

I'm unbuttoning my pajamas. I have trouble sleeping in clothes. "Well, Abbot hardly ever dated while I was growing up. He says American women lack substance."

"That seems a rather sweeping statement," Tim says.

"I think he just doesn't like the sound of an American accent. In any case, now that he's discovered your mum it's our duty to keep them together."

"I think they're both old enough to decide such things on their own."

"Don't be ridiculous, Timothy. Old people need all the help they can get. They've all but forgotten what passion is...but they were once just kids like us."

He grins. "Are you taking off your pajamas?"

"Yes," I say. "And when I'm done I'm going to take off yours."

CHAPTER 93: CHRISTMAS AT BRIGSLEY

There's a knock at the bedroom door, it's six AM. "For the love of God, Abbot," Jacob moans. "It's Christmas please let us sleep in til seven."

Bea comes in carrying a tray. "It isn't the bloody butler."

"Bea!" Jacob says. "Where's Abbot?"

"In bed eating breakfast. I had to get up at five to beat him to the kitchen to make it. Here's something for you boys."

She kisses them both. "Happy Christmas."

"Thanks mum!"

Jacob reaches for a piece of toast. "I can't believe he let you cook."

Bea scoffs. "That man has had his own way for too long." She notices the necklace which is the only thing Jacob is wearing. She touches it lightly. "It's been a long time since I've seen that piece of greenstone... It looks good on you." She stares at the naked lads in bed. "Hurry, both of you get dressed and come downstairs. I want to open my presents."

***

Abbot is poking at the fire. He's wearing a bulky Christmas sweater, sweat pants and UGG slippers. Jacob begins making some espressos for them. "You let her cook breakfast?"

Abbot looks up from servicing the flames. "I've found there is little profit in trying to argue with that woman."

Jacob offers the espresso.

"I guess you've met your match."

Abbot sips from his demitasse. "It would seem so."

"Okay," Jacob announces. "I want the veil to be lifted on the secret Ashlock Christmas project."

Tim comes over beaming. He has a basket with a dozen individually wrapped presents for Jacob. He also has a single present for his mother and one for Mr. Abbot. Jacob begins ripping the paper off to discover a trove of silver framed photographs.

A picture from their trip to Paris, one with Jacob, Coach Lir and Ethan at the Trials, a picture from Mudball, another from Halloween. And then older photographs of Abbot teaching him to ride a bike, and one with his mother and father together, and many others from times long past.

"A mantle should be crowded with happy memories," Timothy explains. Jacob is completely choked up. "You're very good at Christmas surprises."

His mother holds a photograph of Henry and Timothy as boys, while Abbot is looking at a photo of Jacob hugging him at the swim meet.

Jacob arranges each photo carefully on the mantle. "You next, sir." He hands Abbot two packages. The first contains the diamond cufflinks he wanted.

"These are perfect," he says. "But what's this?" He opens the book and fans the pages next to his nose. "Ah, it smells like my childhood. I adore Lewis Carol. Thank you, my boy."

"Happy Christmas!"

"Your childhood smelled like a musty old library?" Bea asks.

"I love the aroma of books, Mrs. Ashlock."

"You need to get outside more often."

The butler hands Jacob a gift. Inside is a Conway Stewart Westminster Teal pen. "It's very Gothic, and so English," Jacob says, showing the pen to Bea and Timothy.

"A serious writer deserves a serious pen," Abbot says.

Jacob hands Bea a package. She glares at him. "I hope whatever is inside this fancy box isn't going to make me cry," she warns.

Jacob looks at Tim. "Better not open it then, mum."

"If it helps, I can tell you that I didn't spend a dime on it."

She opens it and finds a beautiful strand of antique pearls. "My lord," she says.

"They were my mother's," Jacob says softly.

Abbot smiles, fastening the necklace around her neck, "They were his mother's favorite."

"I can't," Bea says, holding back tears.

"You must," Jacob whispers. "They've been sitting in a safe gathering dust for ages. I'm never going to know another woman who deserves to wear them more than you."

Of course, that gets her waterworks flowing. There's a lot of hugging and kissing until finally Timothy turns to Jacob. "So where's my present?"

"Ah, I nearly forgot," Jacob says. "Yes, there is something here." He gives a big Harrods box to Timothy, who quickly opens it up, revealing a polished oak music stand. He doesn't exactly look disappointed, but it wasn't what he was expecting. "It's a music stand," he finally says.

"You should play something for us!"

Timothy seems distracted. "Yes," he mumbles. "I've been working on a piece for you."

Jacob smiles proudly. "For me?"

"Umm hmm," he runs to his room and brings out some handwritten sheet music and his violin case. Abbot and Jacob exchange quick glances.

"It's titled, *Jacob's Ladder* and is supposed to..." He unlatches the case and stares at the instrument. "Hey, this isn't my...oh my God."

"I hope you don't mind," Jacob says. "It's used."

"How old is it?" Bea asks.

"It was handmade in 1703," Abbot answers.

Timothy hasn't taken it out of the case. He's only placed his index finger lightly against the polished top.

"It's...it's a..."

"*Stradivarius*," Jacob finishes. "Supposed to have a really nice sound. Why don't you play it?"

"I can't breathe," Tim shouts. "I can't breathe!" He runs out the front door and into the snow.

Abbot turns to Jacob. "He seems aptly surprised."

Bea is staring at them. "You two really are a pair. Is anyone going to go check on my son?"

CHAPTER 94: TIMOTHY

It's the *Allegretti*. It has a name. The top is spruce and the back, ribs and neck are made of maple. Some of the internal blocks and lining are willow. I never imagined I'd even see an instrument like this, let alone play one.

I hyperventilated and ran directly into a snowbank. Jake is holding me in his arms.

"How could you do such a thing? I'm thunderstruck."

"It's not even that great a gift when you think about it," Jake says mockingly. "It's on permanent loan to Timothy James Ashlock from the Jacob Paul Weston Corporation. We had to do it that way because of taxes and insurance and a bunch of other boring..."

"I can't," I say. "What if I lose it, or worse, break it? People steal these because they are so rare. My God, how much is that thing worth?" It's getting hard for me to breathe again.

"Calm down," he says. "It's a hunk of Italian wood. Only someone with your gift can make it into anything special...and it's insured if something happens. It is rare and precious...just like you."

"How much?"

He scoffs at me. "It's not polite to ask the price of a gift..."

"How much?!" I yell.

"I'm not going to tell you."

My God, I think, it really must be an ungodly sum if he refuses to answer. "Look," he says quietly. "It's a white Christmas."

And he's right. It's so incredibly beautiful outside and I hadn't even noticed. A blanket of snow has fallen during the night so the world is silent, glistening and white. "A serious musician needs a serious instrument. Now, I'd certainly like to hear my song. *Jacob's Ladder*, is it? I love that."

"Okay," I say. "I've just got to thaw out my hands first."

CHAPTER 95: ABBOT

Mrs. Ashlock has bought me a new wardrobe in London. I find most of her choices both comfortable and refined. Perhaps she knows me better than I know myself.

Timothy has been warming his hands by the fire while Jake is roasting marshmallows beside him. These boys seem so happy together. It pains me because I know that at some point I must discuss Eton with him. My instinct tells me that he will detest the idea of transferring schools again, and will dramatically lash out... which is why I'm waiting until after the holiday to broach the subject.

Timothy approaches the open case with reverence, he shakes his head and then gently cradles it. Lightly he touches the bow to the strings.

"We need to get to know one another," he whispers. He practices a few short warm-up scales.

"How does it feel?" Jacob asks him.

"It's good," he says. "Light, and tight." He adjusts his hold on it.

"How much is it insured for again?" he asks me.

"Eighteen million."

Timothy closes his eyes. "Jesus Christ."

Jacob frowns. "I thought we gentleman didn't discuss crass dollar amounts..."

I frown right back. "If he's mature enough to play it, he's mature enough to know its value."

Suddenly Timothy soars into his original composition and we are rapt. It's breathtaking. Spellbinding. There is sadness and joy as he shifts and moves with the raw emotion. The music fills the cottage and we watch him, eyes closed, feeling his way through the piece, altering the tempo, slowing it. There is such yearning and also, in every single note, hope. It is genius. Jacob was right. This is money well invested. If anyone deserves to possess this instrument it is Timothy Ashlock.

When he is finished we stand and applaud...and just then we hear knocking from all around us. It's the sound of a dozen knuckles rapping on a dozen doorframes.

"What on Earth?" Bea exclaims, looking around.

Jacob is standing next to Timothy near the fireplace.

"That would be Tommy Walker, our resident ghost," he says. "Apparently also a music lover."

CHAPTER 96: TIMOTHY

I find that I can't bear to have the violin out of my sight. It has it's own special environmental case which requires my fingerprint to open, but I don't want to lock it away. I love seeing the instrument...the wood seems to glow.

It's Boxing Day and I may have the cottage to myself for a few hours which means I can gloriously practice in peace. I yearn for solitude but dread loneliness. Abbot has been organizing papers on our table all morning.

"Master Timothy, these are ready for your signature."

I look at the many contracts and forms. "What's this?" I ask. "Am I selling my soul?"

He sighs. "You are becoming vice president of a corporation and taking possession of a valuable instrument. Mrs. Ashlock I will also require your signature on a few forms since Timothy is under eighteen."

I sign everything without reading a single word. I trust Abbot and, of course, Jake. Also the Ashlocks are poor and the Westons are rich so I doubt they are trying to take advantage.

"Are you a lawyer then as well as a butler?" Mum jokes.

"I know my way around contracts and bank statements, Mrs. Ashlock."

Jacob is bagging up presents to take to Coach Lir and a few others at the Aquatic Centre. "Do you want to come into London?"

"I'd actually prefer to stay here and practice if it's all the same."

Abbot puts the contracts in a leather briefcase. "I will electronically send copies to the bank immediately."

"Very good," Jake says. "And what are your plans today, sir?"

Abbot folds his apron. "Mrs. Ashlock and I would like to see the Oxford property. I thought we would make an assessment on what needs to be done."

"I'd like to move in next week," Mums tells him.

"That's fine," Jake says. "But I was thinking we might all want to ring in the New Year together...someplace warm."

This is the first I've heard of a trip. "Where?"

"I'm weary of seeing all my good friends in foul weather. What about Byron Bay in New South Wales."

"Australia?" Mum says excitedly.

"It's summer down there," Jake notes. "Think it over. Will you two be spending the night in Oxfordshire?"

"Yes, and I'm afraid we will be monopolizing Ethan's schedule. Were you planning on giving him time off since it's a holiday?"

"No, he's keen to work until you're safely back in the States."

"Hmm, he's a good chap. We should figure out a nice bonus for him."

"I'm a step ahead, my friend. I took care of that during the Eton meet."

"You'll never guess who's coming up the walk," Mum announces.

"Who?"

"Your killjoy of a Headmaster and his wife."

Jake answers their knock immediately and welcomes them inside.

"What a pleasant surprise," he says warmly.

"We noticed how wonderful the cottage looks," Mrs. Rothwell says. "And I just had to see how you decorated the interior."

"Happy Christmas, Kitty, and to you Headmaster. We have Mr. Abbot here to thank for the decorations."

Mrs. Rothwell is enthralled with the sparkling tree and other fine decorations. "It's glorious," she says earnestly.

"Can I offer you an espresso?" Jake asks.

"Espresso? How continental."

Mum hasn't left her perch near the front window, and the Rothwell's haven't yet acknowledged her. She watches the couple suspiciously.

"Weston, I really wanted to wish you all the best at Eton next term," the Headmaster says, extending his hand. "We will certainly miss you around here."

Jake's smile freezes just for an instant as he shakes Rothwell's hand and looks toward Abbot.

"What?" I say.

Mr. Abbot holds up a hand. "Nothing has been finalized yet..."

The Headmaster wickedly smiles. "I hate to contradict you, Mr. Abbot, but the signed transfer papers are on my desk. I spoke to the elder Weston on Christmas Eve."

Jake's eyes narrow. "It's certainly kind of you to drop by. My father mentioned that White Oak is a bit too run down and common for a Weston to take seriously. It's good to see the situation has been resolved." He smiles.

Rothwell turns his gaze to me. "Looks like you'll be moving back into St. John's house, Ashlock."

I grab Jake's arm. "Is this some kind of horrible prank?"

He winks at me. "Don't forget to pick up a copy of *The Sun on Sunday* this weekend, Stillman. I think you'll find it enlightening."

"Yes," he answers, smoothing his beard. "A reporter has already called me asking for a comment. Apparently a photo of your wealthy bruised bum found its way into their offices."

"I hope it makes the cover," Jake replies, lightly slapping his own arse.

Suddenly all the windows begin to rattle. Mrs. Rothwell's eyes widen.

"Restless spirits," Jake says.

"Barbara, we should be on our way," Rothwell says heading out. She quickly hugs Jake good-bye. "I'll miss you, you scoundrel," she whispers in his ear.

***

When the Rothwells are out of earshot Jake turns and yells in Abbot's face. "How could you know about this and not warn me? You've betrayed my trust!"

The butler stands firm. "Jake, calm down. You're not being exiled to the Yukon. For the love of all things holy, it's Eton! And it's only a tube ride away. I was waiting until after Christmas to discuss it, but that horrible man likes to stir the pot..."

I go and stand next to my mum who grasps my hand, hot tears are welling in my eyes. Somehow I knew all of this was temporary. I'm wondering if it was all cloud-built.

"Timmy," he says looking my way. "Don't worry. This isn't over yet."

Abbot wears a worried expression. "I tried to convince your father to let you stay on here, but his mind was made up."

Jake is in a rage. "How hard did you try? I think you approve of this plan."

The butler sighs loudly. "If you must know, yes. Eton is a better fit for you...in my humble opinion. And you should take a moment to consider the positives."

Jacob begins to pace. I've seen this before. "Positives? Losing all my friends? The home I've made here? The love of my life?" He shouts, pointing at me.

Abbot continues to dig in. "It's less than a full year...and a little separation may actually strengthen your relationship."

"He's right, Jake," I say, my voice breaking. "You belong at Eton...I thought so as soon as I met you."

He spins around. "You've all gone barking mad! I'm not transferring and that's final. I'm calling my father to sort this out." He comes right up to me, and I watch the veins pulse in his corded neck. He takes my face in both his hands and kisses me hard. When I open my eyes to look at him he whispers, "I'm not losing you."

I nod. "Do you want me to ride along to Stratford?"

He grabs the bag of presents. "No," he says. "Stay. We've got to get used to being apart. It's going to *strengthen our relationship*," he says acidly toward the butler.

Jake storms out of the cottage and we watch the Mercedes fishtail in the snow as he speeds down the road.

"I've never seen him quite like that," I comment.

"He's furious. Let him be. He just needs some time to work it out in his brain."

I sit down in front of the fire, suddenly very tired. "Timmy," mum says. "Don't fret about it. It's all going to be fine."

I look at her and Abbot standing next to one another. "You'll be tucked away at Oxford, Mr. Abbot will be across the Atlantic, Jake will be at Eton and I'll be in a turret room in St. John's. The future seems a bit lonely for us all."

***

Ethan took Mum and Abbot to Oxford. I've been practicing the violin for hours, until the callouses on my hand have started to crack and bleed. It almost takes my mind off Jake transferring...almost. I sit down by the hearth and stare at the dying fire. This may be my last two weeks in Brigsley Cottage.

I jump when there's another knock at the front door, I don't want visitors. I find Sam on the threshold holding a package. She's wearing a white angora sweater and a short black skirt.

"Samantha Milford," I say. "What brings you over the bridge?"

"You do," she says quickly. "Aren't you going to invite me inside?"

"Of course, where are my manners. Please come in."

She hands me the package. "For you."

I start to unwrap it. "You didn't need to bring me anything."

"It's Dickens. Since you have such a fondness for books..."

"How thoughtful."

She's looking around. "This place is nice. So, where is Jacob?"

"Uh," I mumble. "He's in London. I expect him back..."

"Oh, so we're all alone."

"For the time being," I say. "Can I get you something? A glass of wine?"

"Do you have anything stronger?"

She's licking her lips and her cheeks are flushed. "We have cognac...and maybe some scotch."

"Scotch sounds good."

I pour two glasses and hand her one. She downs it in two gulps, and I pour her another. "So about that Eton swim meet. Last time we were together you certainly didn't seem gay..."

This girl is as direct as my mother. "It's complicated," I mumble.

"Is it?" she asks. "Give me the tour...show me around this posh cottage. What's upstairs?"

"Just a bedroom and a bathroom," I answer while she is climbing the stairs, snooping around.

She jumps on Jake's bed. "It's cozy up here. Sit with me."

She grabs my hand and pulls me toward her. I can smell that warm and spicy fragrance she wears. It's a bit like coffee and white flowers.

"So it's complicated," she says, taking my hand and placing it on her bare thigh. She slowly pushes it up under her skirt and then we begin to snog.

CHAPTER 97: JACOB

I threatened to drop out, to run away, and finally to kill myself. My father wasn't having any of it. "The best goddamn school in Europe is giving you a full scholarship. The next King of England is an Eton grad...the least you can do is go look at the place and talk to some people."

He has a point, I suppose. I'm trying to work out an angle where Timothy gets enrolled too... and I still have Matthew Colton's number.

When I get back to Brigsley someone has parked a cheap Hyundai in our driveway so I have to park up the road. Timothy's violin is sitting in the living room but I hear loud pop music playing upstairs. It's odd because Tim is not a Top Forty aficionado. Maybe he's doing some cleaning.

When I hurry in to my room I see a quick flash of naked flesh and hear a startled, wholly feminine scream.

"I beg your pardon," I say, and rush back down the stairs.

"Jake!" I hear Tim yell. "Jake, wait!"

But I'm already outside...The truth is I can't get away fast enough.

It's not like I didn't tell him to do this, but I don't think I implied he should fuck some bitch in my bed on Boxing Day. I'm choking back tears. God damn him.

It's only sex, I remind myself, but that just makes it worse. My phone keeps vibrating but I know who's calling so I turn it off. I pull over to the shoulder and look something up on the laptop. At least I have a game plan.

CHAPTER 98:   TIMOTHY

I'm the weakest person on earth.   I look over at Samantha who is slowly getting dressed, and I'm not altogether sure that she wasn't planning for something like this to happen. She certainly doesn't seem disappointed that it did.

"Happy now?" I ask.

"What the hell are you talking about?"

"Get out."

I'm starting to sob and I've texted him and left voice messages but he's obviously ignoring me. I'm afraid that in his current mood he might do something rash so I call Mr. Abbot.

"Master Timothy," he says. "Your mum and I truly love this house. It has so much English charm. We can't wait for you to come and see it."

I try to compose myself. "Sir."

"Are you alright?"

"Oh, Mr. Abbot," I sob.   "Jacob and I had...a misunderstanding. A kind of a row. He's stormed off in the Mercedes and I believe he's turned off his cell."

"That sounds like him. Try to calm down. Did you leave a message?"

"Yes," I explain. "Uh, three voicemails and ten or eleven texts. I'm worried sick."

I hear him breathing on the other end of the phone. "Timothy, that might be perceived as...frantic. Please don't call Jacob again today... that will only encourage his misbehavior. Let him sulk and he'll come running home; just stop giving him attention. I can track him through the GPS in his car, so hold on and I'll tell you where he's gone."

I hear Abbot put me on hold. I didn't know he could track the car...I wonder if Jake knows that.

"He's in Kent. It looks like he's going toward Botany Bay."

"Oh," I say, stopping to blow my runny nose. "Yes, he's probably gone to speak with Tommy Walker's mother. That makes sense. Do you always track him?"

"Yes," Abbot says. "I'll keep a watchful eye and let you know when he's heading back to White Oak."

CHAPTER 99: JACOB

Olivia Walker is a frail gray woman who seems altogether happy to have a visitor.

"What can I do for you, young man?"

"Good afternoon, Mrs. Walker. My name is Jacob Weston, I'm a student at White Oak Academy."

Her face lights up. "You're a fair bit away from home. Would you fancy a cuppa?"

"How kind of you. Yes, that would be appreciated."

She invites me into her flat. "It must be wonderful to live so close to the sea."

"She looks toward the window as she puts on the kettle. "Ah, yes, though it isn't often that I get to walk by the shore. I'm turning seventy-five in two days."

"Many happy returns." I look at her bookshelf and notice a photo of Tommy. It's eerie to see an image of him. He looks so alive, and mortal.

"What brings you to Botany Bay?"

I point to the picture. "Your son Tommy does."

"I don't understand, dear. He's been gone for more than forty years."

I look at my shoes. Perhaps it's wrong to disturb an old woman with this strange business.

"I live in the same cottage Tommy used to share. The fact is I've seen his spirit, ma'am. I think he wants me to find his killer."

She smiles weakly. "My Tommy was different."

"He was queer."

"Well, yes, he liked boys. I thought that was fairly common in boarding schools."

"It is," I admit. "Boys liking other boys has been around since they laid the first brick at Oxford."

"I think he fell in love at White Oak. He never talked about it. When he first went missing I hoped in my heart that he had jumped onto a ship and was still alive somewhere. Maybe living a happy life in Greece or Morocco with his lover. Someplace warm and bright. It's a terrible thing to bury an empty casket."

"He loved a boy named Tyler," I said. "Did you know him?"

She shakes her head nervously. There's something about Olivia Walker. I don't think she's lying to me outright, but she's clearly holding something back. She knows much more than she's saying.

"I wonder if you kept his yearbooks?"

"I think so, yes. I never threw any of Tommy's things out. I'm a sentimental old woman."

She rummages around in back and I hear her opening drawers. She comes back holding the 1976 annual.

"Thank you." I quickly flip through the book and it naturally falls open to a well-worn page. There's a sepia-toned photograph of Tommy with his arms around another boy, both of them smiling proudly at the camera. I read the caption.

I think I know who killed Tommy Walker...I just don't know why.

CHAPTER 100: TIMOTHY

It's getting late, I'm alone, worried and sad. Billy and all the other lads are still gone for the holiday break but they'll be straggling back in the next day or so. I lock up the violin, storing it under the bed, and then I decide to get plastered.

At half past eleven the phone rings and I fumble to answer it. "Hullo?"

"Timothy, is that you?"

"Yes, Mr. Abbot. How is my mother?"

"She's well. Have you been drinking tonight?"

I find that question hysterically funny. "Indeed I have, sir. Vigorously."

"Okay," he says. "Steady on, lad. Jacob is at Eton. His car hasn't moved for several hours so we can assume he's staying the night. It's probably a positive development."

"Ha!" I shout. "For who? He's shagging that handsome toff swimmer as we speak."

"Now, now," he says calmly. "Things will look different in the morning."

I start to sob again. "This is all my fault."

I hear my mother grabbing the phone. "Timothy James Ashlock stop your whinging! I raised you better. Go drink a full glass of water and take two Tylenol because you're going to have a wicked hangover in the morning. Do you want Jake to see you hunched over the toilet honking your guts out?"

"No ma'am."

"So do what I say and go to bed."

"I love you, mum."

"Don't be a baby. I'll see you in the morning. Stiff upper lip."

She hangs up the phone and I crawl into bed where I toss and turn. It was my hope that I'd just pass out drunk but unconsciousness evades me. Brigsley feels cavernous, dark and cold. How quickly habit becomes addiction, I muse. I honestly miss just sleeping next to him. I'm safe when I can hear his breathing and feel his warmth and the slow steady beat of his heart.

It's early morning but still bleak and gray when something startles me awake. I sit bolt upright in bed, covered in cold sweat. I look to the doorway and Jake is standing there, naked and smiling. He smells strongly of pool water.

"Blimey Jake, you frightened me," I mumble. "Come to bed; I can't sleep a wink without you." Seeing him back home makes me secure enough to doze off...until Blackmore bursts through the bedroom door.

"Hurry," he says, opening the curtains. "Get dressed, my boy."

"What?" I say, still groggy and tired. I turn to look for Jake but he isn't in the room. "Professor, what are you doing here?"

"Fetching you, of course. I'm sorry, Ashlock, truly I am..." he's handing me sweatpants and a New York University sweater from a pile of Jake's clothes in the corner. I put them on even though they are too big. I look silly. "The police want to speak to you right away."

"Police?"

Blackmore holds my shoulders. "I'm afraid there's been...an accident, this morning at Ducker."

The words he's saying are finally starting to sink in. "Jake?" I say. I grab my phone and sprint down the stairs. "Jake!" I yell to the cottage. I run outside, barefoot in the snow. The Mercedes is parked in the driveway. I touch it's hood and it's still warm. Then I'm running fast, I'm sprinting and slipping up the hill toward Ducker. My head is spinning, my feet are cold and I see the two parked police cars with their lights wildly flashing in the fog. "Jake!" I yell again.

A fat cop tries to stop me but I'm nimble enough to run past and get inside. "Hey," I hear him shout. A small crowd of adults is standing solemnly near the pool's edge, and then I see him. He's nude and facedown in the water.

"No!" I scream.   I'm running to him when two uniformed police grab my arms and hold me back.   "Jake!" I yell. "My God, Jake!"

"Is this him?" I hear someone say in a low, rumbling voice. "The boyfriend?"

"He's the flatmate," Rothwell answers.   I'm beside myself.   I can hear someone uncontrollably crying and then I realize it's me.   The stranger with the low voice is wearing a brown suit and an ugly tie.   "Timothy," he says.   "My name is Owen Forrestal.   I'm an Inspector from the Metro Police Service."

"I'm going to be sick," I say, breaking free and running into the locker room.

CHAPTER 101: ABBOT

It's eight AM when he calls. I turn to Betty sitting beside me in the backseat. "It's your son," I say. "Looks like the boys are getting an early start."

"That's good to hear," she replies.

"Good morning, Timothy. How are you feeling?"

I can hear him crying and other indistinct voices in the background. "Mr. Abbot, sir, please come quick. I'm at Ducker."

"Yes, we're in the car. We should be back in about a half hour..."

"Hurry, sir. Please hurry."

"What's the matter?"

"It's Jake."

"I see his car is parked back at White Oak. Have you two made amends or are you still arguing?"

I listen to him crying.

"My boy, you're obviously upset. Put Jacob on the line please."

"That's just it, sir, I can't," he says choking. "Jake is dead."

I grab the armrest tightly as the blood drains from my skull. Betty takes my hand; I'm feeling unequivocally faint. I clear my throat.

"Timothy, listen carefully. Is that the police I hear with you?"

"Yes, sir."

"I want you to hand the phone to whomever is in charge so I can speak with them. This is very important though: do not let anyone move Jake until we get there. Do you understand?"

"Yes, Mr. Abbot. Please rush."

I hear him explaining and handing off his phone.

"This is Inspector Forrestal, MPS, to whom am I speaking?"

"My name is Blake Abbot," I answer. "I represent the Weston family. We are en route to the scene, please make sure that no one moves the body. We will want a complete forensic examination by our own specialists."

"Then I suggest your specialists get here before the East Berkshire Coroner arrives from London and takes him away," he says rather dismissively.

"Is foul play evident in the case?"

I hear him sigh. "Not at this time. It appears to be an accidental death or a suicide. The boy simply drowned."

"It isn't accidental, Inspector Forrestal, and there is nothing simple about this. Jacob Weston was almost certainly murdered. Please alert a Detective Chief Inspector from the Major Investigation Teams immediately."

"Understood, Mr. Abbot. The Headmaster would like a word..."

"Tell him to sod off. I have important calls to make."

I hang up and turn to Betty. "I'm afraid we have terrible news." I lean forward toward Ethan. "There's an emergency at White Oak, I need you to drive there as quickly as possible. Please make haste, Jake needs us."

"Buckle up," Ethan says, and I see him wiping away tears as the car sharply accelerates.

I call in a favor at Cambridge to get the best forensic scientist in the UK helicoptered in immediately. Her name is Dr. Leta Kelly.

I'm worried that news of this tragedy might leak on social media, so the next call I place is to Paul Weston's private number.

"Abbot!" he shouts into his phone. "Can't tell you how right you were about the weather here. It's a nightmare in Bali."

"Paul," I say. "I need you to sit down."

"Did you just call me *Paul*? I guess you really are on vacation. What can I do for you, *Blake*?"

"You must travel to England as soon as possible. Your son, our Jacob, is dead."

The line goes silent.

"How?"

"Drowned. The police are saying accidental...but I fear he's been murdered."

"Abbot, get the best people on this immediately. Fly them over from the states if you must, but get to the bottom of it. My son was a world-class swimmer so I'm not buying that he drowned. I want the truth. I'll tear that fucking school to the ground brick by brick if I have to, but someone is going to pay for this in blood...do I make myself clear?"

"Perfectly."

"Book the usual suites at Claridge's for us. What about the..." his voice begins to break, "the funeral," he finally says painfully.

"I know what he wanted, sir. Leave all the arrangements to me."

"One more thing, Abbot."

"Sir?"

"His computer, his phone, his bedroom...I'm relying on you to go through everything and remove or hide whatever might prove embarrassing to the Westons. I want my son to be remembered as a scholar and an athlete...nothing more."

Ah, I think, at last. There's the Paul Weston I know so well.

CHAPTER 102: ROTHWELL

"Inspector, a word please."

He's had his rozzers blockade Ducker with yellow and black tape and two additional patrol cars have arrived filled with uniformed men.

"What can I do for you, Mr. Rothwell?"

"Between you and I, a tragedy like this can be devastating to a school. Luckily, many of our pupils have not yet returned from the holiday break. My fear is that a high profile student such as Weston will draw unnecessary media attention."

"Um hmm," he says, distracted by his tablet. What a cabbage.

"It would be my preference if everyone involved referred to this as a tragic accident, not a suicide."

He looks at me, grinning like an idiot. "Mr. Rothwell, the *Met* isn't referring to this as anything at all yet. How you spin it for the media is your own affair."

"And when can we expect your investigation to be wrapping up so we can get back to some normalcy?"

He laughs at me. "You have no idea how many phone calls I've fielded from Scotland Yard this morning, sir, all from gentlemen with higher pay grades than mine. This is not some London street urchin found dead in an alleyway...When the son of a billionaire has gone for a Burton you can expect a first rate shit-show, Headmaster, and certainly an inquest to follow. So, if you'll excuse me, I've got to go meet the helicopter that's going to be landing on your lawn in the next five minutes."

CHAPTER 103:   LETA KELLY

I'm not fond of helicopters. They have a tendency to crash, especially if there is weather. We land on the snowy Great Lawn of the White Oak campus and I'm quickly ushered into the swimming facility where the boy was found.

I have my medical bag and another case of instruments that I might need for the postmortem exam. I've never met this Inspector but he seems competent, and he's kind enough to help carry my stuff.

"Right this way, Doc."

I see Blake Abbot off to the side with a woman and a young, dark haired boy who is barefoot and wearing clothes that are two sizes too big.

"Excuse me, Inspector," I say.

"Owen," he answers.

"Yes, thanks Owen, can you just put my things down near the side of the pool."

Blake is already making his way to me. "Leta, I'm in your debt. Thank you for rushing to us."

I take his hand.   "I'm sorry we are seeing each other again under these circumstances...and I'm terribly sorry for your loss."

He shakes his head slowly. I can see this is taking a toll on the gentleman. "Who's in charge?" I ask him.

"Forrestal, the Inspector who came in with you, for the time being. DCI Bridges is on his way from New Scotland Yard to do the interviews."

I nod.   Carl Bridges is one of the smartest and most senior investigators dating back to when the Major Investigation Teams (MIT) were first formed. No one is screwing around with this case.

"They are saying it's suicide but..."

I hold my hand up to stop him.   "Let's see what the evidence says. Is that boy his partner?"

"Yes."

"Get him some shoes and get him out of here, and that goes for you too. I promise to take good care of Jacob."

"Thank you, Doctor," he says, grasping my hand.

I go to the side of the pool and bend down to take a closer look.   He was in excellent physical shape.   The gluteal muscles are horizontally bruised, possibly from a beating.

"Okay gents," I say.   "Who's going to help me get this boy out of the water?"

CHAPTER 104: TIMOTHY

Jake is gone.

The three of us are back at Brigsley without him. It's still decorated for Christmas, which seems like a cruel joke. I throw a crystal ornament into the fireplace but watching it break doesn't bring me much satisfaction.

Mum has got out some boxes and is starting to pack away Christmas before I have the chance to destroy it all.

"You should go to bed," she says.

"I'm not tired."

Mr. Abbot is darting around the place obviously searching for something. "Why don't you tell me what you're looking for."

His eyes shift my way. "His phone and laptop."

I look at the table and sideboard. "Since they aren't in here, my guess would be the car. The keys are on the mantle."

"Thank you," he says going out to look.

"I'm glad you've stopped crying," mum says.

"To be perfectly honest, I don't know if I'll ever cry again. I feel dead inside."

She nods her head. "I've known that feeling."

Abbot returns with the devices which he sets on the table. He puts on his glasses and turns on the laptop. "The password is..."

He shakes his head. "I don't need it." I watch him quickly punch in several lines of code. Blake Abbot is a fascinating old bird. I'm wondering how he'll hack the phone since it's on facial recognition and that face won't be opening it's beautiful blue eyes ever again.

He pulls a USB cable out of his pocket and connects the phone to the computer, then he's typing something else in.

When he's done he puts the cable back in his pocket and wipes both devices down with his handkerchief.

"May I ask what you just did?"

He looks at me the way he did when we first met, making some kind of evaluation. "I archived and moved everything on his phone and computer onto a private storage cloud, then I scrubbed both devices clean. They will continue to run data destruction, overwrite and sanitization algorithms until nothing can ever be retrieved."

"Wouldn't some people think that was tampering with evidence?"

"Perhaps. What do you think?"

"I don't care," I say. "But the detective will find blank drives rather suspicious. I do find it interesting that you removed your own fingerprints."

"We are going to have to work together to catch his killer, Timothy."

"It won't bring him back," I say quietly. I can hear mum weeping as she works. It's not even one PM but it feels much later.

"I'm going to have to search through all his belongings before the police and his father take this cottage apart piece by piece. Is there anything I should be made aware of?"

"What?" I ask. "Like sex toys or a stash of gay porn?"

He frowns and looks toward my mum. "You're not going to make this easy for me, are you?"

"Any porn he might have had you've hidden in your cloud. He has a journal that he handwrites in, the old fashioned way. You should hide it or burn it. We have a secret liquor cabinet...there's a false bottom in the pantry. He's also hidden nearly a pound of marijuana there. There aren't any sex toys...we used our imaginations in that area."

"Have you read his journal?"

Jesus, I knew that question was coming. "Of course I have. It doesn't help our murder hypothesis...every other page is about suicide."

In ten minutes Abbot has thrown the weed into the fire along with several evergreen branches. He's poured a good amount of fine liquor down the drain and collected the bottles, but the half-full Louis he places near the espresso machine.

"Put his electronics back in the car, if you don't mind."

"Should I wear gloves?" I joke.

"That won't be necessary. Do you have an envelope for his journal?"

"Yes," I say, fishing a large manilla out of a drawer. He addresses it to mum at the Oxford house. "Have Ethan come round. He'll take all the empty bottles and other things with him in the trunk of the Rolls. We'll have him mail this package also."

"Why didn't you pour the cognac down the drain?"

He sighs. "There are only so many crimes one can commit in a single day. I imagine the detective will be here soon to ask you a lot of embarrassing questions. May I ask you one?"

"Of course."

"Do you think Jake took his own life?"

I can see the utter grief etched into the butler's face.

"Mr. Abbot, I know he didn't. He was murdered."

"How can you be so sure?"

"Because he made me a promise," I tell him, and for the first time I see tears in the old gentleman's eyes.

CHAPTER 105: CARL BRIDGES

I hate helicopters, especially in the winter, but it's all a part of this fabulous job. Jacob Weston drowned at White Oak Academy this morning so I'm going to find out how a seventeen-year-old champion swimmer managed to end up with his lungs full of water.

The family flew in Leta Kelly from the School of Clinical Medicine at Cambridge. She'll be working with our coroner, Patrick Doyle, but let's face it, in this racket she's a rock star.

The first Metro chap on the scene was Forrestal. He's a decent Inspector so there's a chance he didn't fuck things up beyond repair.

"Inspector," I shout when I enter the scene.

"Chief," he says, shaking my hand.

"Did you take photos as soon as you arrived?"

"Yes sir. We've uploaded them to the file."

"Witnesses?"

"None. Still dark and foggy out when the floater was found, no one about."

"Who found him?"

"Groundskeeper called it in at seven-ten AM. He keeps supplies in here. Chief, we ran a check on Norbert Paddy Lester. He's got a record."

I smile. "Good catch. Make sure he doesn't wander too far. The doors were locked?"

"Apparently."

"Get me a list of everyone with a key." I'm looking through the images on my tablet. "The boy was naked?"

"Yes sir."

"Where was his swimsuit?"

Forrestal is looking through his notes. "He has four Speedo jammers in his locker. Very expensive gear. All of them were dry and sitting next to his street clothes."

"Bag everything in the locker and send it to the Yard. If we wrap this up fast I'll buy you a case of whiskey, Owen. I've already had three MPs contact me about this boy. What's your gut tell you?"

"The lad offed himself."

"Okay," I say.

***

I walk up to Kelly. She's a knockout. Dark red hair, amazing figure, freckles for days. She's so far out of my league it's like we aren't even playing the same game. Doyle has finally arrived and they are comparing notes.

"Doctors," I say.

"Hello Carl," she says brightly. "I heard you were joining the party. Isn't this case a bit beneath you?"

"Son of a billionaire, Doc, so no. What have we got?"

"Seventeen-years-old, eleven and a half stone, 190 centimeters tall. Athlete, almost no body fat."

"Time of death?"

She is peeking at her tablet. "I did a core temperature reading. We estimate he'd been in the water about four hours when we arrived, give or take. Pool water is twenty-eight degrees celsius. I'm putting it at five-thirty AM."

"I concur," Doyle says.

"Pretty early in the day for a murder," I say.

"Pretty early for a swim too," she counters.

"Cause of death?" I'm being overly optimistic here.

"He was facedown in the water," Patrick says.

"So I guess drowning is a possibility," I say sarcastically.

"One possibility," Leta answers.

"How many others are there, Dr. Kelly?"

She smiles. "A whole bunch Detective Chief Inspector. We won't know till we open him up and get the toxicology report back."

Doyle is nodding his approval.

"So," I say, "we're going to go the whole route on this one. Full autopsy with tox screen, complete documentation and no cutting corners. Are we thinking accident, suicide or homicide?"

She shrugs. "That's your department, *Handsome*. I'm just a doctor trying to cross all the tees. I will tell you that he got his ass beaten pretty badly. The injury is nearly two weeks old and the bruising is still evident."

"That mystery is already solved," I say. "Headmaster flogged him. He admitted it to Owen Forrestal. Apparently a story coming out in the *Sun* about it."

Leta is packing up her things. "You boys and boarding schools."

"What does that mean?"

"It's the twenty-first century and these toffs have parents who are paying top dollar for the luxury of having their children abused...but what do I know?"

CHAPTER 106: ABBOT

Detective Chief Inspector (DCI) Carl Bridges has taken over the case. He's a thoughtful man in his early fifties with a shock of gray hair and a Mediterranean complexion. He enters the cottage and immediately starts taking mental notes.

"Clearing away Christmas already?"

"We've lost our festive mood," Betty says. She hates coppers of any stripe.

"And you are?"

"Mrs. Ashlock. I'm Timothy's mother so I'll be in the room when you ask him any questions."

He nods. He sits across from Timothy near the fire. "Have you been smoking pot?"

Timothy laughs in his face. "Don't be daft."

He looks at the hearth. "What kind of wood are you burning there?"

"It's yew," Timothy says flatly.

He smiles. "It certainly has a lovely aroma."

"Would you like an espresso DCI Bridges?" I ask.

"That would be brilliant," he says. "You're the butler, Mr. Abbot, right?"

"That's correct."

"Would you like to save us all a lot of time and confess? I mean, it's usually the butler..."

"You have an unusual sense of humor, Mr. Bridges. May I remind you that we just lost a family member."

"Of course, and I'm deeply sorry for your loss. So, who in this room is related to the deceased?"

"He was my boyfriend," Tim says.

"You lived here together?"

"Yes."

"It's cozy. I saw a video of you boys kissing on the internet."

"You and two million other people," Timothy responds. He sips the espresso.

"Did Jacob have social media accounts?"

"I'm sure you already know the answer to that."

"Hmm," he says. "I understand you're a musician."

"That's right."

"Would you like to play something for me?"

"No."

"Well," he says, tugging back his unruly hair, "I suppose we should get down to the nitty gritty. Where were you last night?"

Timothy stares into the fire. "Here."

"All night?"

"Yes."

"Were you alone?"

"I was."

He looks toward me. "And you Mr. Abbot?"

"Mrs. Ashlock and I were in Oxfordshire."

"How did you travel there?"

"By car," I answer.

"May I ask how long you've been employed by the Westons?"

"Twenty-four years."

"And you were the one who brought Dr. Kelly into this case?"

He's clever; he doesn't miss a trick. "Yes, Jacob's father, who will be arriving soon, has requested that I bring on as many experts as are needed to get to the truth."

"Indeed," he smiles. "Scotland Yard surely appreciates all the help we can get. By the way, you do know that you and Timothy here are the primary beneficiaries of Jacob's personal fortune."

"What?" Timothy asks.

"Rich people make wills, Mr. Ashlock, and you figure prominently into Jacob Weston's. Did you sign some paperwork recently?"

Timothy looks over to me. "Yesterday."

CHAPTER 107: TIMOTHY

When this guy finds Jacob's blank phone and laptop there's going to be hell to pay. Abbot is in far over his head with DCI Bridges, and if I'm not more careful I'm going to go to prison for killing my boyfriend. No wonder mum hates rozzers.

"Did Jacob have enemies?"

"How do you mean?"

"People who would like to see him harmed?"

"Yes," finally we are getting to the meat of the matter.

"Can you name anyone?"

"Wayne Kendel, teacher. David Reeve, ex-priest currently a bartender, Chase Hampton, student, Peter Chadwick, student, Paddy Lester, groundskeeper, Jane Rowland, councilor, Stillman Rothwell, Headmaster...and there may be other random homophobes that I'm missing."

"That's an impressive list," he comments, jotting down notes.

"Jacob was an impressive man," I say.

"No doubt. Just one thing more: Did Jacob ever talk about suicide?"

And there it is. "Yes," I admit. "He talked about it constantly."

"So his death doesn't really come as much of a surprise, does it?" He stands up and I start to laugh.

"Something funny, son?"

"I'm not your son, and you're a bit of a prat Mr. Bridges. Why not try reaching for something beyond the low-hanging fruit?"

He looks for a moment like he wants to paste me, then he grins. "Such as?"

Abbot steps in before I go completely mental. "Follow the real money, DCI. Jacob's plotting stepmother and her son are poised to make billions of dollars now that the only blood heir to the Weston fortune is out of the way. Billions with a *B*."

The Detective Chief rubs the stubble on his chin. "Long distance homicide. Difficult to execute, so to speak, but that's a hefty payday. Guess I'll add them to the list."

"Are we done here?" I ask.

"With your permission, I'd like to search his room."

I stare at him and he unblinkingly stares right back. "We've been sharing a room lately, and I was just going back to bed. Perhaps you can come back to toss his cell."

Abbot comes forward. "We would prefer if you wait until Mr. Weston arrives before looking through any personal items."

"Fair enough," the detective says. "I've got some folks to interview. Get some rest, Mr. Ashlock, you look terrible."

"Murdering someone that never shut up about suicide gives the killer automatic cover. You've got to dig deeper, DCI."

I wave to him as I climb the stairs. The first thing I do when I'm alone is call Ethan.

CHAPTER 108: ABBOT

It's a full two days before Mr. and Mrs. Weston arrive in London. Jacob's autopsy has been completed and his body has been released so the funeral will be at White Oak tomorrow.

In deference to the Weston's the investigative team, including Dr. Kelly, has agreed to brief us on their findings in a private function room at the Claridge Hotel.

"You drove them in from the airport?" Timothy asks Ethan.

"Yes," he says quietly.

"And?"

"Not much to say. Posh Americans. Pardon me for saying so, Mr. Abbot, but the wife has a bit of a stick up her arse."

I'm going to miss Ethan Polley. "That is a perfect assessment."

Timothy is gazing out the window as we approach the hotel. "I can only assume that they will hate me on sight."

I touch his shoulder. He is wearing the tailored black suit that I purchased for him. We are both outfitted in Savile Row's finest. It seemed appropriate for two men in mourning who are about to go into battle.

"You must show them no weakness, Master Timothy. Paul Weston is a dangerous man. He's powerful, wealthy and not very bright...and he just lost his only son. We must be kind, well-mannered gentlemen. No outbursts."

"Good luck with that," Ethan says as we exit the car.

***

We find the room which is named *The French Salon*. I booked it because it is both majestic and intimate. It has dark paneled walls and a marble fireplace, as well as floor to ceiling windows with art deco accents. Inspector Forrestal, DCI Bridges and Dr. Kelly are already waiting for us. Surprisingly, Headmaster Rothwell is also in the room. The Weston's have yet to come down from their suite.

Leta walks up and greets us warmly. "You look much better than the last time I saw you," she says to Timothy.

"I'm sorry," he says, "I don't recall meeting you."

She smiles. "You were preoccupied, and barefoot. I'm Leta. I'm so sorry for your loss, Tim."

"Thank you."

"Is there anything I should know, Doctor?" I ask her.

"I'll tell you everything in a few minutes."

Bridges is pacing about the room. "Where are the bloody Americans? Aren't they staying in *this* hotel?"

I walk up to him. "The Weston's will be twenty minutes late. He thinks it's a sign of power to keep people waiting."

"When actually it's just a sign of rudeness," Leta whispers to us. We take our seats.

"We didn't expect to see you, Headmaster," I say to Rothwell.

"Where else would I be?" he asks, and the Weston's arrive with P.H. Caldwell in tow.

"Who's the little man?" Timothy whispers to me.

"A lawyer," I whisper back.

Carl Bridges stands and introduces himself. "Doctor Kelly," he says. "Why don't you handle cause of death first."

Leta stands and folds her hands in front of her waist. "I'm Doctor Leta Kelly from Cambridge and I led the forensic team assisting the Medical Examiner, Dr. Doyle. First I'd like to say I'm deeply sorry for your loss. Jacob was a boy in the prime of his life and in unusually good health so this is a terrible tragedy no matter what determinations are made today." She looks over at Timothy. "I'll be going into some detail, are you sure you want to be here for this?"

"Absolutely."

"Very well," she continues. "We did an extensive examination on Jacob Weston. Perhaps not surprisingly, given where he was found, he drowned. His lungs were over-inflated and waterlogged making it what we call a *wet drowning*. Haemorrhagic bullea of emphysema were found indicating rupture of alveolar walls in the lungs. Do you have a question, Mr. Weston?"

He's holding up his hand like he's in middle school. "Yes Doctor. My son was a champion swimmer...how is it he drowns in a pool he's been in a hundred times?"

Timothy sits forward, intently listening for the answer. "That's an excellent question, sir. Mr. Abbot provided us with a full medical history so I know that Jacob had no seizure disorders. I understand his biological mother died of a brain aneurysm, so I checked for any possible correlation to that, and there was none. Although unlikely for a person his age, myocardial infarction...a heart attack, while he was swimming, is also a possibility, but that didn't happen either.

People who drown usually lose consciousness due to hypoxia, a lack of oxygen, followed rapidly by cardiac arrest. This was not the case with Jacob. In fact, his heart was somewhat unusual, being nearly a third larger and much more muscular than other people of his age, gender and race. So, both exercise and training, as well as genetics, made him the exceptional athlete he was."

"So why is he dead instead of headed for the Olympics?" Paul Weston, ever the charmer.

"Foul play is always a possibility and I will let the Detective Chief go into theories in that arena. I'm a medical doctor and deal strictly with physical facts. Jacob had bruising on his buttocks from an unrelated beating administered approximately ten days ago."

Headmaster Rothwell looks uncomfortable as eyes in the room turn toward him.

"There were no conclusive signs of struggle. There was one bruise just above the wrist of his left hand. This happened slightly before or near the time of death. This injury could have been caused by an inadvertent slip or fall. It was very icy that morning. I'm quite clumsy and get these kinds of bruises all the time.

A full toxicology report takes time to return from the lab, so I'm still waiting for those results. However, the preliminary findings show a blood alcohol content of .09 percent, which is regarded as legally impaired. I will also state for the record that alcohol use is involved in approximately fifty percent of all fatal drownings. I'm very sorry. Are there any other questions?"

DCI Bridges says, "Doc, if he didn't go into cardiac arrest what stopped his heart?"

She nods. "Yes, thank you, Chief. Cerebral anoxia led to irreversible damage. His brain function stopped before his heart did. I believe it was painless."

Paul Weston is rubbing his eyes, while his wife looks rather bored.

Forrestal gets up and stretches. "We'll take a ten minute break and then the Chief and I will give you the findings from our investigation."

Timothy is staring at the marble fireplace. "How are you doing?" I ask him but he doesn't even look up.

"I'm fine."

CHAPTER 109: TIMOTHY

Of course he had been drinking. Drinking and driving, then drinking and swimming. The pretty red-haired doctor comes back up to Abbot and me.

"I'll let you know when I get the full tox screen back. I have a rush on it, but you know, these things take time."

"Thank you. We appreciate your gentle touch."

She smiles and looks at me. "You were brave. I know that wasn't easy to hear."

"Doctor," I say. "The bruise on his wrist, could it have been from hitting it against the edge of the pool?"

I watch her thinking about it. "That's consistent with the placement and angle of the bruising. It's exactly what could have caused it."

"Thank you," I say and we take our seats again as Bridges stands at the head of the table.

"Inspector Forrestal and I did a full inquiry into the death of Jacob Weston, interviewing nearly two dozen people. I'm afraid our findings are not very pleasant.

According to his favorite professor, Mr. Fulton, Jacob had a fixation with suicide and possibly a problem with alcohol consumption. His end of term paper was titled, *The Suicide Authors,* and focused solely on writers who had taken their own life. Jacob considered himself a writer and was working on his first novel.

His councilor, Miss. Jane Rowland, found him to be unstable and at moderate risk of suicide. She had recommended, in writing, further therapy sessions.

Everyone, including Mr. Ashlock who is present this morning, said that Jacob Weston spoke often and at great length about suicide.

Mr. Weston has told us that during his last phone conversation with his son, Jacob threatened to take his own life, less than twenty-four hours later he was deceased. As far as we can determine there were two triggering events.

The first is that he was being transferred from his current school, where he felt comfortable and in charge, to one where he would once again be the odd man out. The second event was that he had a falling out with his lover the day before his death."

I can feel the eyes of the room on me, but I continue to stare at the middle of the table.

"Statistics tell us that the most common cause of death for homosexual teens is suicide, and suicide in general is more likely to happen around the holidays..."

"This is a complete load of bollocks!" I shout. Abbot puts his hand on my arm but I shrug him off and stand up.

"Mr. Ashlock?" Bridges says.

"It's true he drank a bit...to take the edge off. We all do, and so would you if you were trapped at White Oak."

I get a stern glare from the Headmaster. "Plenty of boys are smoking weed and doing a lot of harder drugs to find respite. I'll tell you this though...Jake loved life. He loved swimming, and books and traveling...and he loved me."

I will myself not to become emotional in front of this group. "He was fascinated with suicide, who knows why? It was a hobby and he was an authority on it. So let me ask you genius fucking coppers one thing: If Jake Weston killed himself where is the bloody suicide note? Do you think an expert in the field would forget to write a note?"

Inspector Forrestal has come up beside me, ready to tackle me if I go off my nut.

Bridges gives me that cynical detective look that he's nearly always wearing. "Maybe the note was on the hard drive you erased."

I give a sideways glance toward Abbot. "I didn't erase anything," I say, taking my seat again. "Did you at least interview David Reeve and the other people who hated his guts?"

Forrestal nods. "We did. It's true not everyone loved the golden boy that was Jacob Weston. Most have solid alibis for the time in question. We detained the groundskeeper, Mr. Lester, who has a criminal record and apparently threw a brick through your window. He remains a person of interest, but at Scotland Yard we often go by *Occam's Razor*..."

"Fucking hell," I murmur.

"Which states the principle of parsimony. Simplicity. The simplest theory is more likely to be true. I have here Jacob Weston's personal diary. The subject of suicide comes up fifty-nine times."

He thumbs through the book while Abbot is staring my way. I don't look back.

"And I quote: *I've always thought that drowning would be a lovely way to die.*"

"I've heard enough," Mr. Weston says, getting to his feet. "Thank you gentlemen and lady."

"One moment more, if you please, sir. Since no specific note was found, our official ruling will be: Accidental death by drowning. This will be the cause we are releasing to the media."

I watch Rothwell and Mr. Weston both breathe a visible sigh of relief. At least they're happy.

CHAPTER 110: ABBOT

Paul Weston looks weary. He shakes hands with the investigators and then approaches us. "Abbot, I wonder if you and the boy wouldn't mind meeting us in our suite."

I nod. "We'll be right up, sir."

Timothy is still agitated. "Ethan is waiting for us," he says.

"This shouldn't take long. Be polite."

"What do you think he wants?"

He stands beside me in the elevator. His black hair and black suit against his pale white skin remind me of a handsome vampire from the movies. "I'm not at all sure, but you are correct. He wants something."

We enter the lavish suite of rooms. JoAnne has already removed her shoes and is drinking Champagne and playing with her phone. I'd like to push her off the balcony.

The lawyer is pulling out documents, so this is rapidly going to get interesting. Paul approaches Timothy.

"Mr. Ashlock," he says, extending his hand.

"Mr. Weston. Jake often spoke about you and his step-mother."

Paul glances at his diminutive evil partner on the terrace. "Did he say anything nice?"

Timothy watches JoAnne drinking. "No, not really."

"We've spoken to the banks and we notice that you figure prominently in Jacob's will and in most of his private holdings. I want you to understand that the family does not intend to challenge or in any way deviate from my son's expressed wishes. It seems my boy was quite talented when it came to the stock market...and I never even knew it. You are going to be a wealthy young man."

He looks into Paul Weston's eyes. "What's the catch?"

"You're clever. I can see why he liked you." He motions toward Caldwell, the pudgy lawyer. "We'd like you to sign an NDA."

I lean in. "A non-disclosure agreement. He doesn't want you going public regarding your relationship with Jacob."

"Sir," he says, "more than two million people have seen us kiss on YouTube. Hasn't that ship already sailed?"

Weston shrugs. "So there isn't any harm in signing it and getting rich."

"No thanks," Tim answers, and I've never been prouder. I wish Betty were here to see her son in action.

"I don't understand," Weston says, looking at me for help.

"I don't really care about the money," he says. "And I'm pretty sure Jake set it up so you couldn't fuck with it anyway."

I smile and nod my head because he's right. The entire JP Weston Corporation is legally owned by me. Jacob was the CEO in name only because of his age. I signed every transaction on every contract.

"I'll tell you what I will do, Mr. Weston. I'll give you my word as a gentleman that everything that was private between your son and me will remain private. And also, I'm going to find out who killed him."

Paul Weston looks a bit baffled. "You still think he was murdered?"

"Oh I know so. That bruise on his wrist is meant as a signal for us. He caused it on purpose before he died...it's a hint. *Inadvertent slip* my arse. Jake was about as clumsy as a tightrope walker."

"Abbot?"

"I concur with Mr. Ashlock."

He nods his head. "Then let me know if you need any resources..."

"What?" JoAnne says from across the room. "You can't be serious, Paul. He's not the first teenaged faggot to take his own life when the going got tough and he won't be the last."

"Madam," I say with a steady, even tone. "You are an ignorant, mean-spirited little cunt."

Timothy bursts out laughing, and I think I see the hint of a smile on Weston's face too. Caldwell is giggling and has to excuse himself from the room.

"How dare you!" she shrieks. "Paul, fire this servant immediately!"

"Calm down, JoAnne."

Timothy has gone to the bar and is pouring himself a single malt scotch as Paul closely watches him swallow the drink. "That's uncanny," Weston murmurs.

"Sir," I say. "I promised your father that I would look after this family and sadly, I have failed in my duties. I'm afraid I must resign."

"What?"

"Listen to me, Paul. Ask yourself who has the most to gain from Jacob's untimely death. This horrible little harpy and her brat stand to inherit everything. Do you really want that? Follow the money and it leads directly to the two usurpers in your own house."

"What are you saying?"

"I'm saying that I'm an old man and you are an even older one...but it's not too late for either of us to be happy. Think about it."

"Get out!" she's screaming. "Leave us alone!"

I focus my attention on this diminutive lunatic. "Madam, I've been trying to work out how you accomplished it from 3,500 miles away...a contract killer, no doubt. I want you to know this: I loved that boy from his first breath to his last and I will uncover exactly what happened to him...of that you can be certain."

I collect Timothy and we head toward the open door. "All the arrangements have been made for the service, sir."

Paul Weston is watching us leave. "We'll see you tomorrow at ten AM."

CHAPTER 111: ETHAN

"So, how did it go?"

They both climb into the back of the car.

"Do shut up," Abbot tells him playfully.

Timothy looks in my eyes and says, "Madam, you are an ignorant, mean-spirited little cunt," and then he's doubled over in laughter.

"What?"

"Never mind," Abbot says. "I meant to ask you, Ethan...did you mail off that package we gave you?"

"Umm," I stutter.

Timothy is waving his hand. "It's okay, mate, I'll tell him. I intercepted and cancelled that delivery."

"May I ask why?"

"Because I thought letting the detectives find the journal was preferable to my going to prison for killing my boyfriend...and things were heading quickly in that direction."

"I see your point. Mr. Weston enlisted me to protect Jacob's reputation, but in retrospect it appeared as though we were hiding information...because of course, we were."

"I told you erasing those drives looked suspicious," Tim remarks. "Meanwhile I'm sitting at Brigsley with no alibi after just signing up to be a major participant in Jake's financial affairs. I'm surprised they didn't slap the darbies on me right away."

"I believe Inspector Forrestal and DCI Bridges know that your grief is authentic. Bridges is a very insightful observer, and I don't think he ever really questioned your motives or actions. In the end protecting Jacob didn't change anything. Scotland Yard was always going to assume suicide because even as clever as these investigators are...murder is too big a leap."

"So what's the plan?"

I watch Abbot in the rearview mirror. "Tomorrow is the funeral. My guess is the killer will show up to watch."

"Seriously?"

"If you thought you had gotten away with murder you'd want to sit back and take in all the pain and grief you caused. Who do you think it is, Timothy?"

"David Reeve. He's the creepiest bastard I've ever met...or Professor Kendel. Jake threatened him with a face-down trip down the Thames..."

It's starting to rain so I put on the wipers and the headlamps. "I'm glad I'm not on your suspect list."

"Who says you aren't?"

"What?"

"Pay no attention, old chap. Timothy is in a very odd mood. We don't suspect you."

He's back there laughing. "Drowned at the hand of one of your own swim coaches... that's what I'd call ironic. But even Ethan isn't thick enough to kill the goose that laid the golden eggs..."

I'm watching Tim back there in stitches. Grief does strange things to people.

CHAPTER 112: TIMOTHY

Jake hated funerals, but that didn't stop him from planning his own. Who does such things?

He recently wrote out oddly specific designs regarding what he wanted and forwarded them to Mr. Abbot. It feels like he knew his death was imminent. Bridges would say that's because he planned to do himself in all along, but I think he had a premonition.

I put on the Stefano Ricci blue silk jacket that he gave me for the Paris trip. I don't think Jacob would want me to wear black and mope around.

"How do I look?" I ask Abbot and my mum when I come downstairs. She is wearing a black knit dress and her pearls. As a butler, Abbot has been wearing dark suits for half his life. He calls it his *armor*.

"The jacket he gave you for his birthday," she says. "You look smashing."

Abbot is still deciding. "It's very blue."

"I'm going non-traditional."

"I'm sure he would approve."

I pick up my violin case. "Let's go then."

***

White Oak Chapel is a complete zoo. Hundreds of people crowd the entrance. There are two news vans with cameras and reporters as well as a BBC film crew making some kind of documentary.

"For fuck's sake, Abbot, what is all this?"

The butler sighs. "Part of Jake's grand scheme. He wanted all the media informed and invited...he wrote that he

304

requires a *circus atmosphere* and I'm afraid he planned other surprises.

I put my arm around my mum and laugh. This is so like Jake to make a farce out of his own funeral. He once told me that memorials are strictly about the living...the person laying in the box is inconsequential. I glance over my shoulder and up to the bell tower next to Kyler Library. Just for an instant I think I see someone blond up there watching us. I hold my hand up to him.

We decline answering questions from the pushy reporters and make our way inside the chapel. The Weston's are in the front row, naturally, wearing black and looking confused.

It's an open casket so glimpsing his face again makes my heart skip. We sit right behind his father and step-mother. She looks at us like we're stray dogs.

"Abbot," Paul Weston says, "it's hard to tell, but is my son shirtless at his own memorial?"

"No sir," Abbot responds. "He's nude, except for his jade pendant."

Mum and I both start to giggle. Sweet Jesus. Churches make me nervous. I look around and see most of the people I expected to see sitting nearby. Billy crowds in next to me, his eyes red-rimmed.

"I can't believe this," he says. "I'm gutted. I keep waiting for him to jump up and laugh."

Fulton and Jane came, as well as Blackmore, Matron Finlay and all the St. John's boys. Honestly, everyone looks devastated. Dr. Leta and DCI Bridges arrive together. Deep down I think he senses there is more to Jake's death than meets the eye.

Ethan sits with us too, he's wearing his tuxedo. Then Coach Lir stumbles forward. He's unshaven and wearing a rumpled tweed jacket. The Coach appears to be steaming drunk. Abbot purses his lips together.

"I think we've just achieved our circus atmosphere," I whisper.

"I hope he's sober enough to speak. He's one of the eulogists."

The religious portion of the service gets started. It's a full blown Catholic extravaganza with lots of kneeling, genuflecting and Latin. Jacob loved excess. After hymns and prayers with swinging brass incense censers, candles and the pipe organ... we get down to the speeches. Poor Father Gates looks flustered quoting the Bible in front of a gay, naked, stone-dead teenager. The absurdity has got me laughing inappropriately until I get shushed by Jake's step-mother. What a bitch.

Then the Headmaster takes the pulpit. I whisper to Abbot. "Was he on Jake's list?"

"No," he tells me. "That was the price I had to pay to have the service in this chapel. He had me over a barrel."

I see Kitty crying as Rothwell is up there talking about Jake. It's all blah, blah, blah about what a fine example Jake was and how he epitomized everything a White Oak boy should be. This is everything Jake hated about funerals.

"I'm amazed he could deliver all that tosh with a straight face," I say.

Fulton gets up next and reads A.E. Houseman's: *To An Athlete Dying Young*. When he finishes the poem we're all choked up. Bravo Professor, bravo.

Then it's Ethan's turn. "I was just Jake's driver," he begins, "but he acted like I was his older brother. He sat right beside me on our trips together and we talked honestly about life and love. He knew no class lines or had any prejudice based on status. Gentry or servant, he refused to judge anyone and treated everyone the same. I've never known a finer lad, and I never will again..."

That's as far as Ethan gets before he is overtaken by his own emotions. Coach Lir pats his assistant on the back as he takes the stage.

He holds up a silver flask and stares out at us with unfocused eyes. "He gave me this for Christmas. Had my initials engraved and filled it up with the best damn scotch I've ever tasted...and believe me that's saying something because I've sampled more than a few."

People are smiling as the Coach toasts Jacob and takes a swig. "He was the fastest swimmer I ever taught. You toffs could learn a thing or two from him. I never heard a single word of complaint. No pissing or whinging. He worked his ass off in the water and would do whatever I asked. He was a phenomenal athlete; dedicated, fierce and as fast as greased lightning."

The Coach looks over at him, lying in state. "I see that he's naked and that makes good sense. Might as well leave this world the same way you come in. I used to have a devil of a time convincing him to keep his Speedos on."

I see Abbot smiling and nodding. The Coach looks directly at Paul Weston and gives him a nod. "I'm sorry he's gone. He would have won gold, I can promise you that. He enjoyed it, you know. I'm glad he died doing something he loved...only one thing he loved more and it's always embarrassing when someone dies doing that..."

We all have a good laugh as Billy stands up. I look at our program and then I realize what's been going on. It's Jake's Thanksgiving guest list.

"I loved him," Billy says, wringing his hands. "Not the same way he loved Timmy, but I loved him just as well. We all did. He tutored me when I was failing Latin, and he mended me when I was hurt." The tears freely roll down Redgrave's cheeks.

"Someone told me when they opened him up that his heart was twice the size of a normal person's...but everyone who knew Jake Weston knew that already."

It's my turn.

I hold the violin that he bought me and walk up to the dais. Hundreds of people silently watch. Everyone expects me to break down, or fall completely apart, but I don't.

I go to his polished oak coffin and take a gander. He's beautiful even in death. They've managed to cover up the scar with make-up but the bumpy y-shaped incision still shows. I touch the greenstone on his chest one last time and then I bend down and kiss him gently on the lips. He's cold and hard, like a marble statue. His smell, his softness and his warmth are gone and really so is he. This is just the shell that used to be my best friend...if he's somewhere in this room, it isn't in that box.

I lift up my gorgeous *Allegretti* and I play his song. I play it for all I'm worth because I know I will never perform this piece again. I play it for Jake and I hope he was listening because it sounded pretty damn good.

A lot of people cried, including Abbot and his father, but I didn't. Sometimes you feel something so deeply that tears just don't do it justice.

Mr. and Mrs. Weston stand near the door so they can shake hands with all the mourners. Father Tobias is right beside them. Billy hugs me and he whispers in my ear, "Are you in on this?"

"In on what, Redgrave?"

He winks. "You'll see."

We approach to say our good-byes. "Those are beautiful pearls," Weston says to mum. She touches them lightly.

"Why thank you."

"Have a safe trip home, sir," I say shaking his hand.

"I think he was lucky to know you," he smiles sadly at me. "Stay in touch."

"Madam, you are..." I say nodding to the step-mother but Abbot is pushing me along before I can finish my impression.

Peter Chadwick reaches for Weston's hand. "Jacob was one of my best friends, sir, he was a great teammate."

"That's kind of you to mention," he replies.

"And I was his lover," Chadwick says and winks.

Wait, what?

Colin Hunter is next in line. "Jacob and I were good mates, sir... and I was his lover..."

Jesus. On and on it goes, apparently all the St. Johnnies and many of the other boys are party to the mischief. Ian Wood shouts, "He was great in the sack!" Even Oliver Morgan wryly comments, "I'm *Head*-Boy but Jacob really deserves that title."

Mr. Weston's jaw clenches and his face goes three shades of red. He turns toward Rothwell and shouts, "What kind of a school are you running here?"

The Headmaster sputters, "I'm terribly sorry Mr. Weston, the boys, well they must be overcome with grief."

He shakes his head, looking at Abbot. "I send my only child away to boarding school and I never see him alive again."

I know what the guys were doing was just a dumb prank, but it made me realize that Jake Weston never hid from who he was...and lots of people admired him for it.

Abbot puts his arm around my shoulder as we leave the chapel. "That was the best funeral I've ever attended," he says.

On the walk back to Brigsley I see Miranda sitting under a tree. "Excuse me," I say to the group.

CHAPTER 113:   CROSSROADS

The gypsy child is sitting on a purple blanket and sipping orange juice through a straw. She smiles when Timothy comes up to her, holding his jacket and violin case.

"What are you doing here?"

She sets down her drink. "Waiting for you, of course." She motions toward the church with her chin. "I'm sorry you lost him. He has a special soul. I wish he could have changed his fate, but he was caught off guard."

Timothy sits down next to her and looks up at the clouds, then off toward the bell tower again. "Were you at the funeral?"

"No," she says. "I spend enough of my time with the dead. I hate funerals." She looks at him with her big hazel eyes. "Go ahead and ask me."

"He knew he was going to die, didn't he?"

She offers him some juice but he declines. "We're all going to die...but yes, he saw a glimpse of it, I saw it too."

"What did he see?"

She plays with one of her braids. "He was laying naked in a coffin, a green pendant on his chest."

"I loved him," Timothy says, his voice starting to break.

"He knows."

"Is he okay?"

She smiles and leans in close. "He will be soon," she whispers.

He doesn't understand what that's supposed to mean. "Will I ever see him again?"

Miranda gets up and puts her things into a brown paper sack. "Oh, you can count on that."

Timothy's still sitting. "What should I do?"

"First, get off my blanket," she says and musses his shiny black hair. "Finish the task at hand...trust no one...and protect yourself."

She kisses him on the cheek and skips up the hill, waving as she goes.

CHAPTER 114: TIMOTHY

When I get back to the cottage everyone has changed into normal clothes and is in a hurry. "What's going on?" I ask.

Abbot seems practically giddy. "We're going to the hotel. I hired one of the photographers who was outside the church. He's confident he has images of every face that was at the funeral. I'm going to go look for our suspect."

"Brilliant," I admit.

Mum comes rushing out of the back room. "I thought that man was going to snatch the pearls right off my neck."

"Betty," Abbot says, "don't be ridiculous."

"We both know he recognized them. The fact is I've grown attached to this necklace...it reminds me of Jay."

She gives me a hug. "I've never heard you play better, Love. One day you're going to perform for the Royal family."

I laugh. "You lot are royal enough for me."

"I'm going to go see them off," Ethan announces.

"Who?" I ask. "The Westons?"

"Yeah."

Abbot chuckles. "He just wants to see the helicopter. Please be back in time to take us to the hotel."

"Why don't you come with us to London?" Mum asks.

"Thanks, but I've got some errands to run...and I don't want to be a third wheel."

Abbot scoffs. "What errands?"

I'm heading upstairs to change, it looks like another storm is coming in tonight. "I thought I'd retrace Jacob's steps...starting with Botany Bay."

"That's a very good idea, Timothy. Do you want me to accompany you, it might be dangerous?"

"Dangerous? Mrs. Walker is in her mid-seventies, I think I can handle her. Go have fun in the city. I want to drive Jacob's car and look at the sea."

He nods his head and smiles kindly at me. "I'm very proud of you. Do be careful driving around today...I think we're in for some more weather."

CHAPTER 115: ABBOT

Paul couldn't leave England fast enough, and who can blame him? He told me he never wants to step foot in the UK again. I've paid for the Claridge suite until the end of the week so I thought Betty and I could enjoy it.

We've ordered room service and are having a nice late lunch. "I've got something for you, Madam," I say and hand her the package.

"What's this?" she asks. "You shouldn't be buying me gifts. Didn't you just quit your job?"

"I did indeed."

She unwraps it and beams when she sees the pearl earrings. "These are lovely," she whispers and gets up and kisses me on the mouth. Betty tastes like cinnamon and sugar.

"They match your necklace," I comment.

"Yes, I can see that, Mr. Abbot. I'm not blind. Why didn't you give these to me this morning so I could have worn the whole set?"

I shrug. "It seemed a little gauche to give you a gift before a funeral."

She's laughing at me again. "But apparently gift giving is acceptable right after a funeral."

"Must you taunt me?"

She slaps my shoulder and pours us both some wine. "I'm afraid I must. You haven't been taunted enough in your life. So what are you going to do now that you aren't under the yoke of the Westons?"

I clear my throat. "I've given it some thought, but I'd really prefer to wait to discuss it."

"Wait for what, Mr. Abbot? I'm not getting any younger."

"Wait until I've received your son's blessing, if you must know."

I see her expression soften. "Always the gentleman," she whispers. "Don't get cold feet, because I think you're going to like my answer."

What a bittersweet day this has been. My phone vibrates and I see it's Dr. Kelly calling. "Do you mind if I take this, Betty? It's important."

"Of course."

CHAPTER 116: TIMOTHY

The address was already programmed into the GPS. "Finish the task at hand," she told me. Maybe finding out who murdered Tommy Walker will lead me to Jake's killer. Maybe it's the same person.

I wonder if Jake was frightened right at the end of his life. If he was mad or worried or maybe just surprised. She said he was caught off guard. I wonder if he was thinking of me.

I knock on her door and she answers almost immediately. "My, my," Olivia Walker says. "Another handsome White Oak boy, I presume. You better come in."

She reminds me of my grandmother. I see a photo of Tommy on her bookshelf. He was smaller of course, but he and Jacob looked a lot alike. They could have been brothers.

"I'm Tim Ashlock," I explain. "Jake was my best friend." I watch her put the kettle on.

"He's such a lovely lad. Why didn't he come with you?"

I look out her window toward the dark sea. "Mrs. Walker, I'm afraid he was killed the morning after he came to visit you."

"What?" she gasps. "How?"

"He drowned," I tell her this and she looks like she might faint. "Maybe you better sit," I say, holding out a chair and helping her down.

"Thank you," she says, grasping me with both hands. "You're a dear. It's just a shock is all. Was he your...?"

"Yes," I admit. "I've never loved anyone more in my life. I thought by coming here, retracing his steps, I could find out what he was up to. Maybe there's a clue somewhere."

"Well," she thinks. "He was very interested in Tommy's old yearbook."

I can hear myself gulp.

"Do you think I might take a look?"

"Of course," she says. "I left it on the bottom shelf of the bookcase."

The hair on my arm raises as I thumb through the annual. It falls open to a page with a photo of Tommy and another boy, their arms wrapped around one another. This must have been his boyfriend. I read the caption: *Tommy & Tyler. (Thomas H. Walker and Stillman T. Rothwell).*

"My God," I say.

"Jacob had that same look on his face."

"It's our Headmaster. He was a student at White Oak in the seventies. But why would he kill Tommy? It looks like they're so happy."

I pour us both some tea.

"He didn't kill him, Dear." She stands and goes over to her family Bible and pulls out a thin sheet of paper.

"How do you know?" I ask.

"I should have shown Jacob this," she says sadly. "I almost did, but I guess I was ashamed. My Tommy drowned too."

"What?" I ask, and she hands me her son's handwritten note.

CHAPTER 117: TOMMY WALKER

Dear Mum,

I know this will break your heart, but I just can't carry on. The boys at school are so horrid. They bully and tease, and it's gotten worse with all the fag-masters. It used to just be flogging, but lately they do unspeakable things to me. I've tried to be a good soldier like you and Papa want. I've tried to mind my own business and I've even tried to hide myself away...but nothing seems to work.

There's one lad who was my special friend. Tyler knew what I was facing and I think he loved me a little, even if it didn't last. Yesterday in the cottage he went into a rage. He's a big chap and he kept hitting me and calling me terrible names. He said he never wanted to see my face again.

I've got no one, Mum. I'm so desperately alone here. I don't know why the world is so heartless. I'm sorry for what I'm about to do. I'm not like the other boys...I never will be. I'm going to fill my pockets with stones and walk as far as I can into the sea. Please forgive me.

Your loving son,

Tommy

CHAPTER 118: ABBOT

I step into the bedroom. "Dr. Kelly, how kind of you to call."

"Hello Blake," she says in her usual fast, bright way. "I have some news."

I'm looking out on the rooftops of London. "Is it good news?"

"Hmm," she says. "Probably not. I received the toxicology report back and I was surprised with the results. There was a rather high dose of the benzodiazepine Flunitrazepam in Jacob's system."

"I'm not familiar with that drug, Doctor."

I can hear her shoes clicking across a floor, she must be on the move somewhere. "It's commonly known as Royhypnol, or *roofies* in street terminology."

"The date-rape drug," I say.

"Exactly. It's a dangerous hypnotic. I wanted you to know that I found no conclusive evidence of sexual assault with Jacob...however, he was a sexually active teen and his body was found in a chlorinated body of water...so, it's difficult to determine. Some people take this drug recreationally, and it's not uncommon for it to be used in suicides, particularly in Sweden. I'm afraid it leaves us with more questions than answers. Let me hand you off to DCI Bridges."

It's interesting that they are still in each other's company.

"Mr. Abbot."

"Hello, DCI."

"We seem to have come across a new wrinkle. Any idea how Jacob managed to acquire *roofies*?"

I sit down on the bed. This rabbit hole is getting deeper by the hour. "None at all. I can tell you that he would not have knowingly taken the drug."

"I understand that he was routinely tested because of his swimming career," Bridges says. "I checked the history and there has never been any record of illegal drug use with him. No pot, steroids or anything beyond alcohol and occasional prescription pain meds."

"What are your theories, Detective Chief?" I ask, and hear him sigh on the other end.

"First, I don't know where the drug came from or how it was administered. He could have had a few drinks, popped the pills and jumped into the pool in a deliberate swan song...but that doesn't sit right with me given what I know about the Weston boy. Listen Abbot, I know you scrubbed his computer...the father didn't want any embarrassing facts made public, I get it. Was there a suicide note?"

"No DCI. I give you my word as a gentleman on that."

"So, the alternative theory is that someone dosed the lad. This drug isn't licensed for medical use in the UK, but that doesn't mean it isn't floating all around Europe. He couldn't have taken it and driven from Eton to White Oak without passing out...so, I have a few more questions for the last bloke that saw him alive. He's an Eton toff named Matt Colton. Maybe Jacob didn't drive back to White Oak alone."

"He's a swimmer, DCI. Jacob just met him at the Eton Trials swim meet. We know nothing about him."

"I'm not reopening this case. It's not going to bring Weston back, but I'd like to know the whole truth. You and Mr. Ashlock are still under the impression there's a boarding school killer on the loose, is that correct?"

I go to the bar and pour myself a brandy. "You have a colorful way of putting things, Mr. Bridges. Yes, we think Jacob was murdered."

"Well, I'm going to ask a few follow-up questions to some people. There were two other boys that had keys to that pool. Peter Chadwick and Chase Hampton. Both of those toffs are Head-Boys in different houses...and I know Hampton wasn't fond of Weston."

"Well," I say. "I suppose we'll be seeing a bit more of each other."

"Yes, I was surprised to learn that you didn't travel back to the states with the parents after the funeral."

"I am no longer in their employ."

"Hmm," he says. "Did you resign or were you fired?"

"I resigned."

"All right then."

CHAPTER 119: TIMOTHY

It wasn't a murder at all, just a sad, desperate boy alone in a place where he could find no peace or love. I guess it's no wonder he's a restless spirit. Miranda told us that he was at Brigsley waiting for someone...and now I know who.

I call the Headmaster.

"Sir, it's Timothy Ashlock."

"Ashlock?" he says. "How are you holding up?"

"Fine."

"I wanted to tell you that you played brilliantly today, we even saw you on the news. I know that must have been difficult. Jacob would have been proud. Speaking of which, the Weston's paid for the cottage through next year and they requested that we let you stay on."

Finally a tiny ray of good fortune. "Thank you, sir. That's extremely generous."

"So what can I do for you?"

"Headmaster, I'm just returning from the beach. I drove out to Botany Bay."

I can feel the mood shift. "Did you now?"

"I wonder if you could meet me at Brigsley Cottage around six. I have something to show you...a bit of a surprise really."

"I love surprises," Rothwell says. "I'll see you soon."

***

I'm delayed because of the weather. It takes me three hours to get back to White Oak and I'm exhausted. I walk inside to find a fire in the hearth and the Headmaster drinking tea at our table.

"I was beginning to get worried," he says as I shake my wet things out. "I hope you don't mind that I let myself in...I was catching a chill outside."

"Not at all," I say. "I'm sorry I'm late. The roads are a fright."

"Have some tea, my boy. We should have a nice long chat." He's poured me a steaming cup and I'm grateful for the warmth of it.

"So," he says finally, "how is Mrs. Walker fairing?"

I'm a bit surprised.

"You knew I was visiting her?"

He impatiently taps his fingers on the table. "Yes, I was able to join the dots. You and Weston... quite the sleuths...always needing to turn over every stone."

"Curious natures, I suppose. Why did you never tell anyone you were a student here?"

"Because it's no one's business but my own. Discretion is the better part of valor, young man. A lesson your generation can't seem to learn. Some people did know, of course. Father Hodgson and Paddy Lester were both here when I was a pupil."

"You didn't kill Tommy Walker," I say flatly.

"Of course I didn't."

"You loved him."

He turns his face away. "That was a long time ago. We lived right here in this cottage...this room brings back memories."

My phone buzzes and I can see that Mr. Abbot is calling. "Excuse me, Headmaster," I say, but he jumps up and snatches the phone from my hand and tosses it across the room.

"Hey," I say standing up, but I'm suddenly feeling very odd. I'm dizzy and my movements are sluggish. My legs and arms feel heavy. I look at the china teacup.

"It's rude to be on your phone when you have a visitor," he says. "We don't want any interruptions."

Rothwell is putting on leather gloves and he's taken a length of rope from inside his jacket. I stumble for the door but he grabs me and holds me firm. He seems incredibly fast and strong.

"What you're feeling," he whispers in my ear, "is the effects of the same drug I gave to your boyfriend before I killed him."

I'm so confused and tired. "But why?"

He wraps the rope around my neck and begins throttling me from behind. "I wasn't going to just hand him over to Fetterman at Eton...and I didn't want my boyhood crushes exposed to the world. I have a reputation to maintain in this community, and those kinds of rumors would be embarrassing, to say the least. Jacob called me much the same way you did, asking me to visit the cottage. What masterminds!" he laughs and I continue to gasp for air.

"It was you watching us at Ducker..."

"Very good. I enjoyed watching Weston and I often did, from the shadows. That's how I knew to slip the drug into his water bottle...he always used the same one when he swam." I'm seeing stars and I know I'll be unconscious any second. Then he loosens the rope and lets me breathe again.

"I want this to last," he says. "We need to enjoy ourselves since I won't be able to kill another boy for quite some time... pity, I'm just not getting the same old thrill from flogging bare bums lately..."

He's choking me again. "It was such ecstasy holding his beautiful, naked body under the water and watching the life drain out of him, let me tell you...and he wasn't my first White Oak lad, oh no! Some boys jump out of bell towers, others are pushed."

"You're a monster."

He tightens his grip further. "I have a fetish."

He undoes my trousers and slips his free hand under my knickers. Honestly, I wish I had a shilling for every perverted creeper that tries to debag me.

"The story will be that you hanged yourself because you were grief-stricken over your lover's tragic death...it's almost Shakespearian."

So this is what it's like to die, I think. It's not so bad. I feel a strange euphoria washing over me.

"Playing with you is much more fun than smothering an old priest," he says, laughing again.   He's removed his own trousers and I can feel him pressing against my bum.   Not exactly how I imagined I'd die. Suddenly the windows begin to rattle and a cold ocean breeze passes through the room. About bloody time, I think.

The lights begin to flicker and strobe. "Headmaster," I manage to sputter, "I believe your boyfriend would like a word."

All the windows in the cottage open and slam shut. "What the devil?" Rothwell says, just as the front door bursts open. Tommy is standing there, drenched to the bone, his arms opened wide as if he's waiting for an embrace.

"Tommy?" Rothwell whispers. He releases me and I fall in a heap to the floor while he walks toward the ghost of his past. Rothwell extends his arms, but it's not easy to hug a spirit. I know the adrenalin is the only thing keeping me awake and alive. There's not a moment to lose.

"Headmaster," I say, "I don't believe you've met Harold."

He turns to look at me and I shoot him in the stomach. Rothwell takes a half step back, looking down at the wound as the blood blooms scarlet across his white shirt.

"Students aren't allowed..." he says.

But I shoot him again, the muzzle of the gun flashing. I hit him in the chest and then I shoot again, and again, and again. It's an incredibly easy thing to do. I empty the entire magazine into Stillman T. Rothwell.

He falls face down in front of the fireplace, the pool of blood inching its way slowly toward the rug. That's going to stain, I think randomly. I drop the gun which is still smoking and as hot as a stovetop.

Then I see Jake. He's standing at the foot of the stairs with that lopsided grin on his face, clapping his hands and staring right at me. He doesn't look like a ghost, he just looks like himself. For one brief instant I can smell him again...the warm, sweet odor of his skin and a whiff of his expensive cologne. I hear the applause right before the world goes black and the darkness swallows me whole.

CHAPTER 120: WILLIAM REDGRAVE

I've been in a funk since the funeral...just can't believe he's gone...I miss him. This feeling must be ten times worse for Timmy.   It's another stormy night so I decide to run over to Brigsley and see if he wants some company. Maybe we can get drunk and tell stories about Jake.

When I get down the hill his door is standing wide open and the lights inside are flickering. I run in and slip on all the blood.

"Fucking hell!" I yell, wiping the sticky stuff on my shirt. It's the Headmaster and Tim laying facedown on the floor. Are they both dead? It looks like the aftermath of a duel but why are both their trousers undone?   Whose gun is that on the floor? "Fucking hell!"

I look up and see Jake sitting at the top of the stairs laughing at me. Mother of God, I think, just what White Oak needs...*more ghosts*.

CHAPTER 121: TIMOTHY

I wake up in hospital the next morning with my mum holding my hand. My throat is sore and parched. "May I have some water?" I croak out in a strange voice that is not my own.

She pours me a glass and I take a long sip. "How are you feeling, poppet?" she asks. She hasn't called me that in years.

"I shot the Headmaster."

Abbot, who is sitting beside me, looks up from his Lewis Carol. "Yes you did, fifteen times."

Mum is smiling. "I'd have done the same. I never trusted that slimy bastard."

I'm still dizzy. "He killed Jake, and Father Hodgson, and Finn Williams, and God knows how many others."

DCI Bridges walks in with Ethan and Billy. "How are you feeling, Mr. Ashlock?"

I give him a condescending stare. "Like I've had my stomach pumped and been half-strangled to death..."

"Yes," he says and gives me a slight bow. "I owe you an apology, it seems your theory held merit. By the way, Metro found David Reeve's body stuffed in a dumpster behind a pub in Brixton...you wouldn't know anything about that, would you?"

"Of course not," but I can't hide my satisfaction or my smile. "Brixton can get a bit dodgy... maybe he's also the work of the Headmaster."

Bridges crosses his arms across his chest. "No, we believe Mr. Rothwell was busy being shot to death at the time of Reeve's stabbing. Speaking of which, where did that gun come from? One of the White Oak boys, the Hampton chap, hinted that there may be one about...we looked for it."

"You didn't look very hard, Detective. I found it in Jake's car when I was replacing his phone and computer. I strapped it to my shin right then and there. One can't be too careful."

Abbot motions to the detective. "We'd like to have that revolver back, if you don't mind, purely for sentimental reasons."

He laughs. "Fat chance of that, a Glock 19 is prohibited here. Why don't you buy yourselves some nice hunting rifles." He looks down at me. "It's too bad you're such a fine musician...you'd make a good detective."

"Over my dead body," mum answers.

Bridges scoffs. "I read about another famous Englishman who sidelined in solving crimes. I believe he also played the violin."

"That's fiction, Detective Chief Inspector," I say grinning.

"Just the same." He turns to Abbot, "You'll accompany him to Scotland Yard when he's released here and we can put a bow on this bloody mess?"

"Of course," he says. "May I ask you something of a personal nature, DCI?"

His eyes dart about the room. "You can ask."

Mr. Abbot reflexively straightens his tie. "Are you romantically involved with Dr. Kelly?"

Bridges actually blushes and storms out of the room. Mum and he both laugh. "We can take that as a *yes*."

"I told you so."

Ethan and Billy both hug me tightly. "You're a ledge at the school," Redgrave says. I can only imagine the gossip, and sweet Jesus, wait until the tabloids get ahold of this story. "Nanny says she's never seen so much blood."

Mum is pulling Abbot's sleeve, "I'm not going to Scotland Yard, I've had my fill of coppers."

"Whatever you want, Betty. Why don't you go have brunch at the Claridge and I'll meet you afterward."

Ethan checks the time. "We should get a move on then, Bea. Billy and I will be back to take you gents to the Yard."

"That's a lovely wristwatch you're wearing," mum says.

Ethan winks at me. "Thank you. Found it in the glovebox awhile back with a very kind note attached."

***

"It's ironic," I say to Abbot when we're alone again. "Both Tommy and Jake drowned."

"Hmm," he says, "one in saltwater and one in fresh."

"And all this time we were trying to solve Tommy's murder and it ended up being suicide..."

Abbot finishes my thought. "And Jacob's suicide turned out to be murder."

"I just don't know what to make of it all."

"Life is strange, Master Timothy, but it has a peculiar symmetry. There are patterns if you choose to look for them."

I nod at him and notice that the *Allegretti* is tucked safely away beside his chair. "Thank you for looking after it," I motion. "I was worried."

"Of course."

"Mr. Abbot," I say, finally feeling a bit more like myself. "May I ask you a question of a rather personal nature?"

The butler picks at some non-existent lint on his sleeve. "You can ask."

"Exactly what are your intentions toward my mother?"

He clears his throat. "I'm very glad you've broached the subject. It seems I've fallen madly in love with Mrs. Ashlock. I was going to ask for her hand, but I feel I must first receive your blessing."

"Hmm," I say, very non-committal. "Have you purchased a ring?"

Abbot reaches into his satchel and takes out a Cartier box which I open. The ring is magnificent.

"It's a four carat emerald solitaire in platinum," he tells me.

"That will suffice," I say. "My mother is a simple woman. And does she share your feelings?"

The old gentleman looks wistful. "Luckily for me, I believe she does."

"And will you make her happy?"

He places his hand over his heart. "I shall make it my life's endeavor."

I hand him back the engagement ring. "But how will you provide for her? You are, after all, an unemployed servant."

He looks out the window. "I've managed to set aside funds from investments...and I've recently come into some money rather unexpectedly."

I reach for his hand. "Then you have my blessing, sir. But what is to become of me? I'm afraid I'll soon be rather infamous."

"Yes," he agrees. "The press is already hard at work, I'm sorry to say. You'll have to leave the name Ashlock behind you."

I sigh. "What then shall I be called?"

"Not to be presumptuous, but I was thinking Timothy James Abbot...if it suits you."

"That suits me fine!"

EPILOGUE: TIMOTHY

After I'm released from Scotland Yard we go to France for two weeks. Abbot and Mum are married in front of the Eiffel Tower, where I scatter a handful of Jake's ashes.

White Oak made Professor Fulton the interim Headmaster and he immediately abolished flogging as a punishment. I received a very contrite letter which stated that it would probably be better for all parties concerned if I completed my education at another institution.

"White Oak, it seems, is terrified of you," Abbot says.

"So what am I supposed to do?"

We're staying at the George V hotel in Paris. It's Abbot's favorite because of the amazing food and the remarkable flower displays. Once a butler, always a butler. "Details matter," he's often said...and he notices even the smallest ones.

"I've made some calls. We've enrolled you in a quaint little school in Buckinghamshire for the Lent Halve."

"Buckinghamshire?" I ask. "Isn't that where Eton is?"

Abbot's eyebrows raise. "Yes, that's the name of the school, I was trying to remember it." He grins at me.

"Eton!" I shout.

Mum puts her hand over mine. "Easy, Love."

"You'll be rooming with the son of an Earl. Guilloume Redgrave."

"Billy? Seriously?" I'm over the moon.

Abbot looks up from reading *Le Monde*. He places his glasses carefully in his breast pocket. "Please try to refrain from murdering the Headmaster this time."

"That's sound advice. I should write that down."

I turn on the laptop. I've been reading all the gossip rags and other papers online to see how much traction my story has...thankfully, interest in it seems to be waning so it should be safe to return to England. "I read something I found interesting online on *The New York Post's* website."

Abbot looks intrigued.

"Apparently Paul Weston is divorcing his wife. He's run off with his nurse."

Mum and Abbot both start laughing. "Yes," he comments. "I recall hiring her. Lovely young Asian woman. Karen Hoang."

I nod. "It seems there were a great many beautiful young women in the Westons employ during the last few years."

Abbot is holding mum's hand, the Parisian light sparkling from her ring. "I should think so. I hired a nurse, two maids, a librarian and a tax accountant...all of them the stuff of adolescent wet-dreams. I knew I could eventually lure him away from that passive-aggressive shrew if I threw enough beauty into his path."

"Still," I say, "she'll be a wealthy woman once the dust settles."

He shakes his head. "One does only what one can...she won't be a billionaire, I can tell you that. They were only married for three years and I made sure there was an iron-clad prenuptial agreement. He can thank me for that later."

Mum looks at him. "Why didn't you have me sign one of those?"

He looks at both of us warmly. "Because I didn't need to."

"How much money did Jake manage to squire away?" I ask.

Abbot smiles. "More than 300 million dollars. He had a Trust Fund, naturally, but he was quite gifted at playing the stock market. Almost clairvoyant."

***

Abbot and I are alone in the parlor of the Oxford house. I'm heading to Eton tomorrow and he's helping me to prepare.

I watch him tinkering with the computer. "Master Timothy," he says, "did Jacob set up some Gmail accounts for you to exchange information during your investigations?"

I think back to all the crazy MI6 things that handsome, brilliant boy was doing. "Yes, among a dozen other things including PO boxes and burner phones."

Abbot is staring at me. "And how many times did you check that account?"

"Never," I say. "Why do you ask?"

"Because you have a message from him with a video attachment."

I feel my cheeks burning. "What?"

He turns the laptop so we can both watch it and clicks on the Quicktime file. Jacob's face immediately fills the screen.

"Timmy, look! I'm at Eton." He turns the camera to show a bit of the famous campus at sunset. "I was shocked when I saw you. Furious, upset, cheesed off...whatever. I'm not anymore. Seriously. The truth is no one will ever love you the way that I do. You are my blue-eyed boy."

I'm having a rough time now seeing the screen through my tears. "Hey, I thought we might name the Oxford House: *Brigsley Manor*...what do you think? It has a ring.

I drove out to Botany Bay to speak with Olivia Walker today. Tommy's boyfriend Tyler is actually our Headmaster, Stillman *Tyler* Rothwell...the bastard. I'm inviting him to the cottage so he and Tommy can hash it out.

Abbot, if you're watching this, thanks for everything. Please fill Ashlock in on the business. His fingerprint will unlock the Swiss accounts if my premonition comes true and all this goes tits up for me.

Timmy, I'm sorry for our argy-bargy...I hope you will forgive me. More than anything I want you to make your life extraordinary.

I'm attaching a pdf file which is my novella, *Brilliant Flames*. It's a mystery about an arsonist. Please read it and let me know if you think I'm a decent writer.

I'm spending the night at Eton. That swimmer Matthew Colton is going to show me around...and I hope that makes you extremely jealous!

I'll be coming home early tomorrow morning. I'm going to go for a swim at Ducker and then climb into bed with you! Please change those sheets.

I love you Timothy James."

ABOUT THE AUTHOR

Marko Realmonte makes his home in a sleepy beach town on the Central California coast, where he is followed everywhere by his loving dog, Jasper. When he isn't killing off his protagonists, he is a professional photographer. He is currently at work on his second LGBTQ novel,
The Wizard King.

You can follow him on twitter: @markorealmonte
or on www.markorealmonte.com

This book is also available as an Ebook and an Audiobook

Made in the USA
San Bernardino, CA
10 March 2019